Shiny Water

Shiny Water

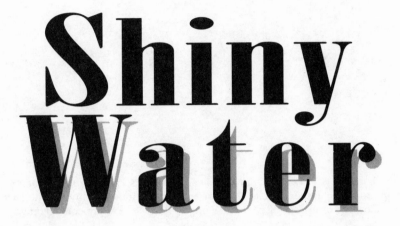

ANNA SALTER

POCKET BOOKS
New York London Toronto Sydney Tokyo Singapore

POCKET BOOKS, a division of Simon & Schuster Inc.
1230 Avenue of the Americas, New York, NY 10020

Library of Congress Cataloging-in-Publication Data

Salter, Anna C.
    Shiny water / Anna Salter.
        p.   cm.
    ISBN 0-671-00310-0
    I. Title.
    PS3569.A46219S55   1997   97-8282
    813'.54—dc21   CIP

First Pocket Books hardcover printing August 1997

10 9 8 7 6 5 4 3 2 1

POCKET and colophon are registered trademarks of
Simon & Schuster Inc.

Printed in the U.S.A.

For my children,
Blake, Jazzy, and Corey

Acknowledgments

· ·

I would like to thank most of all my secretary, Judy MacNeil, for her loving support for all my efforts.

A number of professionals were kind enough to read the manuscript for accuracy. Police chief Russell Lary offered valuable advice on police techniques and procedures. Attorney John Kelly and Judge Julianne Piggotte contributed to the book's accuracy in legal matters. Police officer/writer Massad Ayoud was kind enough to read the book for technical details. My friend, Ardis Olson, M.D., clarified the medical sections and encouraged me throughout the process. Likewise, my longtime friend and mentor, Regina Yando, Ph.D., was supportive of my writing as she has been of all my endeavors since I was a graduate student. I would also like to thank my friend Linda Cope for her encouragement and support. Finally, if my friends writer Elise Title and Jeff Title had not insisted I could do it, I probably would never have written a word.

There was a group of three women intimately involved in the publication of this book, all of whom have a little bit of Michael

ACKNOWLEDGMENTS

Stone in them. My agent, Helen Rees, seemed to know Michael from the start and knew exactly whom to involve. I have the good fortune to have an excellent editor in Dona Chernoff of Pocket Books. Finally, Sandy Gelles-Cole's critique of the manuscript gave the book much of its suspense. More than anyone's, her editing made the book what it is.

Shiny Water

I don't think most people's reaction to finding a dead body on a dock would be to call their kid to come look at it. But that's Mama. She just thought I'd be interested. I was relieved it wasn't Daddy or anything like that. You never could tell with Mama. "Must have had a heart attack," she said.

"I don't think you bleed when you have a heart attack, Mama," I replied. "Maybe he was stabbed or shot or something."

"Girl," Mama snorted, rolling her bright blue eyes heavenward, "this isn't New York City." That was definitive for Mama. People in New York City got murdered; people in Wilson's Pond didn't. This wasn't New York City, so he wasn't murdered.

"The knife," I said, pointing to a knife partly hidden by the body.

"What?"

"The knife, Mama. It's bad for your theory."

"Well, I don't know," she said. "Folks do things different ways." It wasn't clear what she meant. She could have meant

1

maybe some folks in Wilson's Pond got murdered, or she could have meant maybe some folks bled when they had heart attacks. It was hard to know with Mama.

One thing I know for sure. When Mama dies, those diamond earrings of hers will be on the end table. Forty years they've been in her ears, but Mama doesn't hold with burying good diamonds, and she wouldn't trust anybody to get it right.

Some folks think you wouldn't necessarily know when you're dying. Some folks believe in dying in your sleep. But no one who knows Mama thinks those rules apply to her. Mama likes to stare at things from a long way off. Personally, I'm not sure Mama will ever die, because not even God would want to take on Mama.

I rubbed my eyes, the same shade of bright blue as Mama's, and sat up straighter. Funny how when I don't have anything to do, I find myself thinking about Mama. It isn't all that often that I don't have anything else to do, but today my client was late and I was twiddling my thumbs and musing. The mental health clinic in the Department of Psychiatry at Jefferson University wasn't open yet, so I had the whole place to myself.

I am a forensic psychologist—a specialist in court-related psychological cases: child abuse, child custody, battered spouses—and I sometimes get difficult clients. I prefer to see them early in the morning when there isn't an audience in the waiting room.

I had almost given up on my client when I heard noises in the hall—not very friendly noises. They got louder, and I stared at the door to the waiting room as it burst open and my client was brought in kicking and screaming. The two people carrying her barely got through the door before she twisted out of their grasp and crashed to the floor. She came up so fast it almost seemed like she bounced as she made a valiant lunge for the door. One of her escorts, much bigger than she was, grabbed the knob and held it shut. She started screaming, "Let go! Let go!" and when he didn't, she started kicking the door. The other one tried to grab her, but she twisted free again and fell in the process, staying down this time and lashing out with her feet. She started banging her head on the floor while screaming at what I hoped was the top of her lungs.

I ignored her head-banging and spoke to my client's jailers. I practically had to yell to be heard above the screaming. "Pull a chair by the door, sit down, and be as unobtrusive as possible. Don't look at anybody directly. Just read magazines and act invisible." This kind of instruction was exactly the type of thing that could never work with a full audience in the waiting room.

The man and woman sat down, and I looked at my client, who had shown no signs of calming down. Well now, we weren't off to the best start. It wasn't that we had a failure to communicate: She was communicating very well. She had managed to convey with an economy of words her opinion of going to see a forensic psychologist. The court might want to know whether she had been sexually abused by her father as her brother allegedly claimed, but three-year-old Adrienne was having none of it.

Maybe she would have been slightly more cooperative if her mother had been there. But mothers aren't allowed to bring their children to a forensic evaluation if the charge of sexual abuse was made in the middle of a custody fight. If it were a false report, just the presence of mom in the waiting room would be enough to force the child to stick to the story, and if it were a true report, the father's lawyer would use the presence of the mother to discredit it. So Adrienne had come with an aunt and an uncle—distant enough relatives that both parents would accept them as neutral, which meant Adrienne hardly knew them.

Clearly, their rapport with Adrienne was limited—and so was their authority. Adrienne cranked up the volume a couple of decibels. This was an impressive temper tantrum.

To be honest, I love this kind of thing. Challenge smallenge. People who interview adults don't have a clue how tough interviewing can be. No adults I've ever met—and that includes violent Vietnam vets who sat there muttering, "I'm getting those feelings again," psychotic postal workers who thought aliens were giving them more mail to sort than anyone else, and multiple personalities where you could run an entire group with just one person—no adults were as challenging as a table-kicking, head-banging, screw-you three-year-old.

It was my job to take this screaming, out-of-control child and get her to tell me, a stranger, about something that—if it had happened—she had never told anyone about, not even the people she knew the best and loved the most. Adrienne's brother, Andrew, had disclosed sexual abuse to his teacher, but Adrienne had never said anything, even though Andrew had reported seeing their dad abuse her, too. And, of course, I had to get Adrienne to open up without saying anything that would strike anybody involved in the case as being even vaguely "leading and suggestive."

I once sat next to a gifted attorney about to cross-examine a child. This attorney had interviewed hundreds, probably thousands, of clients and opposition witnesses during his lengthy career and could confidently cross-examine anyone from a con man to a college president. "Oh my God," I heard him say as he got up very slowly to cross-examine a six-year-old whose small head barely showed above the witness box.

I understood the sentiment. It would be a piece of work to get this child to talk to me about sexual abuse. It would be a piece of work to get her to talk to me about anything. It would be a minor art form to get her to leave the waiting room. Come to think of it, it would be a miracle if I could get her to stop screaming.

I started walking toward her, alert for a clue as to where her social boundaries were. Children treat social distance differently than adults do. Adults stand the same distance from friends and strangers, the same distance regardless of their mood. But children change their social distance depending on how well they know you and how they're feeling. They'll react if you get any closer to them than three or four feet if they don't know you—particularly if they're upset. Of course, when they know you and like you, they'll drape themselves across your knee and rub your shinbone—something adults rarely do. Needless to say, they don't speak up when adults have intruded on their space, instead, they tend to turn away, avert their gaze, or just plain stiffen when strange or threatening adults get too close.

I had seen a tape of a forensic interview where the therapist repeatedly got too close to the child; each time the child moved away. The therapist—completely unaware of the child's boundaries—chased the child all over the room. At the end of the session the therapist wrote up her diagnosis: Attention Deficit Disorder with Hyperactivity.

I was four to five feet away when Adrienne turned her head away from me toward the wall. I stopped and backed up a foot. It amazes me to see adults who know they're intruding on a child's space just go ahead and do it anyway.

I got down on my hands and knees—if other adults hadn't been there I'd have sprawled full length on the floor—and pulled a large green turtle puppet out of my pocket and onto my hand. "Now, it's all right," I said to the puppet. "She's just a little girl, and she's not going to hurt you. She's here to play in the playroom with me. Now let's see. We have Play-Doh in there and a dollhouse and some puppets and a sandbox on a table. I can't remember everything. She'll just have to look and see what she wants to play with."

Adrienne had stopped screaming while I was talking to the puppet and now turned in my direction. I paid no attention to her. The moment I stopped talking she started to scream again. I immediately balled up my fist and pulled the turtle's head inside the shell. "It's okay. It's okay," I said. "She doesn't mean to scare you. She's a very nice little girl, and she's just here to play and visit and talk some."

Adrienne stopped screaming again and held out her hand for the puppet. I ignored it and continued to reassure the puppet while rubbing its head. Adrienne moved closer, and the turtle's head disappeared again. "It's okay; it's okay," I said anxiously to the turtle and, turning to Adrienne for the first time, went on diffidently, "She's very shy, and big girls are a little bit scary for her." Adrienne held out her hand again, imperiously, as three-year-olds do.

I reached back into my pocket and pulled out a smaller version of the same puppet for her, one that fit her tiny hand. I showed Adrienne how to work the puppet; she said nothing, but sat up and began to play with it.

I had gotten past the distance obstacle, or at least Adrienne had. She had closed the gap between us, something she would never have allowed me to do. The trick was to draw children to you, not intrude on them.

I figured my chances were fifty-fifty. If the large green turtle invited her into the office, she might go now, but then again she might not, and once she had said "no" I'd be in big trouble. The kiss of death would be to start asking questions. "How are you?" is a totally absurd question from a three-year-old point of view. She would not answer a question like that. Strike one. Then if I followed up with "That's a nice dress. Is that your favorite color?" she wouldn't answer that either. Strike two. Then perhaps something like "What's your name?" would go unanswered. Three strikes.

At that point she'd have settled into a no-answer mode, meaning she had decided the rules of the game were that I asked questions and she didn't answer, and she wouldn't answer anything for the rest of the session.

I turned to the door of the waiting room. "Turtle," I said. "Did you hear Ostrich?" I turned the big turtle to look at the door. "I think I heard that silly ostrich. I'll go look." I left the turtle on the floor and went into my office, which was just off the waiting room. I picked up an ostrich puppet large enough to fill a La-Z-Boy recliner and put my entire arm up the ostrich's neck. I hid on one side of the door, and the ostrich peeked his head around the corner of the office and then immediately withdrew. He was quite dashing with his long curly eyelashes and inquisitive look. It wasn't entirely clear how I looked—skinny me crouched and scrunched behind the door. (The last time I did something like this, a group of National Institute of Mental Health site visitors walked by. "Oh, that's just one of the child people," their departmental guide said calmly. "They're like that.")

Adrienne stared transfixed at the door with the disappearing ostrich. The puppet peeked out again. Without a word, Adrienne got up and walked into the office to catch the teasing ostrich, still clutching the small green turtle. I closed the door gently—Adrienne hardly seemed to notice—and left the outside world behind.

Now for the silence. The important thing was not to ask any questions. "Hello, Adrienne, my name is Ostrich and . . ." The ostrich broke off and buried his head under my arm.

"Everybody seems shy today, Adrienne," I said with a big sigh. "The big turtle is shy, and the little turtle is shy, and the ostrich is shy. You just seem like such a big girl to them, and they're a little bit scared." I turned to Ostrich and elaborately reassured him that Adrienne wouldn't hurt him, while pointing out to him all the things that Adrienne might play with instead. I stayed kneeling the whole time so my head wasn't any higher than Adrienne's. Looming over children never fosters a dialogue.

Why don't adults "get" how important size is to children? Totally bizarre. I love the way people always say to pre-schoolers, "Oh, don't worry, he won't hurt you," as a huge dog comes bounding up. I wonder how adults would react to a horse galloping toward them across a field and then rearing up to throw its legs on their shoulders. Would they really be reassured to hear someone say, "Oh, don't worry, he won't hurt you," as the horse sent them sprawling? But then, I seem to understand the kid point of view better than the adult. As my friend Carlotta once said of me, adults still tend to be "grown-ups" to me.

It's hard not to ask any questions, harder than you'd think. I started by mentioning every item Adrienne was wearing, "I like that pink T-shirt, and I have tennis shoes like that except mine . . ." It takes a while to run out of clothes to comment on, especially if you include your own. I had on black dress pants, black turtleneck, and a bright red vest with yellow suns all over it. In my line of work it pays to wear something children find worth talking about. My dangling earrings would be worth a few sentences. Unfortunately, I wouldn't get any mileage at all out of my shoes. For reasons I have never understood, children love interesting shoes. I own one pair of black flats, one pair of brown ones, one pair of running shoes, one pair of dress boots, one pair of warm boots, and a pair of sandals. None of them would turn a preschooler's head.

While I was running my fashion commentary, Adrienne headed for the dollhouse with the action figures, and I switched from fashion consultant to sports commentator. "Wow, that man is sliding down the dollhouse roof," I said, "and that girl is sitting on the couch," verbalizing what Adrienne was doing with the dolls. It was such a play-by-play, I almost added, "and this is the voice of the Boston Celtics," but it wasn't three-year-old humor.

I was prepared to act like an idiot indefinitely, knowing absolutely that sooner or later if I kept talking, Adrienne would volunteer something of her own commentary, but she surprised me by joining in right away. "He fell down," she said. "He has to go to the doctor."

Wow. This child was impressive. She might not have wanted to see me, but it wasn't because she was shy. She had recovered from her temper tantrum, made her peace with being here, and was actually talking, all within a pretty short period of time. She was feisty, a hard trait for me to knock. Feisty would make it easier to figure out what was going on. Piss and vinegar are nowhere near as hard as mute.

I had a hypothesis about what was going on, anyway. I had done my homework and gone over all existing police, mental health, and child protection reports. Mom and dad had both had psychological evaluations for the custody fight that was raging between them.

Mom was either an hysterical paranoid or a paranoid hysteric, depending on your point of view — which is to say, she was emotionally labile, dramatic, and annoying as hell, as well as convinced everything her husband said or did was a plot to get her. The evaluators merely differed on which set of traits they thought were central — as though which was primary and which secondary would change anything.

It was a little like two doctors arguing over whether the patient had died of a heart attack or a stroke. The point was, the patient was dead, and the point here was, the mother in this case wasn't going to win any awards for mental health with either diagnosis.

Dad, on the other hand, fell in the normal range on every test. Of course, that didn't positively mean he wasn't a child molester, since forty percent of child molesters fall in the normal range.

But this was a custody fight, which is the most frequent place where false reports occur (although they don't necessarily occur with the overwhelming frequency the media claims). Putting it all together — a crazy mother, a noncrazy father, and a charge of sexual abuse in the middle of a custody fight — it looked to me like there was a good chance of a false report. That was fine by me.

For lots of reasons, I'm quite happy when I have a false report. It means the child hasn't been abused and that she or he is not going to have to contend with a sex offender in the family, one who might well get custody. Court is like the NFL: On any given Sunday, either side could win.

Who knew these days what would happen in court? In the last case I had lost, a four-year-old child had marched to the witness stand and told in graphic detail what her father had done to her. The father, unfortunately for her, was a pillar of the community and well thought of by just about everybody. The jury decided a nice man wouldn't do such terrible things.

And besides, they reasoned, if the child had been abused, she would have been too damaged to talk about it so clearly. Of course, if she had stumbled and hesitated while testifying, the jury would have said that her nervousness, her inability to look the alleged perp in the eye, meant she was lying.

Finding a report is false these days is definitely swimming downstream with a strong current carrying you. It seems to be what everybody—judge, jury, press, public, not to mention the defense—wants to hear.

On the other hand, finding that a report of abuse is valid is much like putting one's head in a blender and turning it on. Dad always manages to find the lawyer from hell. He always brings so many relatives and character witnesses to court, I feel like I'm running a gauntlet in the halls. As for the local newspapers—well, they are so prejudiced that once one of them printed an account so biased, I didn't recognize it as the case I was in.

So it was okay with me if this child said "no" when I asked her if anyone had ever touched her in a way she didn't like.

But I never got that far because Adrienne almost immediately put the adult male action figure's head in the child action figure's crotch. "Adrienne," I said, "what are the dolls doing?" I kept my fingers crossed that our relationship was now strong enough to tolerate a question.

"He's licking her pee-pee," Adrienne said pleasantly, "like Daddy does."

"Daddy licks someone's pee-pee," I repeated.

"He licks mine," Adrienne said, throwing her legs open and pointing to her white panties, "right there."

Good grief. This didn't sound like a false report. False reports don't involve spontaneous physical displays. They are rarely specific. They have a rote quality about them. They often involve adult language and adult ideas of what is appropriate. With my last false report, a child had repeated over and over, "Daddy did naughty things to me," but could never say what.

I felt depressed immediately. If this was true, it wasn't just bad for Adrienne; this was going to make my life pretty miserable for some time to come. The legal case would go on forever. There would be months and months of pretrial motions and depositions. I'd be on the stand for days, attacked on every conceivable ground. I went on with the evaluation, hoping Adrienne would do something to undo the validity of her initial spontaneous reactions.

Unfortunately, she held her ground no matter what modality was used. I made people out of Play-Doh. Adrienne pointed to the man's crotch and said that white sticky stuff came out of her daddy's pee-pee. In the dollhouse she put the adult male doll on top of the child doll and simulated copulatory movements. Her drawing of a man had three legs—sort of, only the third one seemed to be pointing up. I got more depressed as the session progressed.

2

$\bullet\,\bullet$

Her brother wasn't at all what I expected. He was far more neatly dressed than any six-year-old ought to be and walked into my office with an air of gravity. It had been a week since I had seen Adrienne, but I remembered her energy quite distinctly. I guess I expected a six-year-old version of Adrienne, but her brother seemed to belong to a different species. He looked around my office, saw the child-size table and chairs, and asked politely if he could sit down. I couldn't remember any child asking if he could sit down, much less a six-year-old.

I had planned on doing some psychological testing later in the session, but since he just seemed to be sitting there without making any attempt to play, I decided to go ahead. He seemed comfortable with structure, to say the least. I explained I was going to give him some pictures and I wanted him to make up a story about them. I wanted him to tell me how the people in the pictures felt and what they thought, and what happened before this scene and what would happen next.

The stories I usually get from kids this age are pretty

12

mundane—three or four sentences describing what the person is doing. They inevitably have to be prompted to say what the person thinks or feels, and even then, the answers tend to be brief. "He's happy," they say, or "he's sad."

I gave Andrew the first card, a picture of a boy looking at a toy boat sitting on the desk in front of him. "Actually," Andrew said, "this story is set in 1861. That's a shame, because if it was set in 1860 I would have a perfect story." I waited, stunned, but Andrew said nothing more.

"What do you mean? What happened in 1861?" I asked.

"The Civil War started," he answered. "A lot of people died in that war—837,938 actually. Did you know that two percent of the South died in the war?"

"Uh, no, I didn't."

"Well, they did. Two hundred ninety thousand, five hundred twenty-four Southerners died. It was really a stupid war. It doesn't make any sense. I mean, a kindergartner would know you shouldn't own slaves. It's mean. But the whole South thought it was okay. It seems really dumb. How can people do such mean things?"

"You mean like fighting a war or owning slaves?"

"I mean owning slaves. I think there had to be a war. You just can't let people do such stupid things. My mom says she heard that down South they still play 'Dixie' at football games and wave the Confederate flag. If I was there, I'd go right up and pull that flag down and ask them how they'd feel if somebody tried to own them."

"Then what was perfect about 1860?"

"I didn't say 1860 was perfect," Andrew said, sounding slightly exasperated. "I said I'd have a perfect story."

"Okay, so what's the perfect story?"

"You told me to tell a story about the picture," Andrew explained carefully. "The story is about the boy in the picture. 1860 was before all the bad things happened in his family. He'd be looking at his toy boat and thinking about good things. But he can't do that anymore, because it's 1861." He stared at the picture a minute longer. "Sometimes, he can't even remember the good things." He put the picture down.

"What bad things?" I said. "Things to do with the war?"

"I suppose so," he said vaguely. "Do you have any more pictures?"

It might have been a mistake. Would he have gone vague on me if I hadn't asked the question? On the other hand, telling about the bad things might be the hardest part no matter what I said.

It was tempting to agree with Andrew's ideas, to admire his clearheadedness, to get into an "out-of-the-mouths-of-babes" bit of musing, to be encouraged that the new generation might be a bit fairer than previous ones. But it would all be beside the point. It was Andrew's style, his use of intellectualization as a defense, the fact that he was wildly inappropriate developmentally, that mattered. He was an obsessive kid—a world-class worrier. I had seen a few of them, and they always handled their problems the same way. The books say kids of his age are concrete. They are supposed to worry about whether their baseball team will win or not. They aren't supposed to be capable of abstract thought or abstract worries.

But no one has told kids like Andrew that. They tend to take some large, abstract issue and project onto it their own personal problems. Kids who aren't nurtured at home worry about kids not getting fed in Somalia. Kids who are afraid their parents will get a divorce worry about children being abandoned in Bosnia. Kids whose parents fight all the time worry about the environment being destroyed. Obsessive kids are always exceptionally bright, developmentally precocious, and major-league worriers.

I wanted to think Andrew was just talking about his parents' divorce, but it didn't really sound like it. People were doing mean things to other people, he had said, and there had to be a war. You just couldn't let people keep doing such mean things.

It sounded like the mean things came before the war. Still, who knew? You could interpret his story a lot of different ways.

Things became clearer when I asked him directly about his father. On that topic he was quite concrete and quite precise. He knew that what his father was doing to him was wrong, he said, but he didn't tell anybody because he didn't want to go to jail, and his dad said he'd go to jail if he told. But he walked in his sister's room one night, and his dad had his pants off, and he was standing up leaning over his sister, who was lying on the bed. His dad's face was all red and puffy, and he was rubbing his penis against his sister.

He thought about it all night, he said, before he told his teacher. He had decided he'd rather go to jail than let his dad do it to his sister. She wasn't big like him, he said, and he didn't think she could take it. I realized with a shock he still thought he, and not his father, was going to jail.

"Andrew," I said, "did you talk to your mom about this? Before you told your teacher?"

"No," Andrew said. He straightened out a toy that was sitting a little crooked on the shelf beside him. "I wanted to tell her, but I couldn't."

"Why not?" I said.

"I didn't want to upset her," he said. "She gets upset a lot, and she cries, and then Adrienne gets upset, and she cries, and I don't know whether to talk to mom or try to get Adrienne to stop crying. And then mom tells me to go out and play, but I can't play because I worry about her, and besides Adrienne is still crying."

"Andrew," I said, "I'm going to ask you something very important, and it's very important that you tell me the truth. Did you make this up to help your mom in some way?"

Andrew looked at me in astonishment. "How is this going to help my mom?" he said. "My mom is really mad about this. This is going to make everything much worse."

I looked at the earnest face in front of me, the face of a kid who still thought he was on his way to jail for telling. I hated to be the one to tell him, but nobody was going to jail. I had no doubts that this was a valid report of child sexual abuse, but I also had no doubts that the child in front of me would never be believed in court.

Andrew was right. The problem was the year, although I don't think 1860 would have been any better. There were years in recent memory when a child's report of sexual abuse might have been believed, especially a report that met all known criteria for validity—not to mention one that was corroborated by another child. But this wasn't one of those years.

The problem was the public still expects sex offenders to dress funny and have three-day beards. And most of all, sex offenders should yell "mea culpa" when caught. Sex offenders, according to popular wisdom, would never look anyone in the eye and deny they did it, certainly not convincingly. And sex offenders aren't well educated and they surely aren't wealthy. A group called the IMA (Innocent Man Accused) has published surveys that show the income level and vacation plans of their members. Sex offenders would be poorer, the implication is, and not take such spiffy vacations.

Most certainly sex offenders would surely never engage in aggressive denial, surely not with the kind of righteous indignation that would cause, say, a priest like the one I testified against to sue his victims—all twelve of them—when they first reported. In his lawsuit the priest produced a forty-page, single-spaced, typed rebuttal attacking the children's stories. Eventually, he confessed and admitted to sexually abusing the kids and fabricating the rebuttal.

I had a bad feeling the priest would have nothing on Nathan Southworth, thoracic surgeon, pillar of the community, volunteer fireman, and father of Adrienne and Andrew. He would not show up in court with a three-day beard, and he would deny very aggressively indeed. And this was a custody fight where, popular wisdom held, every report of sexual abuse was false.

But if there would be trouble in court, at least Andrew's mom would be on his side. Ninety-five percent or so of offenders tend to be male, so the nonoffending spouse is usually a mother. In intact families, I hold my breath when talking to mom. About fifty percent of the time she sides with the offender and accuses the child of lying as loudly as her husband did. At least in custody fights, somebody is on the child's side.

3

I had an appointment with Sharon Southworth, the kids' mother, for the next day. I needed a developmental history of the children, plus I wanted to find out what I could about the disclosures of sexual abuse. Had mom suspected abuse before Andrew disclosed it? Had she ever pressured the children or even questioned them about possible abuse? Had she discussed it with others around the children? Hope was fading fast that I could find another explanation for such detailed and graphic stories, but I needed to check out every possibility. I didn't expect any problem with the session, so I walked into it without the hypervigilance I have when I know I'm going into a firestorm.

She shook my hand limply. She was as tall as I am—around five-seven—but rounder, earth mother-like. A granola mom, I thought. The long dark pigtails, the loose dress of a handwoven fabric, the sandals—she brought back fond memories of my hippie days. Of course, in my hippie days I had been poor as a churchmouse, and the luminous, handwoven dress Sharon wore bore no resemblance to my old rough, shapeless counterparts. I'd owned cars that probably cost less than the Native American jewelry around her neck.

Still, wealthy surgeon's wife or not, she had that Vermont back-to-the-earth style about her. You couldn't imagine her in furs. No doubt she went to contra dances, the hippie version of square dances so popular in New England, and bought organic food from a co-op. "The judge insisted I bring the children in. And me, too," she added quickly. "I want to clear this up as soon as possible."

"Well, I'm not sure it's something that can be cleared up exactly," I replied. "But before I talk about my impressions of the children, I want to get some information from you about their history." It proved difficult to get a history. Mom had the information, and she was anything but dumb, but she kept getting off on tangents about her husband. It was going to be, it seemed, one of those deeply bitter divorces.

"Did you have any problems with the pregnancy?" We'd been talking ten minutes, and I hadn't gotten to the first birth. I began to wish Andrew was younger: I'd get through this quicker.

"It was a horrible pregnancy. Nathan was never home. He kept telling me he had to work, but how much can you work, for Christ's sake?"

"He was a resident, wasn't he, at the time? I can imagine it must have been difficult. Surgery residents have a pretty brutal schedule."

"Nathan used work as an excuse for everything. I knew it was a crock. Whenever I'd call, they'd say he was in surgery."

I paused, not sure what she was saying. "What do you mean? Nathan was a surgery resident. Surgery residents tend to spend their days in surgery. What made you think it was a crock?"

"I finally called him on it. I just showed up one day." I hated conversations like this. Sharon wasn't really answering my questions. The train was just going down the track; the litany of complaints was just rolling along.

"So what happened?" Why did I bother to speak? Obviously, she was going to tell me what happened. In this kind of conversation people start asking the question that they know the other person is going to answer whether they ask it or not, just so they won't feel so irrelevant.

"They kept me waiting twenty minutes—plenty of time for him to get from wherever he was. It was comical. I was in the waiting room raising holy hell. He suddenly swept in wearing his little green thingies, holding his hands in the air with these bloodstained gloves on them, and yelling at me to get the hell out. Can you believe it? What a joke."

I couldn't believe it. Was I hearing this right? Had she actually raised such a fuss that he came out of surgery to tell her to go home? Surely, that hadn't happened. The hospital hierarchy would have gone crazy if it had. But who knew? "Sharon, are you saying he actually left the operating room to talk to you?"

"Of course not," she said, rolling her eyes. "Don't be naive. Nathan wasn't in the operating room. It was just one of his little games."

"Sharon, I must be missing something here," I said slowly. "Nathan comes out with greens on, holding his bloodstained, gloved fingers in the air, refusing to touch anything. What makes you think he wasn't in the operating room?"

"You don't know Nathan. That's exactly the kind of scene that son of a bitch would pull."

Sometimes I look at couples, both of them swollen with divorce-hatred, and try to imagine them having a child together. It boggles my mind that people who once had sex together can later hate each other so completely. Then again, lots of people have sex together who hate each other at the time.

The session limped along from one hostile comment about her ex to the next. When Sharon wasn't talking about Nathan, she was pretty rational. She was actually quite precise about the children's developmental milestones, and she had a wealth of information about their growing up.

"Their temperaments are so different," she said, "just like their looks. Andrew has always been a beanpole, and Adrienne has always been built like a little miniature Mack truck.

"We used to take the triple chairlift up Killington in the summer to picnic at the top. The first time I took Andrew up—he was maybe two—he sat there solemnly, hands folded, all the way up and all the way down. I remember marveling that the wind didn't even seem to blow his hair.

"The first time I took Adrienne up at the same age, she refused to get on the chairlift at the last minute. We were waiting for the chairlift to swing around, when Adrienne changed her mind, lay down, and started kicking and screaming. I had to get her up off the ground and sit down in the lift without getting kicked in the face, all in about two seconds. Of course, on the way down, she had gotten used to the lift and it was a different story. There was Andrew still sitting there solemnly, just like when he was two. And there was Adrienne, little blond curls flying, trying to stand up and dance."

Her voice warmed when she talked about the kids, and her face softened so much I found myself smiling. This woman was one kind of spouse and another kind of mother. I looked at her hands. Sometimes the hands tell the tale. Hers seemed to flow, without any aggressive gestures, even when she was talking about Nathan. Maybe her mom side was the real Sharon.

Finally, it was my turn to talk about what the children had told me. "I'm sorry to tell you that both of your children tell a pretty convincing tale of being sexually abused by your husband."

"That's just like him," she exploded angrily.

"It's just like him to abuse the kids?" I said, surprised. This was an unusual reaction. Most mothers, even those who hate their ex-husbands, never expected him to abuse the children.

"Not to abuse them." She sounded irritated. "To set this up."

"Set what up?" I said, confused.

"The false report," she said angrily. "It's obvious, isn't it? No one else could have done it."

"You think it's a false report?" I said, still off balance. "I don't think so. It shows all the signs of a true report."

"God, that man is so fucking clever," she replied. "He's even got you."

God, I thought, had not done these children any favors with either parent. "Mrs. Southworth," I said, "no one would coach a false report against themselves."

"Why not?" she replied. "It's a perfect way to get at me. I listen to the news. I know what's going on. Who's accused of false reports? The mothers, that's who." In a bizarre way, she had a point. There was no question that a mother whose child reports sexual abuse by the father in the middle of a custody fight has a problem. Mom is likely to be accused of coaching a false report no matter what she says or does from that point on.

Sharon wasn't finished. "He just did this to get me. This has nothing to do with our children, nothing at all. He just does one sneaky thing after another, and no one ever stops him. Well, it isn't going to work. I won't let him get away with this."

I wasn't sure where to start. "Even if someone were crazy enough to coach a false report against themselves," I said, "it wouldn't work with someone as old as six. Andrew's got a very good grip on reality, and he's a very bright kid."

"Nathan must have threatened him with something," she replied. "Andrew would never lie unless he was absolutely forced to. That son of a bitch. I'm sure he threatened my sweet child. And why? Do you know why he did this? He just did this to make me look crazy, that's why."

Oh, no, I thought. If he were as smart as she thought, he'd know she didn't need any help on that score.

Six months later, I hated this case. I hated the fact that the kids were screwed no matter who got custody. I hated the fact that their mother was crazy—well, at least unbalanced—and that their father was a child molester. I hated the fact that I was going into court to testify in support of a woman no judge on earth would find credible.

The mothers are always accused of being crazy in cases like this, but most of the time they aren't. Most of the time they are just frustrated and angry because they believe—often correctly—that their children have been molested by their soon-to-be ex-husbands. But I had to draw a case where the mother was just as crazy as they said she was.

This woman was a defense attorney's dream. She had a history of paranoia about the father going back to when they were still married and—if it could possibly be any worse—had accused him publicly of things he didn't do. All of which would have been fine if it were a false report, but unfortunately, I didn't think it was.

I remembered a case that got royally screwed up at Jefferson Memorial, the hospital attached to the medical school where I work. A resident had examined a hypochondriac and concluded—solely on the basis that he was a hypochondriac—that he didn't have a tumor. But he did have a tumor. And nobody took it seriously until it was too late.

"Hypochondriacs get tumors too," the attending physician had screamed at him. "Never forget it," he had said. "Never, ever forget that hypochondriacs and hysterics and all the crazies of the world get the same diseases as everybody else. They don't get an exemption just because they're crazy." And never forget, I thought, that just because mom is paranoid, doesn't mean dad is innocent. Actually, there is a lot of literature that indicates child molesters prefer women who were ill or incapacitated in some way.

But paranoia plays very badly in court. Paranoids sound shrill and crazy. Not so child molesters; they've spent most of their lives fooling everybody around them. Taking on court is just an extension of a process they perfected years ago. They can feign innocence and ignorance and confusion and hurt. Tears roll from their eyes over the injustice done to them.

The last child molester I had testified against was a dentist who kept practicing right up until sentencing. Who knew why the licensing board hadn't acted? Clearly, nobody on the board knew child molesters. The dentist molested a new victim two hours before he went to court for sentencing—where he made an impassioned statement about his innocence. He talked about what an exemplary life he had lived, how much he had contributed to the community, how unfair and untrue this false accusation was. His voice broke in the right places. Several people in the audience had tears in their eyes. Unfortunately for him, the judge didn't.

But if I'm cynical about how easy it was for child molesters to fool people, most people are hopelessly naive. It is simple. Child molesters are monsters. Their nice neighbor-minister-husband-brother-doctor isn't a monster, so, therefore, he isn't a child molester. And that nice man on the stand with tears rolling down his face surely isn't a child molester.

The field is in retreat these days. Anyone who works for or with abused children is automatically thought to be a "child saver," a mythical being who believes children never lie, that all disclosures of sexual abuse are valid, and who relentlessly hammer at nonabused children until, in desperation, they produce bogus reports of abuse. I have never met a "child saver," but I have met the legend many times in court. Like unicorns, sightings are rare but the legend never seems to die.

Much has been written about the "new Salem witch trials." It is said that "suggestible" children today send innocent men and women to prison with false reports of sexual abuse in the same way that lying children in Salem sent innocent folks to their deaths with tales of devil worship. To explain why children today would tell such incredible tales of sexual abuse, defense lawyers and alleged offenders routinely attack therapists, police, social workers, doctors—anyone who has interviewed the child—for "coaching" a false report. But from my perspective, the backlash has it backward: I am the accusee rather than the accuser most days, and therapists are the ones getting burned at the stake.

We couldn't win this case—even with a judge instead of a jury. (Judges should have a little bit more experience seeing through things.) Dad was too credible, and mom was too incredible, and nobody listened to the kids. We were headed down the tubes. Maybe I hated that fact more than anything. The only thing I didn't hate about the case was the kids. I didn't hate the kids.

I had survived the six months of pretrial motions, of depositions and interrogatories, of hysterical phone calls from Sharon, and legal manipulations—survived, but barely. I hadn't seen the children or Sharon since I completed my evaluation, but I had read Sharon's deposition. Kids almost never testified in custody fights, and they weren't going to this time, so they hadn't been deposed.

Six months is the fast track for trying a case, but Judge Fishbein was sitting on family court so the timing was hardly a surprise. Going to court with Fishbein was like heading down a frozen waterfall on ice skates. Nothing slowed a case down in his court. There was no such thing as a continuance. Most lawyers didn't even try. The standing joke was that continuances were easy in Fishbein's court: Just bring a note from your surgeon. The joke died when one lawyer was scheduled for heart surgery and asked to postpone a hearing until six weeks after the surgery. Fishbein told the lawyer he believed he was in a group practice, was he not? Was he trying to tell the court that he did not have a single associate competent enough to try a case? In that event he said, the court would suggest that learned counsel hire someone quickly because he was going to need him to take over the case in his absence.

So I knew there wouldn't be any continuances, and I had been working my butt off to produce the mountains of documents in response to interrogatories. With interrogatories, it seems, the other side can request that you answer anything or produce anything, up to your first-grade report card. Dad's legal team had wanted information about every legal case I had ever been in. They had demanded to know my protocol for evaluating cases of child sexual abuse and every single book or article I had read that supported it. They wanted to know how much money I made from legal cases (not enough by half to justify the hassle). It wasn't clear whether they were going to read all that stuff or whether they just wanted to harass me.

By the day of the custody hearing, I was at least glad to be getting through "the case from hell." Life wouldn't be any better for the kids afterward, but it would be for me. I walked into the courthouse happy to have my bag and briefcase searched. They could have strip-searched me in the hallway for all I cared, I was so anxious to get this case over with.

I stepped into the courtroom just as they were doing arraignments. Once a week all the new cases are arraigned. The judge makes sure the accused hears the charges against them, checks to see if they are represented by counsel, and takes their pleas. Our case was going to be tried in the same courtroom where the arraignments are held and wouldn't be called until the arraignments were done.

In a more urban area, an entire courtroom is dedicated to arraignments, and they go on all day. But this is Vermont, which has a population of five hundred thousand in the entire state. Arraignments in this courtroom take less than an hour, one day a week, and the rest of the time the courtroom is turned over to cases.

I dropped down into a seat in the back and looked around. Arraignment day means a courtroom filled with frightened, youthful faces. The fact is that most crime, particularly violent crime, is committed by young people. I like court less every time I have to face the fact that most people who end up there are young and poor.

I was in the courtroom just to acclimate myself. Courtrooms always seem formal and foreign, even if you've been in them a hundred times before. I come early every time I testify and hang out in the courtroom getting used to the feel of things. I figure you'd walk a jumping course before you took a horse over it. Same thing.

Well, there is one difference. On a jumping course you can see, when you walk the course, how high and how wide the jumps are. They don't move them when you get up on the horse. But in court, you are always riding blind.

A name was called, and the kid in front of me stood. An older man, with the same angle to his shoulders as the kid, rose beside him. Good, the ones whose families come with them always get better treatment. The boy was in standard adolescent garb: old, torn jeans and a rumpled shirt. Maybe it was defiance, but then again, maybe he didn't have anything else to wear. His shoulders were rigid and his hands tightly clasped in front of him—I knew without seeing his face he was doing the adolescent posturing bit—but I was sitting close enough to see that his left leg was shaking.

I was depressed enough already. I slipped out and went looking for my team. We were coming up to bat soon. I found them huddled in one of the little conference rooms off the main hallway. Marv Gleason turned when I entered the door. Marv even looks like an analyst: short, balding, poorly dressed, with a comforting pot belly. Ordinarily, he sort of shuffles along, but today his movements were quick and jerky. "Good," he said on seeing me. "I can't believe you talked me into this."

The face in front of me was contorted by anxiety; I could hardly believe it was Marv. Was this the same guy who was jousting with the entire psychoanalytic world when I first met him? I had met Marv long before he came to Jefferson Medical School—long before I asked him to give a second opinion on whether these kids had been sexually abused—while attending a psychoanalytic conference. I had been looking through the program, trying to find something I could tolerate listening to, when I spotted the title of Marv's talk—"Mother Bashing in Psychoanalytic Theory: Hobby or Habit?" I almost fell in love with him on the spot. I went racing into the session, in time to hear the end of his talk.

He was taking the position that analytic theory was biased against mothers. There was not enough consideration of the role of temperament, of the father's influence, or of external trauma. I didn't know how anyone could argue with him—it was obviously true—but his audience didn't agree.

I could feel a tension in the room that seemed vaguely akin to what probably happened before a lynching—no aggressive impulses here! Marv, the very same man who, at this moment, seemed quite close to a panic attack just because he was testifying at a hearing, was totally unaffected by palpable anger directed at him during the conference. He started cheerfully answering questions.

Now I am known for a certain degree of feistiness, but this was a one-man football team going up against Nebraska. An older man rose to challenge him, an analytic author named Teichner. To the delight of the audience, Marv invited his opponent onstage to debate. Teichner made the mistake of starting off by saying that all children are primarily influenced by their relationship with their mother.

Marv told Teichner his statement was clearly false; he had a case currently that illustrated the opposite. Marv outlined a case in which the mother was distant and unavailable, a workaholic who spent little time with the family. Dad was the primary caretaker and stayed home with the children. Marv went on to describe the dad as smothering, controlling, and living out his unfulfilled fantasies through the children. Surely Teichner would grant that the controlling, omnipresent dad was more of an influence on the children than the mother they hardly ever saw.

Teichner disagreed and gave an impassioned speech on the subject of why mother's absence spoke more loudly than dad's presence. After all, he said, at least dad hadn't abandoned the child. Marv stood up, his eyes twinkling, and apologized profusely for confusing his esteemed colleague. He was sorry, he said, but he had erred in describing the case. Did he say dad was the smothering, at-home parent and mom was the distant workaholic? That wasn't right at all. He had meant to say just the opposite. Yet he didn't for a second believe, he declared, that if he had presented the case correctly, Dr. Teichner's answer would have been any different.

Marv had him. Everybody knew Teichner's answer would have been different had Marv reversed the parents. But Teichner couldn't admit to that—or he would prove Marv's point. Unfortunately for him, by not reversing it he also proved Marv's point.

The audience roared. It didn't matter that they had been ready to stone Marv a few minutes ago. You had to like someone who could pull off something like that. I wasn't sure Teichner appreciated Marv's cleverness, but he stepped up to the podium and skillfully said that psychoanalytic theory would never be moribund with such lively and creative practitioners.

I came back to earth and looked at Marv. The man in front of me in the courthouse was a shadow of the man on the stage that day. "It'll be all right," I said. But actually I didn't think it would. I had known he didn't go to court much, but I hadn't known why until I read his deposition earlier that week.

What is it about going to court that terrorizes some folks? Put this psychiatrist in a debate with the world's sharpest and most vicious academics—and he'd cheerfully hold his own, a veritable intellectual Rambo—but put him in a courtroom with a lawyer with half his IQ, and he'd fold. It had been a serious mistake to get him involved in this case.

Depositions aren't even all that stressful. The opposition's lawyer gets to ask you questions about what you are going to say when you testify. Most lawyers aren't even particularly hostile. No sense in fireworks without a jury present. During the deposition, the lawyer who examined Marv wasn't attacking, but nonetheless, Marv was down to one functioning synapse by the end of the interview. I remember the lawyer had asked Marv for a bibliography of books and articles he would be relying on in his testimony. Marv couldn't remember more than a couple of articles on forensic interviewing. A couple? Marv had given me a bibliography with seventy-five articles on it the week before.

While I was reading the deposition, I thought Marv must have been sick. Then I wondered if he was stoned. But one look at Marv's face today cleared up the mystery. Marv was phobic when it came to court.

Why did he take this case? Well, perhaps I had been a tad pushy. Maybe Marv was one of those people who can't turn down a friend. How was I to know? I'd never asked him for anything before. It was his responsibility to say no. It was my job to advocate for the children. I couldn't quite talk myself out of feeling guilty, but I was working on it.

Court Phobia. You won't find it in the current diagnostic manual, but rumors are always circulating that it might be in the forthcoming one. The entry supposedly reads: "Court Phobia: a well-known and frequent malady first described in the writings of Sophocles. It is thought that Socrates was a sufferer and chose death rather than face further legal proceedings. Sufferers tend to answer questions in high, squeaky voices and suffer from acute amnesic episodes, often with psychotic features. Stigmata are common. Differential diagnosis: Paranoid Schizophrenia."

I have a bad habit of succumbing to black humor, but I decided not to share this with Marv. The term "justifiable homicide" came to mind.

5

N athan's lawyer, John White, agreed to let me stay in the courtroom for Marv's testimony, which was a bit surprising. Usually, the opposition objects to one witness listening to another's testimony, but—I figured out later—maybe the defense wanted me to see what happened.

Marv Gleason was called to the stand. I found myself holding my breath even while he was walking up. Stand up, Marv. Don't scurry. Project some kind of air of confidence, even if it's a lie. I sighed. This just wasn't Marv's arena. The suit he had on could have been okay—if he had pressed it and if it fit him better. Marv's total obliviousness to clothes didn't play well in court. Court is theater, and Marv was a very bad actor: Even his costume was wrong.

Marv got through the direct examination okay. After all, on direct, the interviewer is friendly and you know what the questions are going to be in advance. The real test is cross-examination, and Marv paled when John White rose—before he even spoke.

"Do you consider yourself a child advocate, Dr. Gleason?"

"Well, I . . . yes . . . I suppose so."

"Then you've already made up your mind about a case before you even get started?"

"Heavens, no. I . . . I don't. I mean . . . No, of course not."

"But you've just admitted you are a child advocate, Dr. Gleason. So you're not impartial to begin with, are you? Because you've decided to advocate for the child before you ever even met the child. Isn't that true, Doctor?"

"No, I don't think. I mean . . . no, I wouldn't say that exactly."

"Dr. Gleason, wouldn't you agree that objectivity is important in this kind of assessment."

"Yes, of course."

"I see . . . and are you asking this court to believe that it should consider you objective even though you have decided to advocate for the child regardless?"

"Regardless?" Even from where I sat, I could see Marv was sweating.

"Regardless of the actual facts of the case."

"Yes . . . I mean, no. I mean . . . that's not my understanding . . . I don't . . . I don't ignore the facts."

White paused and looked down at his notes—no doubt to give the judge time to absorb this exchange. Grudgingly, I had to admire his sense of timing. "Dr. Gleason, do young children love their parents?"

"Well, certainly. Well, generally . . ."

"Just answer yes or no, Doctor."

"Yes." I closed my eyes. I knew how twenty questions worked, and I knew what was coming. If-if-if-if-then. "Then" would hit him like a two-ton truck.

"And do you think that young children—certainly a six-year-old as bright as young Andrew—are aware when one parent is angry at the other?"

"Yes."

"And do young children want to please their parents?"

"Yes, of course."

"And is it possible that a child as bright as Andrew could figure out that he would please his mother by refusing to see his father?"

"Well, I . . ."

Tom Gaines, Sharon's attorney, stood up. Sharon might be as hysterical as the test reports said, but she knew a good attorney when she saw one. "Objection, Your Honor. We're not concerned here with what's possible. We're concerned with what's probable, what's more likely than not. Anything's possible."

Tom should have prevailed—he was right—but he didn't. You could never tell with Fishbein. "Overruled," he said. "I'd like to hear the answer." On any given Sunday in Fishbein's court even the *cheerleaders* might win. Was it enough of a misstep for Tom to win on appeal? No, I didn't think so. Fishbein had an incredible capacity to make errors just short of what it would take to get his cases overturned. Nonreversible error—he was a master at it.

"Just answer yes or no." White was clearly buoyed up by Fishbein's ruling.

"Well, I suppose it's possible, yes."

"And is it possible that a child as bright as Andrew would be aware that adults should not touch children sexually?"

Tom stood up again. "I have a continuing objection to this entire line of questioning, Your Honor." Well, of course he did. If one "possible" was wrong, they all were. By making a continuing objection, Tom didn't have to pop up at every question and risk irritating Fishbein, who was easy to irritate.

"Let the record reflect it," Fishbein said impatiently.

Everyone look at Marv to continue. "Yes," he said simply.

"And is it possible that a child as bright as Andrew would figure out that an adult who did so would get in trouble?"

"Well, I suppose so. If he had learned good touch/bad touch at school, yes."

"And is it possible, Doctor, is it possible that this whole sexual abuse charge is not true at all but is a way Andrew has found to please his dearly beloved mother?"

Ah, yes. It is always the same charge these days. The child has manufactured a false accusation of sexual abuse against the father because it would please his mother no end to think he was sexually abused by his dad. Variation two is that mom knew the child was not sexually abused and yet deliberately brainwashed him into believing he was, anyway. In this version mom has no caring, whatsoever, about the impact of convincing a child he has been sexually abused, no thought to how disorienting it would be for a child to think his father committed incest with him. Who cares? Anything to get back at dad for whatever. Such is the malevolence of womankind.

I can't decide which version is more far-fetched. While there are surely false reports, I have yet to meet a mother who was thrilled to discover her child has been sexually abused by her once trusted spouse. On the other hand, I wonder if the proponents of variation two have ever tried to "brainwash" a child into saying "please" and "thank-you." It takes over eighteen years of constant effort, and even then the results are spotty.

"I hardly think . . ."

"The witness is not being responsive to the question, Your Honor. This is, after all, a simple yes or no question."

Marv asked that the question be read back to him—no doubt to buy time. It took the stenographer a few moments to find it in her printout, then she read tonelessly, "And is it possible, Doctor, is it possible that this whole sexual abuse charge is not true at all but is a way Andrew has found to please his dearly beloved mother?"

"I . . . well, I suppose it's possible . . . yes."

It was a good thing we weren't outside. Marv was dead enough to attract vultures.

After forcing Marv to discredit the six-year-old's report, the three-year-old was a piece of cake. The lawyer had Marv admitting that it was possible Adrienne was taking her cues from her brother and parroting him.

It was my turn next, and I was revved: I could feel adrenaline all the way to the tips of my fingers. Watching Marv get drawn and quartered had deep-sixed my depression. I couldn't stand to see someone get beaten up like that. I wanted to say, "Pick on someone your own size." I wanted to get in the ring and start swinging. I wanted a shot at the champ. I always had this strange confidence that I could do better. Sometimes I could.

I almost vaulted the low barrier separating the spectators from the participants, but didn't think it was the right image. Instead I slowly opened the gate. I knew from experience that I was walking twice as fast as I thought — adrenaline worked like that — so I made myself walk agonizingly slowly to the stand. I didn't stoop, but I didn't swagger either. I knew I was onstage from the moment I stood up.

I raised my hand for the oath. Everybody in the courtroom was awake from watching the defense carve out Gleason's liver, and they were curious who was next. Even Fishbein looked over at me and raised his eyebrows. He is a small man, although no one who only sees him in court seems to think that. Like Mama, his manner tends to foster the illusion of size. He has a tall forehead and a crew cut. His crew cut is so old-fashioned it almost looks stylish — sort of a half Mohawk. I kept wanting to ask him if he had been in the marines. I had been involved in a case on a marine base, and it seemed to me every MP there was small and wiry and had a chip on his shoulder.

I settled my face into calm, friendly, and trying-to-be-helpful. I smiled slightly at Fishbein. Nothing too flashy. I get along with him reasonably well because I'm known as a practical type. God help the theoreticians in Fishbein's court. I disagree with half of what he does, of course, but he doesn't know that: It is against the rules to have any communication with judges regarding cases outside what gets formally admitted into evidence.

I sat down and took out my notes. I arranged them in piles for quick reference, leaned forward, and looked up expectantly. Like Marv, I was being put on as a witness by the Guardian Ad Litem since I evaluated the children at his request and Marv had given a second opinion at mine. The GAL is assigned by the court to advocate for the child and represent the child's best interests. Sometimes the GAL does the job well, and sometimes badly. The GAL in this case, Arthur Morrison, was a Cadillac version of a GAL, and it was one of the few bright spots in this case.

Arthur rose. I knew Arthur to be a sweet and conscientious man in his sixties who had attended Jefferson University eons ago. He had left his successful Boston law practice behind when his wife died the year before and retired here, near his old alma mater. Within months he was bored and began working as a GAL on child abuse and divorce cases. That was just what the field needed: someone with a lot of legal savvy who had a Boston-Brahman-senior-partner-prestigious-law-firm manner. When Arthur spoke for a child, he used the same tone he had used when representing Fortune 500 companies, and judges tended to listen up.

I liked Arthur immediately. He had made a dent in my skepticism about corporate America. He had wanted to do something more meaningful than business for years, he told me, but things were so busy, somehow he never got around to it. Retirement and his wife's death had given him the chance. He wanted to make a difference, he said, as silly as that sounded. I didn't have a problem with it. I was glad to see him in front of me.

Nonetheless, it was odd for the GAL to be doing the direct. Usually, either one side or the other—plaintiff or defendant—likes my report. If I say the case is bogus, the alleged perpetrator is happy, and if I say the alleged abuse occurred, the nonoffending spouse is supported. This case was weird because both sides disagreed with my evaluation, and both planned to attack me wholeheartedly on cross.

Mom was still claiming that the whole thing was a plot by dad to make her look bad, and she was furious at me for finding the children's disclosures valid. I was pretty sure her attorney, Tom Gaines, didn't think the whole thing was a plot by dad, but he also didn't think it was a good idea to tie mom into the accusations any more than necessary. He was well aware how often mothers are blamed for child sexual abuse reports that surface during custody fights.

Dad, of course, disagreed with my findings as well since I was accusing him of being a child molester. It all seemed pretty strange to me. I was the only person I knew who could get attacked by both sides in a custody fight.

I glanced around. Arthur stood waiting completely at ease at the podium between the plaintiff's and defendant's tables. Sharon, on the other hand, looked like she was a heartbeat away from an anxiety attack. She was wearing a long silk dress with a discreet print—I'd be willing to bet bought for the occasion. It didn't really look like Sharon, but it looked like a cross between the kind of thing she'd prefer to wear and what Tom told her to wear.

I've thought for years that fashion shows have it all wrong. They show evening clothes, wedding scenes. Someday I'm going to put on a fashion show. Never mind what to wear for the wedding. What to wear for the divorce? What to wear if you're in court for a custody fight. What to wear if you've embezzled money, have a DWI. There are important subtleties here. What to wear to confront the other woman. What to wear if you are the other woman. My speciality would be "he's-running-out-on-me" outfits.

Sharon's attorney should take his own advice. No doubt he had influenced Sharon's dress, but even I—who knew as much about men's fashion as I did about mollusk reproduction—knew he was a decade at least out of style. Hard to be in fashion, though, if you weigh what Tom does. In a world that views fat as a mortal sin, Tom is wildly unrepentant. Going to lunch with him is not for the faint of heart.

On my right were Nathan and his attorney, John White: two peas in a pod. Both were WASP males, both dressed for success, both had efficacy written all over them. Tom didn't have efficacy written all over him, but White would be wise not to take his looks seriously. Tom likes to come in as a sleeper.

Arthur had in front of him a list of questions he was going to ask me. I knew what they were: I wrote them. Arthur looked up at me and smiled in a bemused way. I wasn't sure he was quite yet used to having the witness write the questions. Actually, I've found most prosecutors in criminal cases are pleased. They don't have a whole lot of time, and they usually have a whole bunch of cases. I write the questions because I know what I know and what I don't about the case, and they don't know either one. I had been in the situation before of having answers for questions nobody asked me, and it had not made me a happy camper.

"Dr. Stone," he said. "Could you describe for the court your educational background?" First I had to qualify as an expert. Usually the opposition stipulates that I am an expert, but generally, my side refuses to agree. My credentials are good enough that it is better for the judge or jury to hear them than have them stipulated.

Ordinarily, I couldn't care less about credentials, but in court you buy your credibility with them. So I bored everyone to tears with every last internship, child fellowship, faculty appointment, award, paper, and talk I had ever had or given in my entire professional life. I knew Fishbein had heard it before, but I didn't care. Better to remind him.

Arthur moved on to the interviews with the children. "Do you have a protocol or a set of procedures you follow when interviewing allegedly sexually abused children?" I outlined my interviewing protocol for interviewing alleged victims of child sexual abuse. I emphasized "alleged." I had the transcripts of my interviews of the children with me, and Arthur got them admitted into evidence because they were part of the basis for my opinion. We had agreed he would ask me to read key sections of them to the court and explain my questions and why they were so neutral and so carefully worded.

Then we moved on to the part designed to steal the opposition's thunder. "Did you consider any alternative hypotheses other than sexual abuse that might explain the child's disclosures?"

"Yes, indeed," I said and went over in exhaustive detail every possible explanation for the children's disclosures. I reviewed the possibility that mom had coached the children, the possibility that they had figured out on their own what she wanted them to say unbeknownst to her, the chance that the descriptions came from watching X-rated films. I discussed the possibility they had the right acts but the wrong perpetrator. I went over every alternative hypothesis I could think of and explained why none of them really fit this case.

Finally, at Arthur's request, I ended with a summary of current research on disclosure in child sexual abuse cases and on false reporting. I made every counterargument I could think of and answered each one.

Throughout my testimony I spoke very slowly, which, I knew, would sound to everybody else like normal speed. When I'm revved I can sound like Robin Williams without the punch lines.

Arthur and I didn't make a bad team. We had only worked on a couple of cases before, but the collaboration seemed to get better each time. He kept his part straightforward and direct. He asked me the questions I needed to be asked in order to tell what I knew. Arthur handed me the mortar, and I put the bricks together. This time, especially, I was trying to build a fortress so strong the advancing artillery couldn't dent it. I was trying, as the preschoolers say, to build the brick house and not the one made of straw or twigs, and I was waiting for the wolf.

It killed me that I was having to advocate custody of small children for a woman whose mental health was more or less the equivalent of a whiffle ball. But a nutsy mother was one thing, and a child molester was another. Besides, Sharon's hands stayed with me. She was a damn sight better mother than she was anything else.

Plaintiff's counsel got to examine me first. Sharon had filed for divorce, so she was the plaintiff. Tom Gaines rose slightly in his seat, "No questions, Your Honor." I was taken aback. Sharon had been threatening for months to have her lawyer crucify me on the witness stand. Sharon stared at him glumly. Tom simply folded his hands over his ample stomach and didn't look at her. I had a feeling that they had been fighting over this. But it made sense. Tom Gaines wouldn't let Sharon dictate legal strategy, and clearly, he felt his side should simply stay out of it.

Defense counsel did not pass. Dad's lawyer was the bigger threat, anyway, because he was defending the father, and the father, after all, was the only one being accused of sexual abuse. I had never seen Nathan's lawyer before. All I knew was that his name was White and he was from one of the big law firms in Burlington. He was a tall man with an angular, New England face.

I made of point of leaning forward in exactly the same calm, friendly, and trying-to-be-helpful way I had when Arthur stood up. Marv had made his first mistake before he ever opened his mouth. He had physically recoiled when the defense counsel rose. His body English would have been exactly the same if a giant cobra had slithered across the floor toward him. Of course, he telegraphed instantly to Fishbein that he was on one side and not the kind of impartial expert judges like to see.

I, on the other hand, simply looked calmly at the defense counsel as he walked toward me. I did not glance away, take nervous sips of water, or shift in my seat. I had on my most helpful, I'm-just-here-to-provide-information-and-I'll-be-happy-to-answer-your-questions face.

I knew there were only three ways to attack an expert witness. He could attack my impartiality, he could attack my competence, or he could attack the information on which my opinion was based. In order to do either of those three he was likely to play twenty questions—try to suck me in with seemingly innocuous questions that, if you answered them the obvious and easy way, would lead you straight to the edge of a cliff with no slow way down. White had torpedoed Marv on his impartiality and his competence, using twenty questions in the process. He wouldn't try anything different with me: It would just be a variation.

"Dr. Stone, do you share Dr. Gleason's concern about child advocacy?" Well-phrased. He made it hard to say anything but yes. Wouldn't anybody in my field be at least concerned about child advocacy?

I looked puzzled. "I'm not sure what you mean by the term 'advocacy,' sir, or what Dr. Gleason meant by his answer. If you mean by 'advocate' someone who believes that all children tell the truth and that false reports never occur, the answer is 'no.' If you mean by 'advocate' someone who is concerned about justice for that percentage of children who really are sexually abused, the answer is 'yes.'"

I was ready for the rest of his attack on Marv. "There's nothing in my definition of advocate, sir, that would cause me to ignore the facts. Indeed, whether the child is sexually abused or not is the most crucial issue and determines what I advocate for." But I never got to say it. Defense counsel dropped the rest of his advocacy line. It is a strange profession where you know how well you are doing by the questions you don't get asked.

"Dr. Stone, do you believe Dr. Gleason is a competent clinician?" Interesting. Where was he going with this?

"Yes, indeed."

"And do you have any reason to disagree with his statement that children love their parents?"

"I'm sorry, sir." I looked a little embarrassed. "Again, I'm not sure what you mean. Do you mean do I hold exactly the same opinion as he did, or do I think he has a right to hold his opinion?"

"Let me be clear, Dr. Stone. Do young children love their parents?"

"It depends."

"This is a simple yes or no question, Doctor."

"I'm under oath to be truthful, and I can't truthfully answer that question with just 'yes' or 'no.'"

"Your Honor, this witness is not being responsive to the question."

"That's not clear, Mr. White. If the witness can't answer it with yes or no, you have to give her a chance to be responsive to your question."

He had no choice. "Depends on what?" he said.

"On the circumstances. Most children love their parents and have a very strong bond with them. Some traumatized children, however, do not love their parents. It depends."

"Does Andrew love his mother?"

"Andrew loves both his parents."

"Just answer the question, Doctor."

"I believe I did."

"Would a child who loves his mother as much as Andrew does want to please her?"

"Yes and no."

"Your Honor, surely this is a simply yes and no question. The witness is unresponsive."

Arthur rose. "This witness is being responsive, Your Honor. If the defense will give her a chance to explain her answer, he will find that she is answering the question. Mr. White just doesn't like the answers he's getting. What Mr. White is doing is trying to pressure the witness into partial, incomplete, and inaccurate answers and—given that he's failing on his own—he wants the court to assist him."

I wasn't sure why he came to my defense. I didn't think I was doing that badly. In general, I don't like lawyers to defend me in court. I take it as a sign they don't trust me to handle things on my own. It seemed to me Arthur got his signals crossed. Marv was the one who needed help, not me, and Sharon's lawyer was the only one who had jumped in on that one. Maybe Arthur thought Marv was so hopeless there was nothing to save, but it still annoyed me that he thought I needed saving.

"It has not been demonstrated yet, Mr. White, that the witness is not answering the question," Fishbein said. "I would like to hear her complete her answer."

"Certainly children who love their parents want to please them some of the time. But as every parent knows, they frequently do things they know very well will not please their parents."

"Is it possible, Dr. Stone, that Andrew knew that not seeing his father would please his mother?"

"Anything's possible, Mr. White. It's possible that Elvis is still alive."

"Oh, come now, Dr. Stone. Don't you think the probabilities are higher that Andrew was trying to please his mother than that Elvis is still alive?"

This time it was my turn to pause for dramatic effect. "I don't know, sir. I don't know very much about the probabilities that Elvis is still alive." The bailiff laughed. I took a sip of water. I had to get that "gotcha" look out of my eye. When I looked up again, the twinkle was gone and I was once more earnest and slightly apologetic. I glanced at Fishbein. He was still looking at his notes, but I saw something playing at the corners of his mouth.

The defense switched tactics again. "Dr. Stone. Isn't it true that children are highly suggestible?"

"No, the truth is more complex than that. They're suggestible about some kinds of information — far less so about other kinds. They are fairly suggestible, for example, about what someone was wearing, but far less suggestible about what they did. For example, a child would not be a particularly good witness about what color tie a molester had on, but would remember the details of the assault itself."

"Are you familiar with the work of Sauci?"

"Yes, I am."

"Did he not demonstrate on *Eye to Eye* that children could be easily led into false reports of abuse?"

"I tend to get my information from the scientific literature, sir, and not TV programs. And that program is a good example of why. If you actually read the studies he was describing so cavalierly on TV, you discover that one of them only had a sample size of four. His claims make good media, but poor science."

So go the risks of not fully deposing the other side's witness. White could have asked me these questions in the deposition and known not to ask them in court, but he didn't want to tip his hand. Ambushes, however, can work both ways.

He walked back to his table. "A moment, Your Honor." He shuffled some papers and thought about it. I knew what he had to decide. He couldn't pull off an early knockout. He could either pull up short, cut his losses, and hope he could rebut me with opposing experts. Or he could hammer me for two days and hope I'd cave in, get pissy with him, or do something stupid.

I didn't have a clue which way it would go. It depended on a lot of things: how much time he had allotted to this case, how much money he thought his client had, what other cases were pressing, whether he was just naturally stubborn, and, in no small degree, on whether he thought it would work. If he kept me on for two days and didn't get anything out of it, it would be a disaster for him.

He stopped shuffling the papers and walked toward me. He stood directly in front of me, folded his arms, tilted his head slightly, and looked at me for a moment. I put my palms together, fingertips under my chin, raised my eyebrows in a question, and tried to look benign. I considered trying to look worried, but decided it was probably too late to switch, so I just held the question. It's not good to do anything impulsive in court. Better to hold your ground than get caught between things.

White smiled, nodded slightly at me, too slightly for anyone not looking very closely to see, and turned to walk away. "No further questions," he said.

Suddenly I was free to go. Damn. I wanted to keep going. It is always the same these days. I'm either on for ten minutes or two days. And each and every time I have to get ready for two days, which often leaves me with enough adrenaline left over to throw in a marathon or two. It would take me all day to come down from this.

I had started out the day desperate for this whole sad business to be over, but now I felt as if they threw me out of the ring before I finished warming up. I wanted to climb back in and dance around again, maybe throw a few more punches. I wanted to break a few more tackles. I wanted to play a little more one on one. Court testimony, like they said, was the only contact sport in the social sciences, and I had always liked contact sports.

I spent the next two days listening to experts for the defense. Tom Gaines, Sharon's lawyer, had asked me to sit in and serve as a rebuttal witness. It was typical of this whole nutty matter that Tom wouldn't have dreamed of putting me on as his witness but wanted me to rebut Nathan's—although I understood the logic. Tom had wanted to distance his client as much as possible from the charges of child sexual abuse, which, he was contending, his client had nothing to do with and did not even support.

On the other hand, the defense witnesses had to blame somebody for the reports of abuse. Odds were, they would blame mom, and Tom would need to defend her. It would be hard to blame me: I had documented my interviews too carefully for anyone to claim they were leading and suggestive. Mothers, of course, didn't tape their conversations with their children, so they were easier targets for such claims. Tom wanted a little help from me in countering what he anticipated would be an attack on Sharon.

It was a long two days. The "experts" hammered into Fishbein's head the notion that young children are too unreliable to be believed about anything. After all, they believe in Santa Claus and the tooth fairy. I wanted to shout, "This is stupid. Santa Claus is a cultural lie. We dress men up in red suits and have children sit on their laps. How is a child supposed to know the guy in the beard with the red suit isn't named Santa Claus if everybody says he is? The point is there really is a man in a red suit." But I didn't.

Sharon looked a whole lot closer to getting up than me. Even from behind, I could tell she was deteriorating with every new witness. She was starting to move restlessly almost in an agitated manner. Frequently, she leaned over to whisper to Tom. Several times I saw Tom put his hand on her arm and quietly pat it while he answered her.

Nathan's body English, on the other hand, looked increasingly confident—and well it should. The zeitgeist was on his side, I knew. The backlash had already won the fight for public opinion. And there are always "experts" ready to provide the intellectual scaffolding for whatever people want to hear. What was that "disease" doctors discovered before the Civil War? "Drapetomania," I think—defined as "the propensity of slaves to run away."

The witnesses droned on. There had to be independent corroboration, they warned, to be sure a report of abuse was valid. And their notion of independent corroboration didn't include another child's report. They wanted "hard" evidence, such as photographs or videotapes. Without such corroboration, they claimed, there was no way to know if the child was simply saying what her favorite parent wanted to hear.

Oh sure. Most children think their parents would be delighted to hear the other parent sexually abused them. Besides, it is a convenient theory. Few sex offenders photograph the abuse, so there won't be a whole lot of convictions if corroboration are required in every case. But despite the fact that it

would be open season on children if corroboration was required, the experts sounded good and looked good, and it
wasn't 1860 anyway, so we weren't going to end up with a
perfect story.

The last expert to testify for the defense was a psychologist
named Jamison. He usually comes up to bat last. He is a
cleanup hitter, and it is his job to bring in the runners. They
definitely had several on base.

Jamison is a bulky man who wears a crisp white suit, and he
walks with a cane and a slight limp. That limp always seems to
get worse on his way to the stand. I can never figure the suit
out. Tennessee Williams? *Casablanca?* He sits down slowly,
almost majestically, and he seems to fill the entire witness box.
It isn't just his size. He has an air of pomposity about him that
makes me crazy. Hot air can take up a lot of space.

Jamison has testified in over five hundred cases—or at least
so he said—and in not one of them has he found the child's
word to be credible. Of course not. He is always hired by the
other side, and miraculously, he always seems to agree with
whoever hired him. What am I doing in a profession that has
more prostitutes than Vegas?

"Dr. Jamison, could you list your publications for the court?"

He did. He didn't mention, however, they were published in
his own newsletter. I silently visualized duct tape over my
mouth.

"Have you reviewed all the depositions and available records
in this case?"

"I have."

Sure he had—at $350 an hour. And rumor was, he took his
time reading them.

"Do you have an opinion regarding the likelihood that Dr.
Southworth has sexually molested his child?"

"I do."

"And what is that opinion?"

"This is a classic case, a textbook case of the Spousal

Rejection Syndrome. No doubt little Andrew and Adrienne believe they have been abused, but there is no evidence to support it. Children who have this syndrome are not lying, they are genuinely confused." I doubled the duct tape. You just cannot stand up and start yelling in a courtroom.

Jamison's bald-faced assertion that the kids hadn't been sexually abused would never have flown in criminal court. In criminal court, only the jury gets to say if the child has been abused by the defendant. It is the "ultimate issue," and nobody other than the jury gets to comment on it directly. But even in criminal court, Jamison's testimony would have come down to the same thing. He would have said the interviews were leading and suggestive and couldn't be trusted. He would have implied and the jury would have correctly inferred that he didn't believe the kids had been abused.

"Hysterical and malevolent mothers—and it's quite clear in this case that the children's mother is a very ill woman—often speak so bitterly about the children's father that they convince the children that they were abused even when they weren't. We call it a folie à deux."

What? A folie à deux? A shared delusional system? Now he's saying that the children are psychotic. And the son-of-a-bitch has never even met them. Not to mention that he says kids are wrong in every case in which he testifies. Must be one hell of a lot of folie à deux out there.

Duct tape wouldn't do it. I imagined a glass wall between me and Jamison, of the kind they put around Eichmann when he was on trial. Bulletproof, antiaircraft-missile-proof. There was no point in throwing my little body at him. I couldn't get to him if I tried. Thinking that reduced the temptation somewhat.

Jamison shook his head sadly. "Mothers like this have a disastrous effect on their children's development—disastrous. Custody must be transferred to the father at once—immediately!—and visitation strictly supervised. It is not too much to say"—he lowered his voice—"that the children's very lives depend on the court understanding the seriousness of the risk they face."

I looked at Sharon. She was sitting stiffly, perfectly upright. Her body looked sort of frozen. Tom had his hand on her arm.

Close doesn't count. I didn't leap for Jamison's throat. But I'm not sure I wouldn't have a better chance with St. Peter someday if I had.

The parade of character witnesses came next. Nathan was an outstanding surgeon, they said. He was polite, articulate, responsible, empathic. He could never have abused his children. He wasn't that sort of person.

I have never understood that business. The defense can put on fifty people to say that this is not the kind of man who would do that kind of thing. On the other hand, I have been in cases before where there are five adults who had been molested as children by a particular upstanding citizen, and they were waiting in the wings to testify. They were never allowed to. It would be prejudicial, courts ruled. It might make the jury think he was the kind of man who might do that kind of thing.

Finally, the defense put on Nathan Southworth, surgeon, father of Adrienne and Andrew, and accused child molester. I made myself stay. I made a practice of studying child molesters. I watched how they acted, how they spoke.

Southworth walked to the stand. He is tall with short, dark hair. The Surgery department at Jefferson Memorial has far more control of its residents than does any other specialty. The hair is shorter, the clothes more conservative than anywhere else in the hospital. The atmosphere in Surgery is sort of a cross between IBM, the military, and a good Southern football team. I had a very bad feeling this style would appeal to Fishbein more than Sharon's upscale hippy image.

Nathan wore the expected dark suit, but looking at it I had the feeling it wasn't top of the line in his wardrobe. Lawyers always advise their clients on how to dress. They would know that one of his enemies in this case would be envy. Judges aren't as sensitive about money as juries are, but even judges think surgeons make too much money, which, of course, they do, but the lawyers wouldn't want to remind anybody of that fact.

Nathan sat down and looked directly at the judge—no gaze aversion, no nervous tics. The problem with court, I knew, is that one of its basic premises is flawed. Juries and judges are supposed to be able to figure out who is lying. People who lie aren't supposed to be able to look you in the eye. People who lie should be nervous and fidgety, maybe even have nervous tics.

No doubt that is true of naive liars—people who are new to lying and don't feel that good about it. But it doesn't work at all with most sex offenders. Sex offenders have worked at fooling people for too many years, and they are too good at it.

Victims, on the other hand, are usually nervous and afraid—afraid they won't be believed, afraid the offender will attack them in court, afraid he'll retaliate later. They avert their gaze and have nervous tics.

Nathan's lawyer, White, took him through his relationship with Sharon and the strain residency had placed on it. Southworth was critical of himself and generous with Sharon. I groaned silently. It was the most effective way he could discredit her. "It was tough on Sharon. I was never there. She's right about that. But I couldn't understand why she thought I wasn't working. She seemed to believe that nobody could work that much, and she became obsessed with figuring out where I really was."

I knew, sooner or later, White would ask him about the day Sharon told me about. "That was probably the most embarrassing day of my life. I hadn't told anyone at work about the problems we were having. Sharon called frequently, so I'm sure the secretaries knew something was up, but I just never commented on it.

"I was doing a thoracotomy. Well, I was assisting Dr. Crookshank, who was the attending in charge, when a nurse burst into the operating room. I was so startled I almost dropped an instrument. I don't know what I thought was going on, but what she said was probably the last thing I expected. She said that my wife was in the waiting room demanding to see me and screaming that they were lying to protect me and what should they do?

"Crookshank looked at me for a moment, then said that if my profession was too much of a burden on my private life, then maybe I should make some changes or he would. Then he told me to go out there and take care of the problem.

"I bolted. I didn't want to hear any more. I headed for the waiting room. I didn't even change. I'm sure I didn't handle things well. I was mortified, I was furious, and I was afraid my career was over. Sharon was really upset and screaming, and I wasn't far behind. I just kept yelling at her to get out. Well, you can imagine the looks on the faces of the people in the waiting room. The whole scene was quite fantastic. I had nightmares about it for months, and every time I did an operation after that, I'd keep surreptitiously glancing at the door waiting for someone to burst in." Nathan looked down as though the memory still embarrassed him.

Judge Fishbein was leaning forward, listening attentively. He was so absorbed he had even stopped taking notes. Of course. What busy professional man wouldn't empathize with another busy professional man about a crazy, out-of-control wife?

Judges rarely identify with career criminals. The lifestyle of criminals—the job instability, street drugs, their lack of education and ambition, the lack of responsibility or concern for others—all of it seems foreign and reprehensible to judges. But the man in front of this judge was well educated, articulate, responsible, highly skilled, and seemingly concerned about others—even his crazy ex-wife. He wasn't anybody's idea of a sex offender.

"I couldn't believe it when I heard she was claiming that I sexually abused our children." Southworth's voice broke. "Some of the things she had accused me of before, well . . .

seemed strange to me . . . but I knew she was under a lot of stress. But I would never have believed that she would involve our children."

Son of a bitch. I shook my head. I had interviewed Nathan Southworth when I assessed the children to get his side of the story. He knew Sharon didn't believe he molested the kids. He had admitted to me—while denying his guilt—that, wherever the accusations came from, they hadn't come from Sharon.

But that, of course, was before the legal team figured out their strategy. Nothing, but nothing, plays better in a child sexual abuse case than "coaching." So now he was devastated when Sharon "involved the children" by "coaching" a false report.

Judge Fishbein announced that court was recessed for one hour and that he would render his decision when court reconvened at four o'clock. No other judge would have done it that way. Cases in other judges' courts languish for months before a decision comes out. But Fishbein liked to dispose of a case on the day it was concluded.

Sometimes he got it right. When he did, being in his court was a glorious experience. Cases were tried promptly. There were no delays. Decisions were rendered instantly. Long-winded lawyers were warned. If they persisted, they were told to sit down. If a case was just meandering along, Fishbein demanded a written summary of what every witness would say and refused to hear half of them. He told lawyers how much time he would allot for them to present their case, and by God, he made them live within his limits.

On the other hand, he didn't always get it right. And when he was wrong, he had the same degree of stubborn, arbitrary high-handedness that he did when he got it right. I didn't have a good feeling about Fishbein and this case. From his point of view there was nothing, absolutely nothing, about Nathan that said "sex offender," and I had a feeling he didn't take what kids said all that seriously. It would have taken a thoughtful judge, a careful judge to see behind the obvious. There was more to this case than a crazy mom, a "normal" dad, and a bitter custody fight, but that's what it looked like at first glance, and Fishbein rarely took a second. Justice was swift in Fishbein's court, but not always sure.

It was a long hour. The folks involved in the case wandered the halls—an hour was too short to go anywhere—but nobody said much. Promptly at four, the clerk walked in and said, "All rise." Fishbein walked through the door, sat down, straightened out his robes, and looked directly at Sharon.

I didn't think it was a good sign, and it wasn't. I expected trouble, but the decision was worse, far worse, than anything I had imagined. I shut my eyes while Fishbein read it. It didn't help. I knew Sharon wasn't going to get sole custody—Nathan was likely all along to get the kids fifty percent of the time. But who would have thought Fishbein would actually take the children away from Sharon and give them to Nathan full-time? He gave Sharon only a few hours of visitation a week.

It was all over in a few minutes. I gathered up my things to leave. I decided to move slowly toward the exit to avoid riding down with the folks who had just been in court; I just couldn't talk about the case anymore.

Arthur was holding Sharon and walking her out. She was crying and looked confused. It was painful to see. I reached out and touched her shoulder as she went by. She didn't look up. I don't think she even felt it.

As luck would have it, I didn't wait out everybody. I came up to the elevator just as Nathan Southworth was emerging from the rest room. We stepped on the elevator together, just the two of us, and the ride was silent and awkward. Just before the doors opened, without looking at me, Nathan spoke. His voice had a flat sound to it, curiously devoid of all the warmth it had had in court. "This behavior isn't immoral, you know," he said. "It's just illegal." Then he stepped out.

7

. . . .

I drove home, glad no one was with me. I hated being polite when I didn't feel like it, and I didn't feel like it. Outside, the green Vermont hills rolled by, plus old farmhouses and dairy signs. No billboards, just discreet exit signs. Food this way. Gas that. Contra dancing over here. Vermont is full of contra dancers—droopies from the sixties, a friend calls them. And they are fiercely environmentally correct. The bright sunshine mocked my mood, reminding me one more time that nature— whom I have a few issues with—doesn't care whether you win or lose, or live or die for that matter.

I, on the other hand, hated losing. Maybe I got that from Mama. I surely didn't get it from Daddy. He pretty much stuck with the bottle. Beyond that, nothing mattered all that much.

I turned in the driveway leading to the large Victorian house where I have my private practice office and where I used to live. For a few years I shared it with Carlotta—after my marriage dissolved—and kept a home office there. Carlotta is a "touchstone" friend, one of those people you are friends with before you marry and after you divorce. I am prone to buddies anyway, male or female; it seems easy to me to be like a ten-year-old chum. I'm not sure I know that much about being anything else.

Last year I quietly moved my residence out of the house. Most people I know didn't realize I had moved to an isolated house in the country. Carlotta still lived in the town house, and this afternoon she was out back on the deck. She looked closely at me when I stepped up. "You lost," she said quietly and turned back to the grill.

"God wasted that frame on you." I slumped in the chair and looked up at Carlotta's six feet. It was what I always said when I wanted to put off talking about something. And I was right. Unbelievable that God had put six feet on a woman who had never held a basketball in her manicured hands. "Do you know what I could have done with that frame?"

"Sure," Carlotta said. "Same thing you do with yours. Get it beat to a pulp every week by men who bleed from the eyes when they see any kind of ball." In fact Carlotta had done something a lot smarter with it. She had modeled. "The absolutely most stupefyingly boring job I have ever had," she called it. "I could feel the synapses getting wider at every sitting." She had saved all her pennies and gone to law school on the proceeds. The synapses, evidently, hadn't gotten all that wide.

She handed me a glass of ice tea. Her perfectly painted nails were bright red at the base and slowly changed color until they had bright coral tips. I glanced at them. "Is that the latest?" I asked.

Carlotta said nothing. We both know I get irritable when I lose. With Carlotta my bitching always takes the same turn. My entire childhood can be described as "female-jock-tomboy-battles-stupid-Southern-lady-shit," and it has left me with permanent hives whenever I get around things I think of as superfeminine. I was not going to comment on Carlotta's powder blue silk blazer—or the white silk blouse. I absolutely was not. The jeans at least were normal people's clothing.

My childhood wasn't all of it. There was the small question of politics as well. Twenty years ago—in my radical feminist phase—I had read articles on "studied ugliness," taken karate, and debated whether women should read books written by men. Fortunately I decided women could—which was a good thing because graduate school would have been a whole lot tougher, otherwise. Despite all of it—my childhood phobia about "frilly things," my radical phase—I had stayed best friends with the fashion model—who was buying silk blouses and taking Zen courses in flower arrangement at the time I was punching out imaginary muggers.

We are in our forties now, and both of us have mellowed. I wear suits and heels to court. If I still can't make my peace with makeup, I am glad I look all right without it, and I don't mind my long, blond, curly hair at all.

Carlotta became a feminist lawyer who works long and hard for abused children and battered spouses. In my opinion we are both on the side of the angels now—I hadn't thought much of modeling in my radical days. Still, the differences are there, and Carlotta's obsession with the feminine trappings irritates the hell out of me.

"Having company over?" I couldn't leave the blazer alone.

"Jack called," Carlotta said. Jack, in Carlotta's opinion, is a more worthy object of wrath than she is.

"That makes my day. Just don't tell me he's filing for divorce."

"Michael," Carlotta said carefully. "This thing you have for married men . . ."

"Married men have much to recommend them," I replied absently, laying my head on the back of the chair and closing my eyes.

"Name one," said Carlotta.

"Girl, they're the only truly predictable people on earth," I retorted.

"I know plenty of single men who can't commit," Carlotta responded.

"Naw," I said. "You never know. Single men might want to play with real money."

The silence of friends fell. I sipped my tea. Despite my harassing of Carlotta, she is rarely critical of me, and it made me uneasy that she had a thing about my thing for married men. I knew why she dropped it; she knew where my preference came from, and who knew what to say about that?

Carlotta finished grilling the salmon and served it. "You didn't really think you could win, did you?" I never talk about my cases, but this one was all over the papers. "Let's see. Respected thoracic surgeon. First grader and his three-year-old sister disclose sexual abuse. Not a fair match to start with. Then it turns out mom is truly, certifiably paranoid."

"Truly."

"Paper says she was so convinced her husband was having an affair she got a hold of his patient list and called all of the women on it trying to find out who it was."

"She did." This had come out in Nathan Southworth's testimony.

"How could it get worse?"

"Pit-bull defense lawyer—the kind you want to test for rabies."

"That good?"

"Good enough. He was very careful with me. He cut his losses early and bailed out. I think he had me on for maybe ten minutes. I was hoping he'd take a chance and go for it, but he didn't.

"You want to know the kicker? It's a matter of court record now so I can tell you. Mom is so paranoid she doesn't believe the children, either. She thinks dad engineered a false report from the kids to discredit her. She thinks the whole thing is a plot by him. She's furious at me for testifying I thought the disclosure was valid. Arthur was the GAL. He did a good job, but it meant absolutely nothing. Get this. He did the direct on me, and both sides attacked me on cross."

"Jesus." Carlotta shook her head. "But I don't get it. How did it even become an issue if mom didn't believe the kids?"

"The kids didn't disclose to mom. The first-grader told his teacher. The teacher reported it to Child Protection, which, of course, reported it to Arthur as the GAL, who, of course — since he's responsible for the children — asked for an evaluation."

I rubbed my eyes. They were itching. It always happens when I lose. I hate losing worse than I hate frilly things. Maybe I have an actual allergy to losing. "I gotta get out of this business. I think I'll sell hot dogs for a living. I haven't told you the worst. It was an unbelievable decision. Mom lost big time. The judge not only denied her motion for sole custody. He gave sole custody to her ex."

"What?"

"They brought in Jamison. He testified mom was psychologically unfit. Charged her with coaching a false report."

"Jamison always says that."

"Yeah, well this time he hooked a live one. Fishbein bought it."

"When is the transfer?"

"Right away. Mom had an hour to pack. Kids are gone by now. Don't ask me why. Maybe Fishbein was afraid mom would run and didn't want to give her a head start.

"You wouldn't have believed how bad Sharon Southworth looked. She looked literally like someone who had just had a stroke, or at the least, a heart attack" — which, I suppose, wasn't that far off the mark.

Carlotta fell silent, but her face had lost its usual composure. I looked away and studied the living room through the French doors. I don't know how Carlotta lives like this. She has too many "things," for my Spartan tastes. Antiques, prints, rugs, sculptures, everything is immaculately neat, and there are always fresh flowers on the table. And Carlotta always looks like she is dressed for a photo spread. Yet, even when I lived in the same house with her, I never caught her working at it.

"Carlotta, why are we friends?"

"That's easy. Who else am I going to be friends with? You're the only woman I know who doesn't want anything I have."

She said it facetiously—Carlotta doesn't have an arrogant bone in her body—but in a funny way, it is true enough.

I felt better the moment I stepped into my tiny A-frame. I didn't bother to turn on the lights. There wasn't all that much there to bump into. I got something to drink and headed for the deck. The small stream below the deck glistened in the moonlight. Shiny water. I always did love shiny water. Mama never knew how much time I spent swimming alone at night as a teenager. Swam just to see that shiny water drip off my arms and fall, drop by drop, into the smooth black pool erasing the rest of me. Besides, at night the water was almost always glassy, and my fingers would cut it like a knife.

It was mesmerizing, swimming at night. Never could find anyone at home to swim with me, though. They were always afraid of snakes. I tried to tell them: I almost never ran into a snake in the water at night. Even if I did, I felt I had as much right to be there as the snake. No point in telling them that; they wouldn't have appreciated my point of view.

Of course, if I had been the parent, I'd probably have seen it differently. I put the glass down and got up. I didn't want to get into that tonight. I had enough on my plate already.

I walked back into the house, trying to leave the ghosts on the deck. I looked around at the hardwood floors, the blond wood sofa with the white textured cushions, the small but thick and richly colored orientals, the colorful throws—it was all somehow right, and best of all, there wasn't too much of it. I hadn't liked owning things since the baby died. Two hundred and fifty. That is my limit. I never own more than two hundred and fifty things.

It became a game over time. Seventy-five objects in the kitchen. Twenty in the living room. Forty in the bathroom. Seventy-five articles of clothing and personal stuff; forty for the rest of the house. I got to the point I shuddered when I saw single-purpose items. Who needs a waffle iron when you can make pancakes in a frying pan? It became a hobby, sort of.

Like my clothes. I threw out the iron because I was getting too close to my limit, but that meant I couldn't buy clothes that needed ironing, and that turned out great. I threw out all the clothes that did need ironing, and that gave me room for computer equipment. Now I only buy clothes you can ball up in your suitcase, travel to Rome, and shake them out. Of course you have to be willing to listen to the radio to live with a limit, and use the library. Books and CDs. You could use the whole two hundred and fifty just on those.

The upstairs loft had room for only a bed, wardrobe, and rocker. The bed is placed under two skylights on either side of the A-frame peak. I sat cross-legged in the middle and tried to meditate. Nothing happened. Or, too much, maybe; the wires in my brain hummed. My mind felt like the Internet. The day replayed, bits and pieces surfacing like driftwood floating down the river.

Jamison. Fat man in a white suit. A cross between Colonel Sanders and Santa Claus. I have no idea why any judge or jury ever believes him. You would think that testifying for over five hundred alleged sex offenders without finding a single child credible would be a clue. But there he was, spouting off about his five hundred trials to establish himself as an expert, and he got asked, as he does every single time on cross, "And in how many cases did you find the child had been abused by the defendant?" and he says, "None," and nobody thinks that's a problem?

No doubt the booming voice counts and the air of certainty, not to mention the extraordinary number of research studies he cites with absolute confidence — small matter he's wrong about half of them. When you point that out, you sound like an academic nit-picker.

Once I complained privately to a judge that I had been under the impression before meeting up with Jamison that one had to tell the truth in court. She had laughed and said, "Silly you."

But I did. I thought if you lied in the witness box you didn't get your juice and cookies. I thought God came down, pulled you out of the witness box, and sent you straight to hell. I thought you stepped outside and got hit by a bus. But I have been in several trials with Jamison now, and no divine hand has appeared.

In my bitter, vindictive little soul, I still hope there is a special place in hell for those who send small children back to sex offenders for the money the experts made from it, but there probably isn't. Jamison will live a long and happy life, and we'll both be reincarnated as houseflies.

I used to think—when I first started going to court—that court had something to do with justice. What a crock! After a while I began to think of court as theater. That explains Jamison. Jamison makes no sense if you think court has to do with justice, but—bless his despicable little soul—Jamison is a great actor, and great actors always have a place in the theater.

Later, I realized I had changed again. I no longer thought it mattered what really happened in the case. The only thing that matters in court was what you get into evidence. Leave enough pieces out and you make a totally different puzzle.

These days my opinion has dropped another notch. Justice is for sale every day in American courtrooms. Rich people have better lawyers. And better lawyers, like better b-ball teams, usually win. The truth is, if it were me on trial, I'd rather have the better lawyer than be innocent.

I woke thinking I should get on a plane and head straight for the North Carolina outer banks. It wasn't an idle thought. I keep a bag packed in the car, and I've been known to catch a six-thirty morning flight and call my secretary from the road. I felt beaten to a pulp by the loss in court, and I like to move around when I feel like that. Probably I would have gone if it hadn't been a client day. Looking back, I wish I had.

I felt like the car drove itself back and forth to the office. I just kept my hands on the wheel for appearances' sake. So I was totally off in another world when the car phone rang. This was not good. Only a couple of people had my car phone number, and it never rang.

It was Carlotta. "Where are you?" she said.

"Down by Zuckerman's Farm," I said. "What's wrong?" I didn't like the sound of her voice or the abrupt question.

"Stop the car," she said. "Turn around. You're heading into an army of reporters."

"What? What for?"

"Do it now, and then we'll talk."

I turned the car around. "Carlotta, you're scaring me."

"Do you see a side road? What about that one south of the dog kennels?"

I didn't say anything. Panic was beginning to rise. Something very bad had happened. Something that interested reporters. But what? Jesus, you don't think Sharon had killed herself?

I pulled into the side road and stopped the car. "What is it?" My hands were shaking. I couldn't figure out whether to keep them on the wheel or hold them together. Somehow I needed a place for them.

This time she paused. I had no clue what was coming. The truth wasn't even on the list of possible disasters that were racing through my head.

"It's the Southworth case," she said. "The kids are dead. They were murdered."

"What?" I said, unable to take it in.

"There's more. Sharon is under arrest."

This was too much. It wasn't possible. "Sharon? . . . *Sharon?* For the murders? Why?" I said. "She couldn't possibly . . ."

"I don't know all of it, but they were at dad's, and they disappeared from the yard, and they were found back at Sharon's house, laid out in their own beds. No forcible entry. Looks like they were strangled. Maybe suffocated."

"What did Sharon say?" My hands had found my mouth, and I had to move them to talk. My chest had suddenly gotten very hollow, and I was breathing funny.

"Nothing. Reports say when the police came for her she was wandering around the house disoriented. Except one thing. She's blaming you."

The car got me home somehow. I had the presence of mind to notice no other cars had arrived—the reporters hadn't yet figured out where I really live—before stumbling from the car and heading for the stream. The rocks, the stream, everything had a strange luminescent clarity. I could see tiny details on the stream bed distinctly; the colors of everything were exquisite. It felt as if I had been smoking something.

I sat down on a rock. Dead children. Brought it all back up. She was three months old, and it was my first day back at work. I had brought her to the day care, but was having a hard time with the separation. We had been living in a twilight world of breast milk and rocking chairs where my only goal in life was to find the perfect diaper rash medication.

Doug threw a fit about having her in bed with us, so I pulled her cradle up right next to it and slept with my hand through the slats. Doug had wanted a baby — at least he said he did — but he'd spent the first few months acting, maybe feeling, like a third wheel. He'd been busy teaching at the university, anyway. Maybe his workaholism was part of the problem; maybe it wasn't. At this point it was hard to remember when the marriage started losing air speed.

I had no clue I'd be the kind of mother I was. I thought I'd drop Jordan off at the day care a few days after birth and head back to work. Fat chance. A few days after the birth I was totally absorbed. It was something like California instant intimacy only for real. Hell of a job, mothering. It was like some kind of tunnel I had entered. If everything had gone right, I'd probably have surfaced for air a few years later and picked up a newspaper to catch up with the world. Unfortunately, it didn't work out like that; I more or less got caught in the tunnel.

I had always just assumed I'd want to go back to work, but that first day, I was fairly miserable. I was thinking that maybe what I really wanted was to just stay home with Jordan, when the hospital called to say she was dying. Just like that. Of course, she wasn't. She was already dead, but nobody tells you that on the phone.

But there it was. One moment you're living a normal life, and the next moment you've in the twilight zone. I don't remember the drive there, and I don't remember screaming at the doctors, but I guess I did. I do remember hearing "SIDS," but I couldn't seem to follow what the doctor was saying. Since that day, I've understood what aphasia is. People say words, and you can hear the words, but you can't figure out what they mean.

I know somewhere in there I tried to call Carlotta, but I couldn't remember her number. I picked up a phone book off a desk and tried to look it up under "C" for "Carlotta," rather than "Y" for "Young," but I couldn't remember alphabetical order. By the time I finally found the "C"s, I forgot whom I was looking up. I remember a nurse quietly taking the phone book out of my hand.

The rest isn't fuzzy; it's just gone. Was Doug there? To this day I don't know. I have spots of memory like flashbulb shots. I remember exactly where everyone was standing when I looked around trying to find my daughter, caught exactly the look on their faces, but I don't have anything else until I was in the room with her.

I remember seeing her. That's when I really lost touch with reality. She just looked asleep, and I became convinced she was alive and they had simply made a big mistake. I remember arguing with the nurses about it. I remember hearing the sound of keening, which, it turned out, I was making. After that, I don't remember much of the next few days.

Time got very peculiar. Minutes seemed to last for days. The seconds lost their bridges to each other, and each one reigned supreme, each had to be dragged kicking and screaming off stage. I lost my voice, too. I couldn't force it to be big enough to be heard. Great drifts of words, a friend told me later, would just trail off in space, too soft for anyone to hear. It was weeks before my voice got big enough to activate an answering machine.

The phone was ringing in the A-frame; maybe it had been for a while. I walked in and glanced down: twenty-two messages before the machine ran out of tape. I rolled my office phone over to the house when I wasn't there so everybody trying to reach me got forwarded to my home phone. "Michael," the strained voice on the line now said, "I'm so terribly, terribly sorry." I picked up the phone, for the first time tearing up.

Thank God it was Arthur. "Arthur . . ." My voice had gotten small again. "Arthur," I tried again. "This can't be true. My God, those poor babies. What happened?"

"I don't know. The police aren't being very forthcoming. I'm completely shocked by this. I suppose there just wasn't any clue?"

The slight lift of his voice at the end turned it into a question and reminded me that I was the one, not Arthur, who was supposed to spot clues of homicidal tendencies in clients. Suddenly, I felt more alone, not less, with Arthur on the other end of the line.

"I mean, even in retrospect, do you see anything that makes sense of this?"

The need to make sense of things: He'd rather we both be tragically, stupidly, fatally wrong than have the whole thing be random and unpredictable. How people hate things that make no sense. At any point in time there are a handful of serial killers roaming the country while thousands of men batter their wives, some of them to death. But whole forests have been destroyed making paper for books on serial killers, to the point where there are more books about them than there are serial killers. It isn't the probability of being a victim that makes it scary; it is the fact that it makes no sense. Violence in the home, everyone agrees, is understandable.

Arthur filled the silence. "Carlotta said to tell you half the messages on your machine are from your chairman's secretary, who called her trying to reach you. Toby wants to see you today, right away actually."

Toby's secretary confirmed in her low-key way that, indeed, Toby would like to see me right away, if that was convenient. She managed to convey without raising her voice or stating anything explicitly that a helicopter would be preferable, a car barely acceptable.

This was probably not the right time to act on my adolescent aversion to being given orders. It was even reasonable for the chair of my department to want to see me at this point in time, given that both Nathan Southworth and I worked for the hospital. Urgency was understandable. I have to talk to myself like this in order to psych myself up to comply with anything that even vaguely resembles an order.

More than once I had done things not in my best interest because I absolutely loathe being told what to do—particularly by men. I say that, but I'm not sure it's true. Maybe my problem is with men because women don't tell you what to do all that much.

I ran into the edge of the table on the way out, gouging my thigh painfully. A good reminder. It told me I was out of control and didn't know it. I got behind the wheel of my car and then just sat there, trying to ground myself. What the hell did I miss about Sharon? Her MMPI 2 suggested nothing homicidal. None of the testing did. Hysterical, yes. Depressed, yes. Anxious and even paranoid, yes. But aggressive? Hostile? Potentially lethal? No, no, and no.

So what happened? The tests had all kinds of guards against faking. Had she eluded them? But she wasn't smart enough to do that, I didn't think. Was she just naturally talented at deception? And if so, were the disclosures coached after all? But then what about Nathan's comment in the elevator? It hadn't been a total surprise to me. Sex offenders always rationalize abuse, but it was so odd to actually experience one presenting one way in court and then *immediately* dropping it. Some offenders fool themselves with their spiels; it looked like Nathan knew exactly what he was doing. I closed my eyes against the racing questions.

On the way in to the hospital I thought about the upcoming interview. Toby was not likely to be supportive. I work eighty percent in the Psychiatry Department, twenty percent in private practice. That one day a week away means, in medicine, that I am not really full-time faculty. So whatever nominal protection Toby might be inclined to provide would be minimal. Actually, it wouldn't have been much in any case. Toby is universally disliked by the people below him (that is, the entire department) and universally liked by those over him (honchos in the medical center). He likes it that way, and he knows better than anyone the price of alienating Surgery.

Internal status at the hospital is based on how much money the different departments bring in. Surgery is at the top of the heap because surgery scares the ordinary citizen so much that, as a society, we throw money at it. There is a limit to what you can charge for taking pictures of a brain; there isn't much of a limit on what you can charge for cutting into one. The surgeons themselves remind other folk frequently of the enormous contribution they make to the finances of the medical center. Despite their astronomical salaries, they complain often that, in exchange for the measly few hundred thousand they are paid a year, they bring in millions for the center, which actually is true.

And Surgery works differently than any other department. It is far more authoritarian. Surgery is a craft. You can't learn those motor skills out of a book. The right diagnosis, the right medicine in the right doses—all that can be learned from paper, all are more science than art. But surgery you have to learn by watching and by doing.

With apprenticeship comes certain apprenticeship norms. It isn't a crime to kill a patient—that can happen—as long as a resident doesn't make a habit of it. But if Dr. B wants the knots tied one way and Dr. A another way and the resident makes the mistake of tying them Dr. B's way on Dr. A's service, he or she is going to hear about it. And if the resident is ambivalent and doesn't make any decision at all when one is called for, then we are talking total staff meltdown. Right or wrong, surgeons take charge; they don't dither about. The wrong decision is understandable; no decision is unforgivable.

Still, I have a certain admiration for surgeons. Not for the technical work, which I didn't know anything about and which didn't interest me, but because they are honest professionally. They hold the X-rays up at their meetings for all to see. The screw held in the bone or it didn't. The glue stuck or loosened. The patient did or didn't get an infection. They don't make excuses and they don't whine. Maybe they aren't so honest with the outside world or with their patients, but among themselves, they don't dodge and weave.

The problem is, they aren't that great at accepting the limitations of their power. It all has to do with what happens when they back through those doors into the operating room and swing around. Once when I was prowling around trying to understand things, I talked a surgeon into letting me watch a five-hour hip replacement. There I was, freezing—if the patient dies, I guess they want be able to refrigerate the body right away—in my little green gown and my little green booties, coiffed in a green paper cap with a little green mask that mostly hid the goosebumps around my eyes.

I may have lost my identity, but the surgeon gained his. He backed through the doors, swung around, and everyone listened up. His wish became a do or die command. If he wanted a certain clamp, it was in his hand. If he spoke, people spoke back. If he didn't, there was no idle chatter coming from anywhere. Needless to say, he chose the music—classical for the attending, rock for the resident who finished up. He got to start something and finish it without interruptions; that alone put me in awe. No phone calls came in; no one interrupted.

They say surgeons operate too much—that surgeons call for surgery when medicine or exercise or even patience would do better. Some say it's because it's what they know to do; others that they do it for the money. But I know better. Surgeons operate because they are addicted to it, because nowhere else in the world are they treated the way they are in an operating room. That's why this country has all those unnecessary hysterectomies. Unfortunately, they keep trying to reproduce that little bit of magic elsewhere.

So by now Southworth's boss, Crookshank the chief of thoracic surgery, would have been in Toby's office. Probably he had been in there before this. His golden boy, Southworth—one of the only residents ever to be invited to join the staff had been falsely accused of child sexual abuse by that hysterical wife of his, and that stupid non-M.D. female psychologist had backed her claim. But Toby would have put him off, not sure what the court would decide and how the final wind would blow. My track record was good enough that Toby would have hesitated to bet against me. But the hurricane had now hit. And Toby wouldn't be caught outside.

There were two news vans parked outside the hospital. I got a very bad feeling from them. Did Toby have a press release ready—announcing my resignation? Maybe I should take the tunnels.

Jefferson Memorial Medical Center was built in 1850—it was known as plain old Jefferson Hospital at the time. Like all the hospitals of that period, it is a rabbit warren of below-ground tunnels, above-ground add-ons and take-overs. The hospital just kept building, taking over houses that stood too close, adding on squat little brick buildings in between and wherever. You can get from here to there without ever surfacing in any public area if you know how. But knowing how takes time and commitment. The Pentagon is probably easier to navigate. I had been at Jefferson ten years, and I didn't know all the ins and outs. The morgue, for example. I still don't know where the morgue is. They don't put stuff like that on the main floor next to the gift shop. I am kind of curious, but I figure sooner or later I will run into it wandering around the tunnels trying to find

Dermatology or something. I'm not sure what else I don't know about. Probably a lot.

Most people, for example, don't know there are all sorts of special elevators and back hallways hidden away to take surgery patients to and from surgery without running into the general public. A good idea. Do you really want to be on your way to a hysterectomy and run into the electrician who's rewiring your living room?

Also, those elevators are useful in other ways. They make elevator deaths possible—those long slow rides that allow a hopelessly terminal patient to die between surgery and recovery, thus not showing up on the stats as a death in surgery (which the surgeon would not like) or as a death in recovery (which the recovery room staff would not like). Hospitals are small cities. All kinds of things happen there.

Fortunately, at least the tunnels are safe at Jefferson. At the big city hospitals the tunnels are worse than the streets. There were so many rapes at one I'd worked at that nurses weren't allowed to go down to the vending machines without a police escort.

I could have gone in the front door. I'd have to face the reporters sooner or later, but when I can't be directly aggressive, I just can't stop that passive-hostile piece of me from coming out. If Toby had set me up—incompetent forensic psychologist called in to face the music by her indignant boss, with press notified ahead of time—slipping in unseen was only a small victory, but then again, I probably wouldn't see any big ones for a while. I took the tunnels.

Diane, Toby's secretary, was nonplussed to see me standing in front of her with no sign of reporters trailing after me. She'd been there too long not to understand Toby's ways of managing crises. She looked at me appraisingly, maybe not all that hostilely. I kept my affect flat. "I'm here to see your boss." Uh-oh. "Your boss," not "my boss," not "the boss." I've played b-ball too long. I have trouble not slamming into people who slam into me or who I even think are going to slam into me. The only safe thing was to keep my mouth entirely shut. Otherwise, I'd end up with a war on another front. Fortunately, Toby made it easier to say nothing in a meeting of two than anyone I had ever met.

"Come in, come in," he said. He would not be hostile in person, not unless someone else was present.

"Well," he said, "this must be a terrible time for you. What a shock. No way to predict it, I suppose."

I said nothing.

"A difficult business. Something like this happened to me once. I had just finished telling a parent I had read the chart and the prognosis for their baby was good. The baby died an hour later, and the dad came back with a shotgun. He was on one side of the door, and I was on the other. The door only opened from my side. Never forgot it. Haven't reassured a patient since."

I wasn't sure what this story had to do with me, but I think it was supposed to establish rapport. Toby is a lot like a sex offender. He not only wants to screw you; he wants you to say you liked it.

I shook my head appreciatively.

"Of course, this is awkward for the department, and as you know, I wear different hats. I have to think not only of the well-being of individual faculty, but of what's good for the department and of what is fair and objective, too. All too easy to forget those obligations when faced with a faculty member in trouble." He shook his head at what a soft touch he was.

I nodded as though I understood.

"Well, Crookshank was in here this morning. Beside himself. I'm sure you can appreciate his dilemma. He feels terrible for Southworth. Such a tragedy. And from their point of view, such a preventable one."

I wasn't sure how. Dad had gotten all that the court could order. After all, they seemed to be forgetting that I had lost my bid to have mom get custody, although at this point even suggesting mom get custody sounded like a very bad idea. But in the end the court hadn't followed my recommendation, so clearly I had actually had nothing to do with the outcome. I brightened a little at the thought.

"We all agree how terrible it is—one member of the medical center suing another. Very bad PR." I was expecting a blow, but this still caught me by surprise. I think I suppressed the flinch. Even so, Toby got me, and he knew it. He was up by two.

He waved his hand airily. "I know what you're going to say, and I agree. Lawyers are ruining medicine. Half the tests I order these days are unnecessary, just covering my flank. But then again there has to be some recourse for people who are seriously aggrieved. Not, of course, that I'm saying that has happened here," he added, covering his flank. He was playing this very well.

I shrugged.

"In any case, painful as it is, I have to put on my departmental hat and do what anyone else in my position would have to do." His voice grew somber. "You know that I have always been one of your biggest supporters . . ." I looked straight at Toby. How many times had he screwed me over the years? Let me count the ways. He faltered and looked away; he had overplayed his hand, and we both knew it. Two all.

"In any case, in any case, the fact that you did recommend that this woman who murdered her children get custody over someone who—except for the word of two very young children—appears to be a rather stalwart and stable professional does raise certain issues. Crookshank is insisting that we set up a committee to investigate this matter. I understand Southworth will be filing formal ethics charges with the state licensing board as well. I gather he thinks, no doubt unjustly, that your assessment of Sharon was incompetent to the point of malpractice.

"Allegedly," I said.

"Allegedly?" he echoed. He paused, thought it over. "Well, yes, allegedly. Allegedly murdered her children." It hadn't occurred to him there was any question of her guilt. Unlikely as it appeared, it now occurred to him that it was conceivable she was innocent, or failing that, would get off anyway. It did put a slightly different slant on things. Whatever else he was planning to say, he didn't.

"Well, then, of course we'll have to have a psychological autopsy." The investigation of me had suddenly turned into a psychological autopsy, the equivalent of the routine morbidity and mortality conferences held in other departments at any unusual death or complications. "And we'll see how it goes." Toby's natural caution had prevailed. He wanted to make sure I was well and truly dead before he danced on my grave. I smiled and left without saying good-bye.

10

. . . .

Allegedly." It was the only word I spoke in the meeting with Toby, and I didn't know until I said it that I didn't believe mom did it. All morning, I had been poring over mom as murderer, and I couldn't see it. What did we know about women who murder their children? Well, lots and lots of them have already battered the child severely. Some of them are being battered by violent males and aren't in the best of mental health as a result. Some are psychopathic—they don't care whom they hurt; a tiny few are psychotic—the voices they hear don't care whom they hurt. Many of them, however, are just plain mean. Some think they'll find true love if they aren't weighed down by children. "Is she crazy or just plain mean?" is a reasonable question when assessing a mother who has murdered her children.

All of them—whether enmeshed with their children or disengaged—all of them had thinking errors about the children. They tended to project malevolence onto the children: The three-month-old was crying because she knew mom had a bad day. She wouldn't eat because she didn't love mom. But this mother had shown none of that. She might have pathological jealousy toward her husband, and she may have turned Andrew into a parentified child, but she never attributed malevolence to the children.

All of a sudden I needed to find out what the police had on her. I started up the car and pulled out. Where to go? I could go back to the Psychiatry Department and my office there—taking the tunnels, of course—but somehow I didn't feel like it. My private practice office was closer than my house; I'd head there. What evidence did the police have—and how could I find out? Ordinarily, I'd just call up my buddy Adam Bowman (who, most fortunately, was the police chief) and ask him. The police aren't all that careful about confidentiality anywhere, but are probably even looser in small towns. But, brassy as I am, even I knew the front door would be closed on this one. At the moment I was in the center of the maelstrom, and it was "cover your ass" time all the way around. I couldn't even call Adam without it going through the front desk at the station, and who knew who would be on?

I called Arthur instead. For a man in his early sixties, he wasn't a bad b-ball player, and he sometimes joined our weekly game. "Arthur, will you do me a favor and call Adam? Ask him if he's playing b-ball tonight. If he laughs in your face and tells you he happens to have a couple of murders to investigate, tell him the short point guard wants to know."

The pick-up games were on the third floor in the old gym. I arrived early. I like empty gyms. Besides, the older I get, the longer it takes to warm up my shot, not to mention my creaky bones. I took the basketball and felt the rough texture in my hands. I bounced it a few times. The sound of a single basketball echoing in an empty gym was the most stable rhythm of my life. I'd heard that sound for thirty years, felt the raised surface of the ball, stared at the shiny expanse of silent court. I started to warm up. I shot methodically, starting with a position right under the basket—five on the right side, five in the middle, five on the left—and repeated shooting around a semicircle, moving a few feet out each time. I finished at the top of the key. That was about it for my range.

It was a relief not to have to break into gyms anymore. When I was a kid, I broke in so many times the high school coach gave up and opened the gym in the summer, starting when I was in seventh grade. That was a lot better. For one thing, after that I didn't have to play by myself all the time. There wasn't a lot of company when the gym was locked because other kids had more sense than to play in a closed gym when the temperature outside with the breeze blowing was ninety degrees. I never knew how hot it was inside when it was all closed up.

Mama never did understand why I'd want to go shoot a ball through a hoop all day, but then again she rarely noticed I was gone. Mama has never been what you'd call "child-centered." My daddy noticed, but if it made me happy, it made Daddy happy. Carping at Daddy made Mama happy. Not being home to hear the fighting made me happy.

For his part, Daddy pretty much did the same thing I did. He had a part-time law practice, and it was only in high school that I began to realize he didn't exactly have a lot of cases; it was more an excuse to get out of the house than anything else. Thank God Grandma left him a little money so he didn't really have to work that much, or Mama would have had one more thing to complain about.

The first few players started to filter in. Pickup basketball is one of the most egalitarian institutions on earth. We have kitchen help and the college president routinely playing in the same game. We have professors and mechanics and the unemployed. There aren't many other arenas where they play on level ground. Here it isn't how much money you make or how much education you have, it is whether you can get your shot to fall or not.

Someone always showed up who was an organizer type. The big guys got divided up. Us little folk were thrown in after. I liked the looks of my team tonight. A couple of players who liked to pass the ball. A big guy who knew how to set a pick. Nobody who pouted when they lost. Nobody who thought this was World War III. And no run and gun types. There were a few unknowns on the other side.

Charlie, who I think was in Poly Sci, brought the ball up. I set a pick for him at the top of the key, then rolled for the basket. (It always amazes me how many players forget to roll when they set a pick.) He didn't need the roll. Charlie's guard ran into me hard and yelled "switch," but it was too late; Charlie was gone. One-zip. Each basket counted one point. We played to twenty-one but you had to win by two.

I could tell right away that the guy I was guarding thought he had a mismatch. He had a few inches on me, and he turned his back to the basket and started waving his arms for the ball. Someone tried to pass it in, but I knocked it away. I think he thought that was an accident. He started waving his arms again, and this time he got the ball, but he had to go pretty far out to get it. He pivoted toward me, and I was relieved to find he thought he could start his shot at the waist. Hell, I can reach his waist. I stuffed him, and he nearly went ballistic. Not everyone plays well with women.

We headed down the court. The ball went up immediately— we had at least one gunner. My man just turned and scrambled for the basket, which is not right at all. He should have waited to see which way I tried to go around him and then pivoted that way to block me out. It wasn't just that he didn't think too much of me. A well-coached ballplayer would block out a duck. I don't know what the coaching world is coming to; they just don't stress the fundamentals anymore. Ten to one my man wouldn't follow his shot, either, but would stand there watching it, bouncing his head sideways to make it go in.

I brought the ball up. He didn't press, but picked me up at the key. I held the ball for a moment and looked over the court. Joy of joy, a forward crossed under the basket and set a pick for the guy on the other side, who came around and had one shining free moment under the basket all by his lonesome. I had the ball high enough to pass and sent it over my man's shoulder, who, I was pleased to see, didn't have his hands up.

I filed the fact he was playing me dead center. Interesting. Better to overplay someone you don't know to their right since most people are right-handed and drive faster and more often to the right. I decided to go to the right next time since he wasn't favoring it and I, too, was faster that way.

I had completely forgotten about the case and about why I was there. I had even forgotten that anyone was murdered, when Adam walked in. (I can dissociate anything on a basket-ball court.) I kept on playing for a few minutes. Adam didn't look like he minded waiting, and I was in no hurry to leave the court to deal with the horrific business I had to talk to Adam about.

I hit a couple of points: once when I faked upward, caught my man in the air, went around him, and pulled up short. The second time I drove on him (to the right), faked a straight layup, and then reached under his outstretched arms for an underhanded layup. I made a bunch of thread-the-needle passes that did my little heart good. We took the first game twenty-one to seventeen, but I don't think I made a friend.

I went over to talk to Adam. He had chosen a bleacher away from where everybody had left their stuff. He was dressed to play and started putting on his shoes. He always looks good to me, even just putting on his shoes. He has one of those great tennis bodies I love so dearly. He is long and lean, and his body just hangs from his shoulders. He has good haunches. We are both divorced, both in our forties, both fond of each other. I don't know why nothing ever seemed to come of it. We'd see each other all the time when one of us was dating someone else. Somehow, if both of us were free, we managed not to run into each other for months. Every once in a while, I would block him out, feel the heat of his body against mine, and lose my concentration. We were on each other's agendas somehow, but we never seemed to get there.

"What do you have on the Southworth case?" I asked.

"You have more balls than anyone I know," he said angrily. "I can't tell you dipshit about this case."

"Oh, come on, Adam, it'll come out in disclosure anyway."

"Not to you, it won't. Not unless you're one of the defendants." Not funny given that Nathan was supposedly suing me.

"Adam, I don't think she did it. I've got her testing. I've got her interviews. I just can't find it. I need to know, just for me, if you've got enough that I have to buy it."

"You're not getting it," he said. "There are people in this town tonight who would pay a lot of money—a whole lot of money— to anyone in this gym just to confirm we were having this conversation. What are you going to do when you're on the stand and they ask you what we talked about?"

"Lie," I said.

"Lie? You're going to lie in court?"

"I'm going to say we talked about how crazed the media was and what a pain-in-the-butt. That we talked about the fact that we can't talk about the case. How you said it was amazing my shot was dropping, given the pressure, and what a jerk I was playing against." I gestured toward the court as I spoke, as though talking about some play.

"You're sure," he said.

"Adam," I said, irritated. "Between not getting any information out of you and lying in court, I am going to lie in court. I knew these kids, Adam. I can see their faces without closing my eyes. I can't stop seeing their faces when I do close my eyes. And I don't think you've got the murderer. So maybe there's a son of a bitch still out there who likes to butcher children. So maybe I'm wrong. Tell me why. We can't talk all night, or this will look suspicious. What do you have?"

The other players had gathered and were ready to go. Luckily a couple of extra folks had shown up, and I gestured to count me out.

"If you're sure," he said.

11

· ·

W hen I got home there was a note from Jack on the door and a wild rice salad with a subtle sweet-and-sour sauce from Carlotta on the table. I took the note inside to read it. "I'm thinking about you. Sorry about your nightmare case. Want to talk? I'll call when I can." I tossed the note and ate the salad. I ignored the answering machine. I hadn't played back the twenty-two messages from the morning yet so there couldn't be any new ones. The phone started ringing immediately, but I ignored that too.

It didn't make any sense psychologically for Sharon to kill her children. It wasn't even all that logical, but I could see it shaping up to be a nearly impeccable case in court. Jesus, it wouldn't take the prosecutor from hell to win this one; a third-year law student could do it. I was tired and discouraged. After the conversation with Adam on the court, someone had nailed a lid on the basket: I couldn't buy one. I never even got into the flow of the game. I finally quit because I was making a fool of myself.

A long time later I was still sitting on the deck when Carlotta walked in. My muscles had stiffened up. I was still wearing soaking wet shorts and T under my sweats. "Go sit in the hot tub," she said. I don't let anybody else tell me what to do. I don't know why I let Carlotta. I got up and walked around the corner of the deck. The deck is L-shaped with a very small section around the corner. You can see the stream from there and the sky through the overhanging trees. The L is tucked behind the one-car garage and completely invisible from the road. Because it is away from the front of the house—the glass part that faces the stream—none of the house lights reach it at all, and the tiny hot tub was bathed in moonlight.

I stripped off my stale, soggy clothes, noticing with surprise I still had on my basketball shoes, surprise because I never wear my precious basketball shoes on the street; I might wear the tread down and lose traction on the court.

I slipped into the shiny black water, tipped my head back, and looked up at the stars through the filter of the overhanging branches. I thought about all the rivers I had floated down in the dark looking up at the sky throughout my youth. I hadn't been afraid then like I was now. I just naturally thought you had to go some place other people wouldn't go, to have something of your own. I was arrogant, I suppose, in my teenage way. I believed all those folks sitting in their backyards with their barbecues didn't see the same stars I saw—stars so vivid they hurt your eyes, moonlight so bright you forgot it was night. All my life I had been going to places other people wouldn't go, and never once had I been bitten by a snake—until now.

No one else I knew would have called the case my way. People have a way of ignoring kids when it is convenient to do so. The disclosure of sexual abuse would have been rejected despite the fact that it met every criteria for being valid.

The problem was that dad had tears in his eyes when he denied it. He also had money and power and fifty character references. Mom was a personality disorder on a good day.

Most importantly, nothing would happen to you if you voted against mom. A whole lot could happen to you if you voted against dad, even before the kids died. Voting for mom was like stepping in front of a locomotive. She was never going to win this case, not in this day and time, not with the backlash on every television show, not with the average juror believing that four-year-olds can be programmed like computers.

But I hadn't been afraid then, even though I knew we were all going down for the count. What was I so afraid of now? Was it losing my license? That would be a disaster, but it was the kind that usually got my back up, got the "fuck you" part of me going. Was it being thought a total and complete fool? Half the people I knew thought that already. Besides, the thing about losing a child is that it immediately changes your perspective on what disaster is. A friend of mine—a high-level political type—used to fret over the political wars he got caught in. Then he had a bout with cancer. After that, he found committee meetings a whole lot less taxing. "What are they going to do?" he used to say. "Give me cancer?"

I trailed my fingers back and forth slowly in the water and sighed. The problem was I wasn't swimming alone anymore. I was taking people with me, whether they signed up for it or not. And I hadn't got bit by the snake—they had. Was there any chance, any chance at all that something I said or did had helped get those kids killed? Would custody have been trans-ferred if I hadn't supported the disclosure? Probably not. If I had quietly deep-sixed it and written a report that just said it was all a misunderstanding, no court time would have been spent on it at all. So Jamison would never had gotten the chance to go on his tirade about mom coaching the kids. Would she have killed the kids if dad hadn't gotten custody? All of a sudden I remembered something I hadn't thought about for years.

As an adolescent I drove like a maniac on the barren North Carolina backroads. I squealed and skidded around curves, put the pedal to the metal on the long straightaways. One fine summer day I was doing ninety down a long straight stretch when a child stepped out in front of me. She was a long way away, but a long way away is not a long way away when you're doing ninety. I hit the breaks, and the car skidded and shuddered, hardly seeming to slow at all. The child froze in the road. Time slowed: Several millennia passed in the next few seconds. I saw the shanties I was passing as clearly as if I were walking by them. The people out front seemed as frozen as the girl. The car shuddered to a stop within a foot of her. I put my head on the wheel and cried. It had never occurred to me a kid might just casually walk out in front of me. That was it for my racing career; I never drove fast again. If I had anything to do with those kids' deaths, I doubted I'd ever practice again either.

The knot in my stomach couldn't be eased by a hot tub. The stars didn't seem so bright anymore. I got out, wrapped my shirt around me, and walked back inside. I put on a bright Moroccan robe, a hangover from my hippie days, and came back to the deck. Carlotta had made brewed decaf hazelnut coffee from beans and had put out the patio lights, flickering candles that sat on the floor of the deck and kept the late summer bugs away. Her instincts were impeccable, as usual. A hot bath, an old, comfortable friendship, a seat on the deck listening to the sounds of the night. There wasn't much better solace.

"Sit in water long enough," I said, "and things surface."

"What did Adam say?"

So she had been talking to Arthur. He was the only one who knew I had gone to meet Adam. "He said," I replied, "they have a good case, a very good case. It makes no sense, but it's a case that will get a conviction."

"Adam wouldn't do that," Carlotta said. "He wouldn't put together a case he didn't believe in."

"He doesn't have a choice," I said. "You know the Attorney General's office gets involved in all the homicides in our little bitty state. So they sent a lawyer over, as usual, to make sure nothing would screw up the court case. Bottom line is, the

Attorney General wants her charged, and that's it. Besides, even Adam admits she had opportunity, and—to say the least—the lack of an alibi. He's got too much evidence on one side and nothing against it except for one small, ephemeral thing, so intangible he can't even put it in a report."

Carlotta said nothing, so I went on. The woman should have been a therapist. She says more by saying less than anyone I know. "Okay. Here's the deal. Four o'clock yesterday afternoon, the hearing ends. Fishbein has given mom the one hour to hand the kids over. Mom complies. Kids arrive right at five o'clock. Why such a tight time frame? Who knows? Ask Fishbein.

"Dad tells the police later that mom was extremely upset, but trying to hold it together. She unloaded all their stuff, crying the whole time. She gave dad instructions on the latest in routines and all that with tears running down her cheeks. Dad, who's magnanimous, of course, now that he's won, claimed he almost said something reassuring, like he wouldn't be an ogre about visitation. He didn't, thinking he'd just make it harder for her to keep it together. That's his story, anyway.

"Mom finally leaves, and dad reads books to the kids for the next half hour or so. Then he gets a call. He's on backup, and an intern is nervous about an admission. Dad takes the call and asks the kids to go outside and play because they're making noise. He doesn't worry at all. The yard is fenced in. The kids have never wandered off. They go outside, and he never sees them alive again."

I paused, thinking about the implications. Seemed to me it was going to leave a lot of room for what ifs and if onlys. Also seemed it would feel like a bad way to say good-bye. Go outside and play, I'm busy.

"He's on the phone maybe twenty minutes—which the resident he was talking to has verified. When he gets off he goes outside, and they're gone. He thinks they must have slipped past him back inside, but they're not in the house. He's annoyed, of course, and goes to all the neighbors, starting with the ones who have kids. No one has seen them.

"He gets a little more alarmed, but decides they probably tried to walk back to their mother's. He gets in the car and goes looking for them. He drives all the way to the mother's house, but there's no sign of them. He calls her from the car phone, but she accuses him of trying to yank her chain and hangs up on him. He calls the police, and they start looking. When the kids don't turn up, they go to Fishbein for a search warrant, but Fishbein won't do it. The neighbors said they didn't think mom had been out. They hadn't seen any kids. Probably, Fishbein just didn't believe mom would drop the kids off, then yank them back and go home. Didn't sound all that likely. The kids would turn up. This is Vermont. Nothing bad happens, right?

"At six the next morning they go back to Fishbein. The kids have not turned up, and they have found zilch. Everyone is alarmed at this point, and Fishbein reverses himself. He gives them the search warrant, and they show up at mom's. When they open the door to the kids' room, there they are, laid out neatly in their pj's, covers just so, exactly centered in the beds, hair brushed, hands neatly folded, etc. No obvious cause of death. They think either suffocation or poison, but the autopsy hasn't come back yet. Mom's fate is sealed when they discover all the doors and windows in the house are locked, and there's no sign of forcible entry."

"So what's on the other side?" Carlotta asked. "What's this intangible thing that Adam can't put in a report."

"The sound she made when she saw them."

It was a while after Carlotta left that I decided to quit obsessing and call it a day. As I passed the answering machine, I heard Mama's voice. On a whim I picked it up. "Girl, I've called you three times today." Mama takes it personally if you aren't there to answer her call. "I've been hearing about you on the news."

" 'Spect you have, Mama."

"You've got a world of trouble."

" 'Spect I do."

"What'd that woman want to go and kill those sweet little babies for?"

"It's not clear she did, Mama."

"The news says she did."

"They don't always get it right."

Mama digested this. "Well, you're always into something. I'll say one thing for you, though. I'd pit you against a tiger."

It was as close to warmth as Mama gets.

12

. . . .

I suppose the decision to go see Willy started when Adam told me how the kids looked when they died. I had a feeling Willy would know something about that. But on the way, the sense of dread almost turned me around. Most people live their whole lives without knowing the things Willy has to teach and are better off for not knowing. I go to see Willy only when I have to.

I have never understood prisons. Guard towers, electrified fences, razor wire, bars literally within bars, steel door after steel door after steel door—the whole shooting match, so to speak—mystifies me. The system is designed to keep people in who are dangerous. They shoot them for trying to leave no matter what the charge they came in on. Yet one day, they just open up the gates and let them go. Whoa! Are they still dangerous or what? And if they aren't, what was all that paraphernalia for? The routine I like is when they bring a man to the front gate in shackles so he won't hurt the guards on his way out, and then let him go.

I drove up to the outer gate and told the guard I was there to visit an inmate. He waved me on, and I parked and walked up to the inner gate where the razor wire starts, fifty feet from the main building. The gate clicked open. Whoever mans that thing always seems to be awake. You just walk up and click. I passed the sign advising visitors not only against carrying firearms and knives but against carrying sunglasses, aerosol cans, glass bottles, writing pens, hairbrushes, hairpins, combs, purses, billfolds, checkbooks, cigarettes, lighters, tobacco products, tools, nail clippers, nail files, alcohol, drugs, colored handker-chiefs, pictures, cameras, stationery, medication (except nitro-glycerin), more than five dollars in cash, wigs or hairpieces (unless prescribed by a doctor), and nearly every other item a human could be reasonably expected to carry. Luckily, I'm known here, and they don't consider me that much of a risk, so they cut me some slack on writing pens. That is good because otherwise I would have had to borrow one from one of the inmates who are allowed to have them anyway.

I dutifully surrendered my driver's license and my car keys. I understand the car keys, but the driver's license always makes me nervous. Exactly why do they need my driver's license? Do they have a problem with fewer people coming out than go in?

The parade of steel doors began. One steel door. Wait. Click. I stepped through and waited again. That door had to close before the next one would open. I stood impatiently in the fifteen feet of corridor caged at both ends by a steel door. I took a last look at my clothes: long, shapeless, and dark — my kind of prison garb. The next door opened, and I headed for the sex offender wing, where another set of steel doors waited. One of the by-products of working in a prison, I was told, was that every once in a while you walked up to a door in the outside world and stared at it waiting for it to click open.

I found myself wondering one more time why prisons don't work. They work for me. I wouldn't jaywalk for a week after this. If I had visited a prison in my joint-smoking hippie days, I would have parted company with recreational marijuana a whole lot sooner. As usual, I was counting the steel doors as I walked. I always knew exactly how many steel doors there were between me and the green, green grass outside. To the people locked in here, though, prison is just a way of life. To some it is a whole lot easier than making all those choices you have to make on the outside.

I walked into the sex offender wing and glanced at the schedule on the wall. There was a group running so I headed for the group room to see if Willy was in it. The group room was actually the far end of the cafeteria, which had been sectioned off. The top half of the wall separating the two rooms was glass, so I didn't have to interrupt group to see that Willy was inside with his back to the wall.

I opened the door quietly and stepped in. Instantly, there was a quiet undercurrent of tension in the room. Visitors to group are rare: Few people are allowed to sit in. I am because of the work I do.

Not every head turned when I came in—most prisoners were too "cool" to be caught gawking—but you could tell by the electricity in the room that everyone was acutely aware of my presence. It looked like at least half of the prisoners were lost in some kind of internal fantasy: They had that glazed look in their eyes. I knew from experience the agendas would vary. Some would be thinking about conning me to help them get more privileges. Some would be thinking what a notch on their belts it would be if I fell in love with them. Some would be thinking about sex. And some just wanted to knock my teeth in, just to see the look in my eyes.

Every prison has a story about some woman—a staff member, a volunteer, a lawyer, a psychologist who "fell in love" with a prisoner. Before long the woman started working late, and some guard would find a prisoner in some area he wasn't supposed to be in, with or without his pants. If the guard missed it, a snitch would tell the warden. Or a note would be intercepted. The woman would cry and sob and talk about unconditional love. Her boyfriend's friends would talk about bragging sessions late at night, about free cigarettes and sex and promises of help with the parole board.

I never quite get how anybody can be so naive, but then again few women are prepared for the intensity a prisoner can muster. With nothing to do all day but obsess, a prisoner can hone his attention until it has a razor's edge. The focused attention he can shower on a lonely woman can take her breath away. And some of the less desirable aspects of his personality—the violent outbursts, the drug and alcohol problems, the sexual assaults, the living off her—she won't see while he is in prison.

In fact, the last time I was here I had received a note: My comments in group had been brilliant, the prisoner said. If he had met someone like me long ago, he wouldn't be where he was today. Would I send him a list, he asked, of books to read? I would know which ones were right for him. He had started by talking about his sincere commitment to treatment and ended with a comment about my legs. I dropped the note off in the warden's office on my way out. But then, I had been around long enough not to romanticize prison or prisoners.

I remember being a young hippie and sitting under an apple tree listening to Joan Baez sing "Raze the Prisons to the Ground." It sounded good at the time, but nobody who actually works in a prison hums that tune. The first thing you learn when you work in a prison is that a whole lot of the people who are there belong there.

I sat down behind Willy. Any other prisoner in the room would have taken offense at someone sitting behind him, but not Willy. Sitting behind him would put him on edge, just as it would anybody else, but Willy likes that feeling. He has a history, he told me, of molesting kids with their parents in the next room. He is proudest of molesting them in the backseat of a car with their parents in the front seat. He likes the adrenaline rush that taking chances brings. I wasn't, however, sitting behind Willy to feed his psychopathic need for excitement. I was trying to see the group from his point of view.

Willy had stationed himself next to the youngest-looking prisoner in the room. So he was up to his old grooming tactics. He turned to see who had come in, and as he turned back, he exchanged a meaningful look with his neighbor. I gathered the grooming was pretty far along. Child molesters invariably pick the youngest prisoner they can find and use the same grooming techniques they use on children to manipulate him into a sexual relationship. Like heterosexuals, pedophiles often have sex with other men in prison even if they had no interest in them on the outside.

I noticed, too, that Willy had placed himself across from the group leader. No doubt he was setting himself up as a competitor. Mark, the leader, was in an argument with Roger, a thin, middle-aged prisoner, an accountant before he was caught for child molesting. "So you're saying that a four-year-old who says nothing is giving consent?" Mark said.

"Well, he didn't tell anyone, and he could have. I never, ever threatened him. And during the . . . more intimate parts . . . of our relationship he never protested. I would have stopped if he had wanted me to. But there was a chemistry between us right from the start. He begged his mom to spend the night at my house that first time."

"All right, group. Roger thinks the fact that he said nothing means he consented. Let's go further. Let's say he said yes. Is that consent? Can a four-year-old give consent?"

"No," Willy said quickly. "A four-year-old can't give informed consent."

"Willy," the group leader said, getting up and setting up two chairs in the middle of the circle. "Why don't you and Roger come up here and role-play this? What I want you to do, Willy, is to pretend Roger is a four-year-old and to tell him all the things about sexual abuse — what it involves, what will happen to him now and later — all the things he'd have to know in order for the consent to be informed."

It was a mistake from a group dynamics point of view. Willy was always playing junior therapist, and that bit of status gave him a leg up on manipulating other prisoners, but I could see why the group leader chose him. Willy had fifty IQ points on the next brightest prisoner there, and being what he was, he didn't make the same thinking errors the other sex offenders did, so he could see theirs very clearly.

Willy stood up and walked to the center of the group. His face was as calm and genial as ever, but I thought his eyes a bit shiny. I had a queasy feeling that Willy would find a way to get off on this. He always likes having power, and when he does, he uses it to humiliate. My guess was Roger was about to have his head handed to him.

Willy ignored the chair, preferring to stand and pace around the "four-year-old," who looked nervously away. He began, "I'm going to do some things to you, and you need to know what they are so you can decide whether or not you would like me to do them. First I'm going to take your clothes off and touch your body all over. That may not be too difficult for you, unless, of course, you don't really want to have your body touched, especially your penis and your butt; but then again, I don't really care what you want. This is really for me, you see, and not for you, so whether you like it or not isn't actually important.

"Then I'm going to insert my finger in your butt, which will feel quite strange and as though you have to go to the bathroom. This will make you feel embarrassed, but I won't really care about that either." Willy walked around the chair as he spoke, looming over the sitting prisoner and getting more in his face than he needed to.

"And then after a while, I'm going to place my penis in your mouth. Your mouth, of course, is quite small, and my penis is quite large, so it will no doubt make you gag and perhaps feel like you're choking. That won't bother me either. I may keep my penis in your mouth for quite a while and eventually, a sticky fluid will shoot out of it. That will definitely make you feel like you're choking or even suffocating, perhaps make you want to throw up as well. Again, I will not care.

"Finally I am going to force my penis in your butt. Your butt is also much smaller than my penis, so there should be quite a bit of pain. You can anticipate crying or even sobbing. That most certainly won't stop me because you'll be the one in pain, not I. My penis will quite enjoy your tight little butt, and after all, the point of this is for me to have fun, not you. Afterward, there may be lots of bleeding, which should frighten you considerably, but it really won't bother me.

"I'll probably bribe you afterward. Perhaps McDonald's or the arcade. I'll buy you things. I'll shower love and attention on you because I am quite aware that your father is an alcoholic and your mother doesn't have the money to buy you a hamburger. I know it because I researched your family. I prefer children who are desperate for attention so I can be confident you'll keep what goes on between us a secret.

"Afterward, you may feel dirty or ashamed, perhaps as though you did something wrong. At the risk of redundancy, that's your problem. I will make sure you don't tell. Of course, that will mean you don't get any help for your problems.

"This may bother you for years, perhaps even for the rest of your life. You may have trouble being close to people, or trusting them. You may dislike sex. You may be sad a lot or nervous or afraid, but I will have dropped you long ago, just as soon as you started to grow up. Fortunately for me, I won't be around at that point.

"Now that you know what this is all about, come now, do you want to do it?"

The accountant looked crushed. He blinked back tears. "It wasn't like that," he said. "You make it sound dirty and sordid, but we were very close."

Willy put his hands on the arms of the chair where Roger sat and leaned forward into his face. "Stop it," I said silently to Mark. "Stop it right now. You've gotten maximum benefit. The rest is just going to be Willy getting off." But it wasn't my group, and Mark would surely take umbrage at my getting involved in his, so I said nothing out loud.

"You're disgusting," Willy said quietly. "You love him? My oh my. How many 'love affairs' have you had? Two hundred? Three hundred? Five hundred? And how many kids are still 'dear' to you once their butts aren't little and soft and creamy anymore? Once they grow up a little and you can't get a hard-on just thinking about their stubby little penises. No, Roger, quit lying and whining and making an ass of yourself. Everybody here knows what you really are. You're a pervert. You don't love children. You just use them."

"That's enough, Willy," Mark said, stopping it about ten light-years too late. Willy walked back to his seat practically whistling. Behind him the accountant sobbed. It was the ultimate humiliation, to be crying in front of the other prisoners. Most looked away. A few looked like they had spaced out. And there were a couple whose eyes were as shiny as Willy's.

The group leader broke the silence, "Well, the role-play may be painful, but isn't it true that those are all the things a child would have to know to give informed consent? Now some of those things you don't tell kids and other things you can't tell them because they wouldn't understand. So basically the child doesn't have a clue what he's getting into or how it's going to affect him. The bottom line is, no, you don't have informed consent when a child is silent, and no, four-year-olds can't give informed consent for sex."

Group broke up shortly after that, but Willy agreed to stay and talk to me. I had started to sit down when Mark asked me if I had time to talk with him for a moment. I had avoided speaking to Mark thus far, but it looked like I wouldn't get away without it. Willy, unfortunately for me, allowed that he didn't mind waiting, so, reluctantly, I followed Mark outside the group room. "What'd you think?" Mark asked eagerly as soon as I closed the door.

I moved farther away from the door. Willy would surely be listening. "About the exercise? I thought Willy got off on it."

"Well, maybe, but it certainly had an impact on Roger."

"Up to a point," I admitted. I really didn't want to get into this.

Mark paused. "What do you mean 'up to a point'?"

"Well, it got into humiliation, and you know what I think: You can't teach people not to abuse power by abusing power."

"Willy didn't exactly abuse his power. He got a little carried away, maybe, in a way that's understandable. Role-playing is a very powerful medium."

"Mark, he didn't get a little carried away," I snapped. "He's a sadist. He gets off on suffering and humiliation. He had a field day out there humiliating Roger. Making Roger feel like a shit is not going to change Roger's behavior. It'll just make him depressed, and what does he do to medicate depression? You got it, given the chance, he molests little kids. I think the basic exercise is a good one, but, Jesus, stop it before it becomes abusive. All that happened out there was that Willy got an excuse to inflict pain, and he loved it."

Even as the words came out of my mouth I knew they were too sharp. I need to learn to hem and haw better. I hem once, I haw once, and then, if somebody keeps pushing, I just tell the truth. It's a problem.

"You know," Mark exploded, "I think you've got this thing about Willy. I know you think he's Hannibal Lecter or something. But you'd better look at your own countertransference because you're missing another side to him. He can be very insightful about abuse. Maybe he's trying to make up for some of the harm he's done. You should see him in group. He's always calling other people on their thinking errors."

Jesus Christ. Who couldn't Willy suck in? Next the warden would be telling me I was too hard on him.

"Hannibal Lecter! Hannibal Lecter dreams of being as charming as Willy. Look—you know I can't tell you the details—trust me on this, you wouldn't like him any better than Hannibal if you knew what I know about him." I tried to keep my voice down, but my temperature was rising.

I always have more trouble with other professionals than

with clients. I expect clients to be off the wall. There's some naive part of me that expects professionals to know what they are doing. Lots do, present company excepted.

"So, he's got the whole world fooled but you. Is that what you think? You know what I think? I think you're the one who's gotten sucked in. I think Willy's figured out you'll eat up any wild tale he tells, and he's getting a good laugh out of leading you on."

"Mark, he tells me about it because he's got so many people fooled there's no one left to see how smooth he is, no one to 'appreciate his artistry,' as he puts it. Give me a break, Mark. How many people who aren't sadists could get a hard-on describing sadistic acts they've performed on small children?"

Mark tried to keep it going, but I cut it off. I wasn't going to change his mind about Willy. He wasn't going to change mine. I made a running-late excuse and headed back in to see Willy. I don't know if Willy heard the conversation or not. Probably. Who cares? Willy would already know he had Mark conned.

I took my time taking my coat off and putting my things down. I needed to cool off. I wanted to wring Mark's neck, but why? Why am I so down on him? He's no different than a lot of folks. People never want to see malevolence. When it's right in front of their faces, they shut their eyes. He can deal with Roger and all the other "grooming offenders," men who project their own sexual arousal onto the children and believe the children want to have sex with them. Mark wants sexual abuse to make some kind of sense, however weird. He wants everybody to mean well, however much havoc they wreak.

I arranged two chairs equal distance from the door. Willy was still sitting where he had been in group, waiting for me to set things up. No doubt he knew my routine by now. Standard practice with potentially violent folk is to set things up so they don't have to go through me to get out of the room and I don't have to go through them. There are some people — if they knew Willy like I did — who wouldn't think that being alone with Willy was a good idea under any circumstances. But Willy has no history of violence with anybody over twelve (that I know of), and his violence has always been secretive. He only becomes violent in situations where he has total power and control. An open attack wouldn't be his way. Publicly, the persona he presents is quite different.

I looked across at Willy. How many times had I seen him now? I should know. Just count the number of psychic scars I have. I remember first meeting him. It was back before I knew Mark wanted me to keep my nose out of his group. I was telling a guy in Mark's group he was lying through his teeth. You don't beat small children just to subdue them for sex as he claimed. You beat them because you enjoy it.

Willy congratulated me afterward on my acuity. Most counselors, he informed me, were really quite stupid and had no clue about some of the "more unusual" motivations of sex offenders. He offered his services as a consultant. He had some knowledge, he said, gained through his "research" and his interviews with other prisoners regarding the more "unusual motivations." It was obvious to me that what he wanted was an audience to lecture to on sadism. Is the price I've paid since then worth it? I know about things I wish I didn't know about. On the other hand, I like to think I am harder to con because of what I've learned from Willy, although the present case, unfortunately, might turn out to be an exception.

"Dr. Michael." Willy took one of the chairs I had arranged, sat down, leaned back, and folded his arms. He seemed pleased to see me, and I was pretty sure he was glad I had been there for his little performance. Prison is stultifyingly boring, and, no doubt, I brightened his day. Of course, prison is so boring a disciplinary hearing would have brightened his day. He never called me Dr. Stone. Dr. Michael was his way of being just a tad familiar and getting away with it.

I looked at Willy, trying to sort out one more time why he had been so successful at entrapping children. He is a small, portly man with a round, genial face. The unknowing would have called it gentle. He looks like your local minister. He was somebody's local minister.

He has a persuasive charm about him. His open face shows concern at your slightest discomfort. He misses nothing—a shadow passing over your face from an old memory, a slight smile at a pleasant thought. His voice holds all the warmth you ever wanted from your mama and never got. You want to confide in him: Lots of people have—particularly single mothers with eight- to ten-year-old boys.

But my relationship with Willy is a little different. I don't really have a clue how much risk knowing what I know has put me in, but I would not be happy to see Willy out of prison. Given the situation, charming me was a ludicrous thought, but even so Willy always tries. Probably he just wants to keep in practice.

"Mr. Willy." I was pleased that my voice sounded clear. I had the fight with Mark mostly behind me. Being angry is a kind of vulnerability, and being vulnerable around Willy is the worst idea I know.

I looked at Alex B. Willy. Most people just call him Willy. I always call prisoners by their last name, too, but I always add Mr. Even minor signs of respect are important in prison. Self-respect, respect for other people, respect from other people— these are rare and precious commodities in prison. I plan on receiving it, so I always give it. Even in a confrontation with a prisoner, I always call him "Mr."

I knew I shouldn't get into the role-playing exercise. I wasn't here to lecture Willy or to treat him. But it burned me to see him get off on power-tripping while coming across to the whole group as a nice guy. I'd have been all right if Mark had dealt with it, but he hadn't called the fight when the accountant was dead on his feet. I've already had one fight about the exercise. I didn't need another. I could stay out of it if Willy didn't mention it.

"What did you think of our little exercise?" Willy asked.

I made a last, heroic effort to stay away from it. "Mr. Willy, you really don't want to know."

"Oh, but I do," Willy said. "You know I value your knowledge of those morons." I didn't ask if he included Mark in his definition of "moron." I didn't have to. Willy feels superior to anyone who doesn't drop him in his tracks.

"My problem is not with them. It's with you."

"Whatever do you mean, Dr. Michael?" Willy said. "I was asked to participate. Chosen. It's obvious I was the only one in the group who could have made any impression on that particular lowlife. I rather thought you'd be . . . well, grateful that I was using my skills prosocially—as I often did in my former life, by the way. You tend to always emphasize my mistakes, but I assure you I did many good things for children and their families. You never give me any credit," he chided, "for anything decent that I do, and this is a perfect example." The voice was warm and the expression on his face was injured, but the eyes weren't injured; they were wary.

He's right. I never give him credit for doing anything decent with children; as far as I know, he never has. Anything nice he's done has been in the service of grooming his victims.

I played an imaginary violin. "Wrong audience, Mr. Willy," I said. "Save it. It'll play in Peoria. But you can't have it both ways. You can't tutor me as well as you have, and still expect me to buy your press releases."

"You've lost me," Willy sniffed. "Whatever are you talking about?"

"Give me a break," I replied. "You know as well as I do what happened out there today. You got off on humiliating that guy and making him look and feel like a fool. You got a high from it.

"And talk about the pot and the kettle, he's not half the offender you are. How many victims has he had, Mr. Willy? And how many have you? If he's into male children, maybe he has a hundred and fifty victims, right? Should I double that

103

number for you, triple it, or just add another digit? And it was news to him that children don't like to be abused. He never let himself know that because it would have bothered him. But you've always known how much children suffer when they're being sexually abused because that was why you were abusing them. Inflicting pain and suffering is your thing. Did he ever take a knife and enlarge a child's anus? I don't think so.

"You had a great cover out there tonight, but somebody should have asked you the crucial question. Somebody should have asked you how long you've know what you know and why it didn't change your behavior. It would have changed theirs."

I heard the anger in my voice and tried to mask it—all right, maybe the fight with Mark wasn't entirely behind me. I failed so completely I smiled, instead. I have learned over the years that you can say almost anything to anybody if you smile warmly while you're doing it. I needed Willy, and I didn't want to completely alienate him. Even so, I always have trouble controlling myself when he gets into his sadistic stuff.

I needn't have worried; Willy laughed. There are times when, if you call Willy's facade, he just drops it. It is as though he is trying out different parts, and he lets go any that the audience doesn't applaud. He can go from righteously indignant to mildly amused in the space of a heartbeat. It is like a series of photographs I once saw of an octopus changing his color to match a checked floor in the aquarium. There is something disquieting about it.

"There's hope for you yet, Dr. Michael, although you'll have to grant your tutoring was exceptional. Now if I could just get you to see that what you call morality is just another aesthetic decision."

Typical of Willy. He wasn't offended that I would accuse him of getting off on pain and suffering. Given he has no con-science, it didn't seem like such a terrible accusation to him. He thinks torturing small children is an art form, like music or the ballet—simply an "aesthetic decision."

"I'm not into philosophical debates, Mr. Willy. Once an

alcoholic tried to convince me that alcoholism was just an alternative lifestyle. It wasn't worth my time, and neither is debating whether hurting children is a reasonable hobby." I never argue about right and wrong. I know the difference. People like Willy don't. End of argument. "So, how are you and how was your parole hearing?"

"And to think that you're the closest thing I have to a sparring partner. I've fallen onto hard times. I suppose some people say you're refreshingly direct."

"They do."

"And other people say you're hopelessly tactless and lack subtlety."

"That, too. So how was your parole hearing?"

"Ah, my parole hearing. A twelve-year deferment, unfortu-nately." Twelve years! That was unheard of. Willy is in his sixties. He'll be in his seventies before he comes up again for parole. Parole boards inevitably give two-or three-year defer-ments so that prisoners will retain hope. Prisoners are a whole lot easier to manage when they are trying to impress a parole board.

"That's incredible. I'm surprised to hear it's so long."

"You didn't talk to them, by any chance?"

"Now, Mr. Willy. If I had, it would have been in the file, and that very capable lawyer of yours would have found it and told you. I suspect you're very familiar with the rules and regs about these things."

"And I suppose nobody ever makes an informal comment here or there that never shows up in the official record."

"I don't know if they do or they don't. Nobody asked me if I thought you should be paroled."

"And if they had?"

"I would have told them what your better side knows. It wouldn't have been a good idea." What better side? Maybe I had a modicum of tact after all. "I have the feeling, though, that something happened. Something surfaced for them to give you a twelve-year deferment."

"Nothing significant. But Dr. Michael, that's not really what you came to talk about."

I couldn't face it quite yet. Maybe I'd try to work up to it. "Tell me about the double life, Mr. Willy. How did you keep people from suspecting you in your former life?"

Willy hooted. "Come now, Dr. Michael. You must think we are living on the moon here. You are quite the celebrity. Front page in all the local papers—well, you have seen the papers, haven't you?"

I shook my head.

"Well, my dear girl, you have even made the *Wall Street Journal,* although, alas, you are not the main character in their little story of this most interesting case."

It wasn't "alas" from my point of view. Good grief. If this story had even hit the business press, it was everywhere.

"I was surprised at you, however. And a bit disappointed. I thought you understood all this much better than that. To recommend that custody go to a woman who turned out to be a child murderer. My, my, my. I assume that's considered a bit of a faux pas in your profession. Were the press reports accurate? You actually vouched for her mental health and her skills as a mother?" Willy shook his head, a loving father admonishing his foolish daughter. I most certainly did not vouch for her mental health, but I wasn't going to get into it with Willy.

"Actually, there's quite a lot I don't understand, Mr. Willy. That's why I'm here." Willy's narcissism is his Achilles' heel. Besides, what I said was true.

"Well, I don't know that I have anything to offer, but I'll certainly help if I can, dear girl. And I do hope you have some support in this dreadful time—at home, perhaps?"

I raised my eyebrows and looked at Willy. I stopped smiling. I had told Willy unequivocally my private life was off limits and that if he ever got into it I would terminate all contact permanently. This was hopefully not an idle threat since I suspect Willy relies on my company and conversation more than he admits. I had also told him if he tried to contact me

after I broke off contact, I would tell the parole board everything I knew about him. I didn't tell him that if he ever showed
up at my door I planned to shoot him.

Nonetheless, I suspected Willy knew pretty much how much
support I had at home. Prisoners had nothing but time, and a lot
of anybody's private life can be found out through newspaper
accounts, public documents, and so on. Not to mention Willy is
in a vocational program that uses computers, supposedly under
close supervision. The "close" supervision started after several
prisoners successfully ran a credit card scam through the
computer. But I'd bet that Willy has ways of eluding "close"
supervision, and I'd bet he knows more about computers than
the instructor.

The fact that Willy would be in a world of trouble if he
got caught meant nothing. People like Willy make a profession
out of doing things that would get them in a world of trouble if
they got caught. Molesting, torturing, perhaps even killing
children—hard to think he did all those things without knowing
he'd have a problem if he got caught. Using the computer to
satisfy his curiosity about me is pretty minor after that.

But whatever Willy knows about me he has never used
before. Now here he was—hinting, edging toward that line.
Which could only mean he must think I really needed him if
he's willing to play around like that. Well, I do, but the
adolescent, make-my-day-fuck-you-Willy part of me is bigger
than any other part. I wasn't feeling even halfway patient with
Willy's nonsense today. If Willy tried to use my need for
information to get even the slightest edge over me, I would
walk. Maybe he knew that; maybe he didn't.

I continued to stare at him without a trace of warmth until he
spoke. "Well now, I believe you needed help with something?"
A conciliatory tone but with something—annoyance, maybe
even anger—curling around the edges of it.

He hadn't been able to call my bluff because I hadn't been
bluffing. Which is good, because I'd lose if I started bluffing
Willy. I'd have walked not just because of my adolescent

aversion to being controlled but because I know better than to let Willy lay even a single psychological finger on me. Give that man a finger, and he'll have me by the psychological throat in a nanosecond. It is not a good idea to let little things go with people like Willy.

"Yes, Mr. Willy, I do have a question." I figured I might as well come out with it. I stopped staring, but kept my voice formal. "Who would dress the children neatly in their pj's, comb their hair, place them exactly in the beds, fold their hands just so?" Adam had given me an unforgettable description of what he found when he walked in the room.

"Well." Willy sat back. "I wouldn't know, of course. I never took anything that far."

"On the contrary, Mr. Willy. I think you are very thoughtful about these issues, and I think you have an extraordinary capacity to put yourself in the minds of others and imagine how they might have felt—in the same way the FBI profilers at Quantico do."

It was such a thin cover. It amazes me every time that Willy goes for it. But it fits in a way. Willy wants to brag, and to brag properly, it has to be absolutely clear that you're not telling tall tales. Willy likes the cover to be thin so that his audience can smell how close to the truth of his own life he was getting.

"I could do better with pictures."

"Absolutely out of the question. No pictures."

Willy pouted. I went on. "I'm just asking for the psychology of it. What would such a person be thinking and feeling? Why do it that way?"

"Umm." Willy leaned back and looked away. He didn't say anything for a few minutes. "Well, you might be tempted . . ." His tone changed. He seemed remote. I noticed the fatherly tone had dropped from his voice like a stone. He had a slight smile, and his eyes got shiny again. "You might be tempted to think it was for show. To upset others with a parody of parenting. A nice, subtle touch, perhaps, but there are . . . other ways . . . to leave a child's body that will upset others."

I was not, absolutely not, even going to speculate about what Willy meant by that last comment. I didn't want any pictures in my head. I looked down at my notes. I don't like Willy to see when he gets to me; he gets off on it. But I didn't need to worry. Willy was in another world. I didn't have to look at his pants to know there was a bulge. Willy had been convicted of child rape and aggravated assault—some of his victims had been badly hurt—but his fantasies go beyond what he was convicted for. I could never shake the memory that there were two unsolved murders in his county—both nine-year-old boys.

I looked at him. This man looked so normal. It was easy for him to get invited into people's homes, easy to get access to their children. When one kid finally told on him, many of the parents of other children he worked with wouldn't even let their children be interviewed by the police. Despite his guilty plea, a number of them still maintained he was innocent, and some even wrote him in prison. And worse, if he were released tomorrow, the same thing would happen all over again. People insist on believing the bad guys look and talk like bad guys and the good guys are easy to spot: They are warm, sincere, and charming.

As I waited for him to come back to earth, I had a bizarre fantasy. I wanted to freeze Willy where he was and reach out and touch his face. Could that be real skin? Could this be a real person? Could I understand something through touch I had never been able to grasp by listening?

He went on. "No . . . No, I think it was for his own private pleasure. There is such sweet control in it. Maybe he dressed them and combed their hair and got them all ready first. But no, it is far sweeter once they're dead. You just have such control. Probably he made one watch, though, while he did the other." He sighed.

I couldn't deal with any more. "Mr. Willy, I just have one question. Is that way of leaving a body consistent with a desperate, panicky mother killing her children in fear or in some crazed state?"

"Not in fear or panic, no. The kids were definitely done by a sadist. Only a sadist would have such a loving ritual at the end of it. Forgive me, Dr. Michael, but you are such a limited student. You never seem to grasp the loving part. But what makes you think mom isn't a sadist? How do you know you didn't miss her? You would have missed me, you know."

It is what brings me back time and again. I could have met Willy on the street. He could have been my next-door neighbor. He could have been my minister. Maybe someone like him is my client. I'm not sure I would have any more clue than anybody else about the Willys of the world. I likely would have missed Willy, and I didn't know about mom.

"The problem is, Dr. Michael, that you want to believe I'm one-of-a-kind. But that is very naive. I am not as unusual as you would like to think." He was most certainly not as unusual as I would like to think.

As we left the room, Willy threw off his exit line. "I suspect plastic bags over the heads, myself. You get to see the child's face, and it is very satisfying. Also, if you're careful, you get to stop it before they actually die and do it all over again."

I froze. The medical examiner's report wasn't in yet, but there were no obvious marks on the bodies. Poison, maybe, Adam had said. Or suffocation.

On the way out I tracked down one of the other offender therapists and asked what happened to Willy's parole. "Oh," she said. "Willy self-destructed. He tried to sell some child pornography on the unit, and someone turned him in."

I almost smiled. Typical of Willy. Living on the edge. Driving the adrenaline up by taking chances. Prison is too boring to feed his need for thrills. He would have to make his own action. "Um," I said. "That was enough for a twelve-year-deferment?"

"Sure," she said. "Writing about the warden's eight-year-old daughter helped. But they might never have gotten ahold of it if he had stuck with the straight stuff. We've got some guys here who would have bought it and kept their mouths shut—you know, guys who are talking-the-talk instead of walking-the-walk. But he got into taking her eyeballs out with a screwdriver, and we don't have anybody on the unit right now that appeals to. I think the worst, most violent rapist we have would have turned him in."

That was reassuring about the unit, but nothing was reassuring about Willy. I carried him with me down the highway. I needed a ritual to get him out of my head. I needed an exorcism. I could see why Mark needed not to know that people like Willy existed.

It was Willy who changed my mind about capital punishment. I had a knee-jerk liberal reaction to the issue until I met Willy. I am still a liberal, with two exceptions. For one thing, I would personally throw the switch on Willy and anyone like him. For another, after my first session with Willy, I bought my first gun.

Mama would say he is meaner than a snake.

13

By evening I was a long way from Vermont, in a skiff heading up the North Carolina part of the Inland Waterway. All my folks live somewhere in these parts, and I was on my way to have dinner with Mama. If the skiff had had a rearview mirror, I would have seen Cousin Wilbur's cabin in it. The cabin sits on the banks of a cove off the Inland Waterway. Cousin Wilbur wouldn't see it that way. To him the duck blind—his pride and joy—sits on the banks of the cove. The cabin is just an appendage and support unit. It is a simple cabin except for one grand gesture: a huge stone fireplace that takes up most of one wall. To most people the cabin—simple or not—would be a whole lot more important than the duck blind, which is nothing but a small platform with rushes nailed to the sides that hunters sit in to shoot ducks. But that is Cousin Wilbur.

I was staying there—at the cabin, that is. I always stay there when I come home—at least I have since Daddy died. He wouldn't have liked it. He always wanted Mama and me to get along. It didn't turn out that way. These days Mama and I are like two heads of state. We don't like to meet up accidentally, lest we start World War III. We need the right setting, the right time, the right ritual, and most of all, the right buffers. We had agreed I'd come for dinner. I expected I wouldn't be the only guest.

The wind had died as it often does in the late afternoon, and the Inland Waterway was a single, long mirror. The boat seemed to just slide along. Here and there in small coves, sailboats making the New York to Florida run had dropped anchor for the night. The smell of barbecues wafted across the water, and folks on docks and boats and porches waved as I went by.

Half of them were relatives. One way or another, most of my people live on the water. It is just something my family does, and it is still possible — if you don't mind not having neighbors, if you don't mind driving forty-five minutes to get to a grocery store, if you don't mind living seven trillion miles from the nearest minor sign of civilization — to live on the water without a lot of money. You can tell how well off my relatives are by how close they are to civilization. Waterfront lots in town are increasingly something only out-of-towners can afford.

But the distances are deceptive because they are land distances. In fact, my relatives are mostly closer to each other by water than by land. They tend to take boats back and forth across the Inland Waterway, Neuse River, Core Sound, Bogue Sound, wherever they are. So it was only business as usual to take the skiff down the waterway to Mama's for dinner.

I waved at the bridge tender at Core Creek, the father of a high school boyfriend, and headed on up toward the sound. I had picked up a school of dolphins, all bobbing in and out of the water in their rocking horse rhythm. The lead dolphin was huge with scars covering her torso from who-knows-what shark battles. In the middle of the pack were two dolphins in perfect synchrony, diving together, surfacing together. Between them was a tiny baby dolphin totally out of synch. His little body just wasn't long enough to keep the same rhythm. The out-of-synch bobbing was comical from a human point of view, but I doubted the dolphins felt that way. Humor is probably species specific.

I don't know why I wasn't exhausted. I'd left the prison and driven straight to the airport. Why not? Melissa, my secretary, had cancelled all my clients for the week. It didn't seem fair to ask them to run a gauntlet of reporters. And so much for confidentiality. Anyone who came to my office was likely to end up on the six o'clock news.

I had no airline reservations, but I knew all the local flights by heart, and there was one leaving for Boston in half an hour from the time I left the prison. From there I'd picked up something to get to Carolina. That's how I like to do it. Grab the travel bag in the trunk and go. I don't keep pets and I don't keep plants just so I can leave without bother. The planning thing has never worked for me.

I have to admit I'm a little vain about my ability to travel. I keep enough stuff in my knapsack for any length trip. What do you really need? You wear a pair of jeans and a sweater, carry another pair of pants, two pairs of shorts, three T-shirts, two shirts with a collar, one bathing suit, one set of pj's, and a dress. Any place that needs a warm coat isn't a place you ought to go. Everything goes together. Everything is wrinkle-free. Everything can be washed out in the sink, and everything fits in a knapsack. I always feel a little smug watching people struggle with big bags at the airport. I had picked up my ticket and changed into my jeans with five minutes to spare. Now here I was, home, on the Carolina water.

I always seem to come back here when I get disoriented. It's my way of grounding myself, of starting over. I don't know why it works like that. I don't like the South, never have; I left it as fast as I could. But an expatriate Southerner is still a Southerner, and home is home. Everybody has some place that resets the clock.

The flight from Boston landed in Raleigh. I could have taken a puddle jumper from there to Wilson's Pond, but I preferred to rent a car and drive. I get the feel of things that way—good and bad. Things are poor outside the research triangle of Raleigh, Durham, and Chapel Hill. I passed lots of shacks and rusted cars. There are endless Stuckey's and too many stores with people outside dressed up like peanuts or candy bars or whatever—the South believes in personal advertising. Too many signs that say "Southern spoken here." At least they have taken down the billboard outside Smithfield of the Ku Klux Klan member on a rearing horse—bed sheet and all—holding a burning cross. That had still been up when I was a kid. Nothing like having the Nazis in your backyard.

But there is another South beyond the poverty and the Klan and the Stuckey's, and this was it. Fresh Southern vegetables cooked with fatback—heart-attack bait, but better-tasting than the watery, pallid stuff served up North—the South where I picked fresh figs off my grandmother's tree and rode in my uncle's shrimp boat at dawn watching the sun lay a golden ribbon across the glassy water. The South where I sailed a Styrofoam sailboat, of all things, for years as a teenager, up and down bank-protected waters collecting sand dollars and sea urchins and oyster shells with colors cast lightly across the ridges.

Mama's house was coming up. It's a big white house on a hill with a porch running across the front and down one side. It was lit up tonight to beat the band—as Mama would say. As I pulled up to the dock, I noticed a disquieting number of other skiffs; it looked like most of my relatives were there. I wasn't sure I was up to dealing with the entire clan tonight. Up at the house I could see tables set up outside on the porch.

Uncle John was down on the dock holding a glass and watching the sunset. He's a big man with large, gnarled hands, rough from hauling in nets from his own shrimp boat. I threw the bow line of Wilbur's skiff up to him, and he tied a couple of half hitches around a piling. I scrambled out the back and tied up the other end.

"Girl," he said, "I've got some great blues for you. They're running good this year." From now on I probably wouldn't hear my name twice. Michael just isn't a good Southern name. It should have been Sally Ann or Anna Carol or Mary Beth. For years I couldn't figure how I got the name Michael. Cousin Wilbur finally told me my daddy was drunk when I was born and thought I was a boy.

Mama hates it. Even when I was a preschooler, she and Daddy were still fighting over changing it. I don't know why, but it was the one time I can ever remember Daddy standing up to Mama. I never have figured out if the name meant something to him or whether he just finally got his back up.

Mama didn't give up easily. When I was a teenager, she tried to get me to change it. She had an impact: She completely ended any ambivalence I had about the name. As usual, though, Mama got the last say. For as long as I could remember, everybody in the family had just called me "girl."

"I'll be happy to look at them, John, and I'll be happy to leave them right where they are."

"Come on by the fish house before you leave. You can take a mess back with you. They're the best fish you'll ever taste."

"It'd be a waste of good fish, Uncle John. I hope you think more of your fish than to send them with me." I not only go to the same places when I come down; I have the same conversations. John and I have played this duet dozens of time.

"I don't know what happened to you, girl, not liking seafood. I can't believe you come from around here. Somebody didn't raise you right."

"You can take that up with Mama."

"Your Mama is a good woman."

I find it interesting that people frequently feel the need to tell me Mama is a good woman. My daddy, God rest his soul, was the sweetest man in the county, but no one thinks they have to remind me of that.

I walked on up to the house. There was a huge buffet of fried

116

chicken, sweet potatoes, collard greens, sweet peas, butter-beans, sweet corn, black-eyed peas, and cornbread. Well, actually that was just the edible stuff. There were also mountains of various disgusting sea critters better left unnamed.

"Lawd, girl, I wanted to bring you something." Aunt Sally was at the sea critter table. "But I don't have a thing in the garden. The only thing I've got is some collard greens, and they ain't nothing special. They'll be better come January. My sweet potatoes aren't in, and most everything else has gone by."

"You don't have to have anything for me, Aunt Sally. I come to visit you, not the cucumbers."

"Well, I worry, girl. You aren't nothing but skin and bones. Come home for a while, and we'll put some meat on those bones. How long you here for?"

I had to smile. I could come down here with the entire news apparatus of the Western world temporarily deserting, say, something along the lines of the O. J. Simpson trial, to focus on the Southworth case and know for a fact that the only question anyone would ask me would be, "How long you here for?" I'm not sure what my family has against questions, but I think it has something to do with the family attachment to certainty.

Mama, particularly, has degrees of certainty: ordinary certainty—"I reckon he's sorry he ever got mixed up in that crowd"; extra certainty—"I'll tell you one thing. He's sorry he ever got mixed up with that bunch"; and dead certainty.—"You can say what you want, but it was a sorry day when he got mixed up with that mess, and that's the word with the bark on it." But Mama doesn't have anything you might call uncertainty.

I found Mama sitting in the porch swing, sporting a sequined sweater. "Girl," she said, "It's about time you got here."

"Good to see you too, Mama. You're looking good."

"You got some food?"

"I'm about to."

"Well, help yourself. You're not going to find any better

shrimp anywhere than those shrimp right there. John brought them straight off the boat, and I do believe the scallops are as good as I've ever tasted."

"I don't like seafood."

"Of course you like seafood. Everybody likes seafood."

"Mama, I've never liked seafood."

"You can't not like seafood."

"We have this conversation every time, Mama. I have never liked seafood in my entire life."

"Well, just taste one of those shrimp. Just try one."

"In my lifetime, Mama, I have tasted so many 'just-one-shrimps' that I can close my eyes and bring up the disgusting taste of shrimp at will."

"Well girl," Mama said patiently and slowly like she was talking to an idiot, "you can't just not-like-seafood."

I moved off to the edible table. I did not want to blow up at Mama the first three minutes I saw her, and I was not that far from it. It amazed me. Defense attorneys could hammer at me on the stand for days, and I would smile sweetly and answer their questions, but Mama could yank my chain within sixty seconds.

Mama went back to her story, and the family went back to their own personal art form: conversations without questions. "Well, that nor'easter just came out of nowhere," Mama allowed. "It was as pretty a morning as you could find. John took me over to the banks to troll for some of those blues they been pulling out by the bushel barrel. And we did have right good luck. But right after lunch he says to me, 'I don't like the look of that sky,' he says. 'I think we better head back through the bar while the gettings good.' Well, I hadn't paid a speck of attention to it with the blues biting and all, but I looked up, and sure enough, there were some real dark, mean-looking clouds coming in. I liked to died. I knew right away we'd be lucky to get home. Well, I tell you one thing. I pulled in that line right smart. And we took off like a bat. By the time we got to the bar, we had five- and six-foot breakers over the bow."

"Well, if that don't beat everything," Aunt Sally said. I knew without turning she was shaking her head.

"I don't know why you're going on about five- and six-foot breakers," Cousin Wilbur retorted. Yes, Cousin Wilbur, go for it. Cousin Wilbur has a bit of cantankerousness in him. He knows the sea as well as anyone, so I guess he felt he had a right to speak. He had gone into the military because he figured it was the fastest way to retire to the water. Twenty years later, just like he planned, he retired and started full-time fishing, clamming, crabbing, hunting, and the like. He is one of the few folks who can cross Mama, and I love him for it. "I've come through the bar when I lost a thirty-foot sailboat in the trough in front of me. Couldn't see hide nor hair of her, not even the mast, and she'd be right in front of me. Five- and six-foot breakers ain't nothing special."

There was a dead silence. Story topping is not all that common, at least not around Mama. I turned around and saw Mama looking at him evenly. Then she leaned forward, put her elbow on the table, and got in his face. "Well, I 'spect if you go out in the things you go out in, anything can happen. You momack that little boat of yours to death. But I don't treat things of mine the way you treat things of yours." I had a bad feeling that comment had to do with more than boats and that I wasn't going to like it when I found out what it meant.

"I'm not talking about going out when the coast guard has a small crafts warning up and any damn fool with half a brain would know to stay home. I'm talking about going out on a day as pretty as you please and have a nor'easter blow up in your face. That's a little different."

Cousin Wilbur didn't say anything. Mama's threat to talk about whatever-she-knew-about-that-I-didn't must have got to him. I sighed. Mama is five-one and slight, but I bet if I polled the entire community there wouldn't be anybody who thinks she is that small. If she just had Carlotta's frame — what a hell of a ballplayer she would have made.

14

. . . .

The dark speck on the water kept getting larger—and so did my sense of unease. I tried to reassure myself that there were lots of places it could be going. Even if the boat was coming for me, that didn't necessarily mean anything was wrong. But once someone calls you up and tells you two children have been murdered, you get a little phobic about news. A motorboat heading wide open at eight o'clock in the morning toward Cousin Wilbur's cabin, where there is no phone, looked like news. I sat down on the dock and waited. There wasn't much else to do.

Bitterly, I hoped this wouldn't mess up my day. I had lunch packed. I had the clamming fork in the skiff. I had on my old tennies that I wore to walk on oyster beds. I was wearing a bathing suit under my shorts and T-shirt, and I was headed for the banks. I was going to poke around: fish a little, boat-ride a little, clam a little, swim a little, and walk on sandy beaches-without-another-single-soul a little. All the time I'd let my head freewheel.

120

I have discovered I can take my head out of gear. Just slip a gear, and I have roughly the IQ of a jellyfish. I call it freewheeling. Interestingly though, I get a lot sharper perceptually. Ordinarily, I can't remember where I've left my car keys, but free-wheeling I seem to see everything and remember a lot of it. It won't work for something like court. I am practically aphasic when I'm freewheeling: I have to work to understand language. But afterward, all sorts of things come up: new ways of looking at a case, strategies for court, methods of getting a shut-down kid to talk to me.

The speck was no longer a speck. It was, in fact, Aunt Sally's son Paul on the family speedboat. I was going to be royally pissed if I didn't get to go to the banks today.

"Michael," Paul yelled. The younger generation couldn't exactly call me "girl." He pulled up at the end of the small dock and jumped out to hold the boat. "There's two phone calls for you. Carlotta somebody called and wants you to call her back. She says its urgent. Somebody named Melissa wants you to call, too. She says its urgent. I'll take you over if you want to go."

I thought for a moment about not going. Not knowing might be better than knowing whatever it was. But it was Carlotta, and it was Melissa, and they'd asked me to call. And if I didn't go, it would probably be something I could have done something about. So I climbed on the speedboat with Paul. I didn't particularly feel like talking, but I hadn't seen Paul in a year, so I had to say something.

"How's it going?" I ventured.

"It's going good." he said, revving up the boat as he wheeled it toward home. "The football team won the conference championship, so that was kind of a big deal, and I'm getting psyched about getting out of here and going to college next year." He is a big kid with an easy manner and an open face.

Of course it would be Paul who volunteered to pick me up. He always does everything right. Other kids like him, teachers adore him, coaches chase him. His parents have no clue about the kind of pain and misery that kids can bring. Everything comes easy to Paul. He is a gifted athlete, and if the team won the conference championship, he was a lot of the reason. His parents hope he'll play college ball, but I know he won't.

He doesn't have the killer instinct. He is just too nice a guy. He is like a lot of good high school athletes who win on their natural abilities but who fade in college because there they face people who would kill them to win if not for the fact that it would incur a penalty—the kind of people who wouldn't pick up their sailors if they fell overboard in a transatlantic race if not for the fact they'd be disqualified if they came up short. Paul likes to win. Maybe he even loves to win, but he doesn't despise losing. In the end, he thinks it is just a game.

"How's your girlfriend? Are you still seeing Jennie?"

"No, that was getting too serious. It doesn't make any sense if I'm going off to college in a year and she'll still be here." It was what every parent would want to hear. He is a kid with a plan— a sensible kid, a kid with a future. But my fanatical little soul hoped that, some day, Paul would find something he wanted badly enough to break all the rules.

We pulled up at Aunt Sally's dock, and I jumped out and walked up to the house. There are gardens on both sides of the house, and container plants everywhere on the dock and the deck. Aunt Sally is one of those folks who live to garden, and things blossom and bloom in all directions. She waved from the direction of the beans.

I called Carlotta. If it was going to be bad news I'd rather hear it from her. "What's up?" I said.

"It's nothing terrible," she said.

The relief made me light-headed.

"The police are here. They have a search warrant." Carlotta's ordinarily smooth voice was ruffled.

"What? What? To search our premises? For what? For my records? Why did they get a search warrant for my records? They could have used a subpoena. Did they think I'd hide them?" My voice was rising.

"No, they're not even looking at your records. They're

looking for a book," Carlotta said, "or at least something in a book, but I think a specific book."

"What are you talking about, Carlotta?" I was practically yelling. "Why would the police want a book? What book?"

"I don't know. Adam isn't here, and the officers who are won't say anything. And there's something else you should know. Jack came by last night. He just knocked on the door, and I was cooking, so I let him in, and he talked for a while. He thinks you're avoiding him because he won't leave his wife. He's been trying to reach you to tell you he's decided to leave her."

"What!" This time I did yell. "I don't want him to leave his wife." Through the window I could see Paul and Aunt Sally turn their heads at my screaming. "Tell him not to leave his wife, Carlotta. I've been avoiding him because he was talking about leaving her."

"I can't stop him from leaving his wife, Michael. And anyway, I don't want to get in the middle of this."

"You put yourself in the middle of it, Carlotta. Why were you talking to Jack to all hours instead of telling him to take it up with me?"

"Because he's tried to take it up with you, and you wouldn't call him back, and I didn't say I talked to all hours."

"I was just fooling around, Carlotta. I don't want him to leave his wife."

"Well, there're real people out there you're fooling around with, not blow-up dolls."

I was livid. "So now you're judging me. What gives you the right to judge me? What is this Puritan thing you have?" Then I stopped. I have a bad temper, but I reach a certain point and hit some kind of icy calm. When I spoke again I was chillier but calmer. "This is not about Jack. It's about a lot of other things, but let's stick today with the fact that the police are stomping through your house and my office without anybody's permission, and that feels lousy. And neither one of us knows what they want or what it means."

There was a pause. "You're wrong. It is also about Jack, but, I'm sorry, now isn't the time to bring it up, and, yes, I find them going through my things unbearably intrusive." Carlotta had righted her boat also.

I called my secretary. Melissa informed me that the police had been at the department office as well, and the only thing they had gone through had been my books. What was this? What did they think I had: *Guide to a Double Murder* or *How to Suffocate Two Children Without Leaving Marks?*

A wiser woman wouldn't have called her buddy, the police chief, right away. A wiser woman would have wanted to be in a better frame of mind. But I only have two rules about my temper: I never blow up in court or on one. Other than that, things depend on the circumstances.

I called him. In retrospect I think Adam was probably waiting for the call. I was so angry I felt as if I were mainlining adrenaline. He knew who was on the line because I had to announce myself to the sergeant on the desk. "Chief Bowman," he answered. It was a message, but I ignored it.

"Oh, that's good, Adam. Now it's Chief Bowman."

"Can I help you, Dr. Stone?"

"Better yet. Sure. I'd like to know why the police are searching my premises."

"I'm sorry, but I can't divulge that." Adam's voice was formal and distant. I couldn't detect even a trace of our usual camaraderie in it. "But I would like to talk with you at your earliest convenience."

"About what? Do I need a lawyer?"

"Everybody's entitled to a lawyer."

"I asked if I needed one."

"You know how the police feel about that. Only people with something to hide need people to hide behind."

"Adam, what is going on here? Is it the custom of the police to obtain search warrants without first ascertaining whether or not the person would voluntarily permit the search? What on earth made you assume I wouldn't cooperate with a murder investigation of two small children? Not that I have a single clue what on earth you could possibly expect to find in my office, anyway. And why are you hinting around that I might have something to hide? And while we're at it, what is this Chief Bowman–Dr. Stone shit anyway?"

"Dr. Stone. This is a murder investigation. I plan to do everything by the book. Every single thing that is done or not done and the way it was or wasn't done is going to end up in court. A lot of questions have been raised already about the fact that you and I are friends. I don't think it is in anybody's best interest for me to be forced to withdraw from this case. And I would personally be very annoyed if I had to. The point is, Dr. Stone, that you were out of town and we needed to search your office. Before you jump down my throat again, let me ask you whether or not you would have cleared our going into your offices—or whether you would have asked me to wait till you got back and then tried to pry out of me what we were looking for."

I thought about it. Of course, I wouldn't have just cleared it. I would have wanted to be there. "I'm not so sure from my point of view that I wouldn't prefer you got taken off the case," I grumbled. "At least I could have you on my side."

"I am. But until this case is over, I'm going to dot every *i* and cross every *t*, and it's Chief Bowman to you."

Adam has such a strangely effective way of being angry. I don't understand how he does it. I felt like apologizing, although, of course, I'd never actually do such a thing.

15

I pressed my face against the glass as the plane took off. I've never gotten over that business of things getting smaller as the plane goes higher. Clouds, smouds—once you are at forty thousand feet, nothing interesting happens. But taking off and landing, you feel a little bit like God looking down on the goings on. That blue car passing the white one: Who is in it, and where are they going? And will they ever in their lifetimes cross the people in the white car's path again? And if this is their one and only look at each other, do they know to look carefully, that they are seeing something they will never see again?

The clamming fork had had to go. There was nothing to be done about it. I couldn't very well play on the dunes all day with the police formally requesting an interview and searching my office. So now I slept. I had learned over the years to sleep like a stone once the plane hits the clouds. And learned, too, to wake up as the flight attendant announces landing.

I decided to go home before I went to the police department. The state of the house would tell me something about where I stood with Adam. I was more nervous than I would ever admit when I drove in. No signs of disturbance. I walked around to the deck and looked through the window. Absolutely no sign the police had been there. I punched the air with my fist, kicked my shoes off, and danced barefoot to the kitchen to get a glass of ice tea. I was feeling better. Whatever Adam was after, either he didn't need it very badly, or he didn't think I had it, or—better yet—he trusted me to tell him if I did.

Adam knew I had retreated to a house in the country, one that I passionately wanted to keep private. A police raid on that house would have been the end of my privacy, so, somehow, he managed to use his search warrant on my old house where my office was. Carlotta lived in the old home, of course, but I would bet that search warrant had my name on it, and not Carlotta's.

I put on my Dr. Stone clothes: long black skirt, white ribbed turtleneck, checked suit jacket. Conservative. Respectable. This was a role, just like being in court, and it requires a certain kind of costume. I didn't know why I was so nervous about this police interview. It couldn't be any worse than testifying in court, and I did that all the time. At least, I'd get a clue what they were looking for from their questions. Of course, there would be the usual fight over the records and over revealing my client's confidences. But both Adam and I could sleepwalk through that by now. He was the only police chief in town; I wasn't the only forensic psychologist, but I was probably the busiest. We'd sung this duet already. And somewhere in there he'd have to tell me what book he was looking for, and, if I was lucky, he'd tell me why.

I walked in the front door of the police station. I didn't know the officer on the desk, and he didn't seem particularly excited to see me, which somehow pleased me. I'd like to be as minor a part of this case as possible. Adam came out, formally thanked me for coming, and led me to an interviewing room. He asked me immediately if I minded if he taped the interview. I didn't, but the whole thing was getting more mysterious all the time. What on earth did he think I knew that was worth taping? A senior detective named Jonathan joined us and sat down across the table.

Jonathan has a fireplug body, square, immobile face, short, marinelike haircut, and biceps that looked like the kind they use to advertise dumbells—I've never understood why most of the world's weightlifting seemed to be done by cops or convicts. He looks like a caricature of a cop, which means, of course, that most people don't take him seriously. I do. He is a very savvy cop: an ex-Boston cop who used to work organized crime. He is, in fact, Adam's most experienced detective. What on earth was he doing in this interview?

"Good to see you, Jonathan." I reached out to shake his hand. "Good work on the Rouleau case." Jonathan's face didn't change a whole lot, but his eyes warmed up a bit. The Rouleau case had been interesting. A woman had come in to see me for depression in the middle of a divorce/custody fight case. Her husband didn't want to give up his girlfriend, but he didn't want to let go of the marriage, either. His wife had finally had enough and had filed for divorce. By the time I saw her she was worn down by her husband's continual crying jags, his marathon two A.M. phone calls, and his suicidal threats.

The next time I saw her, I hardly recognized her. She had been sitting up all night with a loaded gun in her hand. Her husband had broken in the house that afternoon, raped her, photographed her in obscene poses, then demanded she get $100,000 from her wealthy parents and give the money to him or he would distribute the photos. Adam had been out of town, so I called Jonathan. She was too frightened to agree to go to the police, but she agreed to talk to an officer "friend" of mine off the record. Jonathan had come over with his best strong-competent-male-rescues-frightened-victimized-female manner, which, I admit, irritated me to the point my jaw almost locked.

Nonetheless, he did calm her down and talk her into formally going to the police to sign a complaint. I hated that male-rescue routine. On the other hand, I wasn't that fond, either, of seeing my client so traumatized her voice was an octave higher than normal. There are times to take gun courses and times to call the police.

All at once I felt the weight of the being-interviewed-by-the-police thing. In all my years in court, they had never been asking questions about me; it was always about someone else. With the spotlight turned on me, I felt small and exposed and as if I wanted to meekly protest my innocence even though I wasn't being accused of anything. I wanted them to like me. That kind of feeling infuriated me so much it would make me insufferable.

Adam cleared his throat. Damn it, he still looked good, even while getting ready to interrogate me. I looked at his hands. I was not going to think about his hands.

"Thank you for coming in today, Dr. Stone. We just have a few questions we'd like to ask."

I said nothing.

"Please state your full name for the record."

"Michael Stacy Stone."

"And your address?"

I told him, sort of. Well, he didn't say home address, he just said address. Adam looked at me. He could consider that a lie, since we both knew they were asking for my home address. I wondered if he was remembering our conversation in the gym in which I had cheerfully planned on lying in court. Was he wondering if I'd lie to him as well? I tried to look sincere and reassuring.

"Do you know Sharon Southworth?"

"Yes. I believe that is a matter of public record."

"How did you meet her?"

"Chief Bowman, it is a matter of public record that I did a custody evaluation on Sharon Southworth's children and met her in that context. Now, that is all I am going to say about Ms. Southworth. The ethical rules for psychologists prevents me from revealing any information about a client without either the client's permission or a court order."

"May I remind you this is a murder investigation?"

"Then it shouldn't be difficult to get a court order. Although," I added, "much of what you're interested in may be in the transcripts of the case already, which are — as you well know — a matter of public record."

He had to ask. I had to decline. Neither of us had a choice. The cops would go for a subpoena. I wouldn't oppose them, not this time. It was all routine. But it didn't explain why Jonathan was here. Something important had to be going on because Adam wouldn't waste his time.

Adam continued. "I understand your position, Dr. Stone, but I'm not entirely sure Ms. Southworth ever was your client. It is my understanding that the children were your clients, so I'm not sure that she is entitled to privilege on her own. And given that the children were your clients, I'm sure Dr. Southworth, who had custody when they died, would be willing to sign a release." I was sorry to hear him raise that whole issue. He could be right, and I knew it. I wasn't sure whether I was required to keep information about Sharon confidential or not. In truth, she had never been my client.

He went on. "But be that as it may. For the moment I am not challenging you. If we need more information about your relationship with Ms. Southworth, I will go for the subpoena. But I am going to ask you some very specific questions about Ms. Southworth that I believe have nothing to do with any professional confidences. They are simple observational questions, and I would like you to think before you refuse to answer them."

This was not routine. It was not the duet I knew. Worse, it sounded like a genuine request.

"Are you aware of any books Ms. Southworth may have been reading recently — aware by noticing books at her house when you made a home visit, by hearing any off-hand comments by her or others?"

Books she had been reading? I thought about it. "I don't know if I'm allowed to answer that," I said. "I will need to get a consult." Had she been reading any books? I couldn't remember anything like that.

"I would appreciate it if you would get back to me on that. I have other questions in that line."

"Like what?"

"Like any information you may have on where the books came from, on her opinion of the books, things like that. Information on whether any particular books seemed important to her."

Carlotta said they were looking for a book. But why? This was getting weirder and weirder.

"All right," I said. "I will get back to you."

But Adam wasn't finished. "Have you read *Beloved?*"

"*Beloved?* By Toni Morrison?" I was thoroughly lost. "Yes, I have."

"Do you own a copy of it?"

" "Yes, actually, I do." Melissa didn't know my craziness about not owning things and had given me a copy for my birthday. I had loved it so much that I hadn't been able to bring myself to get rid of it.

"When did you acquire this copy?"

"Last January. January sixteenth." I started to go on and then shut up. I didn't have to explain how I knew when I got it. Besides, what did this have to do with anything?

"Do you know where that book is now?" The atmosphere was suddenly charged. I became aware that he and Jonathan were completely still.

"I don't know. I had it in my office for a while to read when I had a cancellation or whatever. I think I took it home when I finished. I'm not sure. But what is this about, Adam?" I was so befuddled I slipped back into our usual casualness.

"Bear with me," he said. "Think carefully. When was the last time you saw that book?"

"I don't know. Like I said, I remember having it in the office, but I think I took it home sometime earlier this summer. I can't remember seeing it at home, though, so I'm not sure what I did with it."

"Did your copy have any writing on it? Any underlining? Any identifying marks of any kind?

"Sure," I replied. "I underline things I like. Sometimes I make comments in the margins."

And then I stopped. I knew what *Beloved* had to do with the case. I didn't know where they found it or how they tied it to Sharon Southworth, and I certainly didn't know why they were interested in my copy, but I knew what they thought it had to do with the murders.

"Oh, my God." I said. "That can't be." My mind was flying. If it were true, she did kill them. But how could that be? And somewhere I kept thinking I had talked about *Beloved* with somebody connected with this case months ago. But whom? I didn't think Toni Morrison was going to like this.

I was so preoccupied that at first I didn't see Adam had put a photostat of a book page on the table. I picked it up and could feel the color leave my face. It was a single page, torn out of a book. I knew what it described without reading it. I looked at it for a very long moment. I put it on the table and smoothed it out carefully, very carefully, though it didn't need smoothing. No one spoke. I tried to look at the page. I tried to think about what it meant. But I felt as if I were freewheeling. My brain seemed to have slipped a gear without my consent. I did recognize the handwriting in the margin right away—well, I know my own handwriting even brain-dead—but I could barely read the three words written there. "Murder as love?" I slowly read. Whatever that means, I thought. I stood up. "Excuse me," I said. "I have to go."

16

. . . .

I headed for the car at warp speed. Adam hurried after me. "I'll go with you," he said. I ignored him. To be truthful, I only half heard him. I just wanted to get home. He caught up with me at the car and stepped in front of me when I started to open the door. "You can't touch it," he said. "Do you hear me? You can't touch it."

"All right, all right," I said. "Just get out of my way."

"I'll drive," he said. I must have looked a little disordered.

"You most certainly will not," I said. "If you want to drive, drive your own car. Now move. I want to go home."

"Okay," he said and flew around to the passenger side. I guess he thought I'd leave without him.

I drove straight home, to my real home. Ordinarily it was not a long drive, it didn't take more than fifteen minutes. But this trip was taking light-years. I'd retire before this trip was over. The light went red. I wanted to kill the spotlight designer who had me trapped there when there was no one else in any of the other three directions. This is progress? They can't figure out a stoplight that lets the only car at the intersection go? The light should have changed by now. It must be broken. How long before I can just give up and go? If Adam hadn't been with me, I'd have just run the damn thing. Millenna passed. The light changed.

We didn't talk. My head hadn't slowed down since I saw the page from the Morrison book. Did Sharon really kill them after all? Did her crazy, paranoid little mind seize on *Beloved* as an excuse? Why my copy? Did she take my note in the margin as permission? I could kill the bitch. But then I tend to be down on child murderers in general. How could she drag me into this? I didn't want to be within one hundred miles of this thing.

"This goddamn thing has been one shock after another," I said to Adam. "I hope you don't have anything else in store for me." He didn't comment, which was not at all reassuring. And then what he had done hit me. "Jesus, Adam, the book was crucial evidence," I said, as much to myself as to him. "I can't believe you didn't search my house. You really went out on a limb." He just shrugged. Great. On top of everything, I owed him big time. Next to owning, I hate owing.

I flew into the house. I wasn't sure where to look for the book; I just don't leave a lot of stuff lying around. Maybe it was in those piles of legal cases I brought home from the office. "I'll check upstairs," I said.

"I'll come with you," Adam replied. It looked like he wasn't going to leave my elbow till he got that book in his little evidence bag.

I started pulling legal papers off the pile next to my bed and, in my frenzy, almost missed it. The paperback was smaller than the legal papers and had fallen behind them.

I just looked at it. Adam didn't need to warn me about touching it. I had no impulse to pick it up. Somebody who had killed two children had touched it. I'd much rather be nose to nose with a cottonmouth water moccasin in the middle of a moonless night than touch that book. Adam had his hand within inches of my arm. So much for trusting me. When he saw I wasn't making any move to grab it, he slowly pulled out a pair of rubber gloves and put them on—eyeing my arm all the time.

Ordinarily I would have been miffed. I know enough not to touch evidence that might put a child murderer away, and Adam ought to know that. But I was too fixated on the book to get into it with him. I noticed that, even with the rubber gloves on, he picked the book up by the edges.

"What page?" I asked.

"One forty-nine," Adam answered, gingerly turning the pages. There it was: a ragged edge where 149 should have been. I shook my head in disbelief. Still in a crouch, I rocked back on my heels and stared at the jagged edge. Nobody said anything. I had the feeling Adam was looking at me, but I couldn't take my eyes off the book long enough to find out. Finally, I heard myself say, "I'd like some tea."

I got up as Adam put the book in a plastic bag, and I remembered Willy's comments. He couldn't be right. Nobody would put a plastic bag on a child's head and make another child watch. Killing children is nonsensical enough, but to make another child watch? There isn't that much meanness in a swamp gator. There isn't that much meanness in an Outer Banks pony. There isn't a snake in the world that has enough venom in it to do a thing like that. Am I really related to a species that has that much malevolence in the gene pool? Being reincarnated as a housefly might be a step up.

17

. . . .

Mostly, I am an ice tea person. Almost nothing ever gets me to the hot tea stage. Men never do. Most court losses don't; they just make me mad. But this case. If this case kept going, I'd need a samovar.

I sat on the deck thinking. I just wanted to be out of this thing. I didn't want to be responsible in the tiniest, most miniscule way for the murder of those kids. I certainly didn't want a book of mine to have inspired anybody. I wanted to know that if I had never been born, it wouldn't have changed anything: I had no responsibility for their murders. But it wasn't bad enough that my testimony might have cost mom custody, which maybe got the kids killed. Now I had to worry about her getting ideas from my books, or worse, my comments in the margin.

"It reminds me of the chicken bones," I said out loud. Adam looked up from his tea. Behind him I could hear the rush of the stream and see the trees turning dark as the dusk settled in.

"Time out," I had said to him after the book was safely in a plastic bag. "Time out. What if you and I have a cup of tea. Just sit on the deck and drink our tea and try to sort this out. Off the record."

"Absolutely, definitively off the record?"

"On both sides, Adam. You can't use things you hear from me, either."

"Deal," Adam had agreed and had gone off to fix the tea while I changed out of my work costume.

Pulling off my blouse, I sighed. I had had fantasies of bringing Adam here. Fantasies that involved hot tubs and moonlight shining through the skylight in patches on my quilt. Instead, with this case going on, I'd be lucky if I could get him to call me by my first name. I could not imagine him on the stand admitting he was having an affair with one of the principal witnesses, and I couldn't imagine him lying. I had to smile. The more unavailable he got, the more appealing he became. They write pop psychology books about people like me. I put on earrings. You never know.

"What do chicken bones have to do with anything?" Adam was still waiting.

"I had a client who showed up early one day while I was eating lunch. I told her to come on in and excused myself to wash my hands. Three years later, she got mad at me and came in one day and threw chicken bones in my face. I didn't even know what they were. She had stolen the chicken bones from my lunch and had frozen them to keep some part of me near her. It was pretty sick.

"I'm just not sure what territory we're in here. Is it an accident she stole my copy of the book? Did she hear me talking about it with someone? Is it a message to me? Therapists just don't believe in accidents about stuff like this. But I can't make any sense of this. Where did you find the page?"

"In her diary," Adam said. "It was just stuck between the pages. But it's odd. There were no other references in there to the book or anything related to the case. In fact, the rest of the diary is pretty mundane. 'Called mother.' That sort of thing. It's not what you'd consider deep."

"Are her fingerprints on the page?"

"No, they aren't, which is part of what makes me uncomfortable with the whole thing. And why I'd have broken your arm if you had reached for the book. Although," he said, "it isn't one hundred percent clear the lack of her prints means anything. Fingerprints don't take particularly well on paper."

"But if Sharon Southworth's fingerprints are on the book, it's a done deal."

"Maybe. Even then, fingerprints aren't everything, but I'd say things would be looking pretty grim for her—unless she can buy O.J.'s defense team. On the other hand, it would be interesting if her fingerprints weren't on it and Nathan Southworth's were."

This really was crucial evidence. I raised my eyebrows and sighed. I had calmed down a bit, and I was having trouble again seeing Sharon as the murderer of her own children. Then again, a lot of people probably felt that way about Susan Smith. Who the hell was it I was discussing *Beloved* with? I was sure it wasn't Sharon. No matter who did it, *Beloved*—my copy of *Beloved*—was in the middle of it. What son of a bitch wanted to drag me into this?

I was more and more amazed that Adam hadn't used his search warrant on my home. But I wasn't going to raise it; it might get sticky.

But Adam did. "It wasn't that big a deal," he said. "The only person who had a stake in destroying the evidence would have been Sharon Southworth—and she was in jail. If it was anybody else, they wanted the evidence to be found."

The wind lifted the ends of my hair. I closed my eyes and listened to the resonance in Adam's voice. Some voices just dripped testosterone: Elvis Presley's and Bruce Springsteen's and, for my taste, Adam's. They made the estrogen swim in your ears. You could get high on that amount of estrogen.

"While you were searching the wrong house, what if I had given the book away? Handled it? Burned it?"

"You were out of town by then."

"What if I'd had it with me?"

"Then the search warrant wouldn't have done me any good."

"I don't understand why you waited so long to come looking for it. You must have gone through everything that first day."

"We did. We found it that afternoon. But I didn't recognize your handwriting right away."

All of a sudden I sat bolt upright. This business of putting pieces together had just blown up in my face. "Adam, did they get in my house? How do I know she, whoever, got into the book at the office?"

"You don't," he said.

"But I lock it," I said, trying to calm myself. "I lock it, and there was no sign of forced entry."

"Doesn't have to be," Adam said, peeling a tangerine. "Do you lock it when you're in it? Do you always lock and unlock the door every time you go in and out?"

"No," I said, my heart rate going up, this time without benefit of estrogen.

"Well," Adam went on, "it wouldn't take much. Say you're in the shower, or out back in the hot tub. Our perp walks in, filches the page, and he's off. Or she's off."

I looked down into my tea and took a sip. I found it interesting that I was using both hands. I closed my eyes and shook the thought off. It didn't have to be that. He, she, whoever, could have gotten the book from the office. They could have ripped the page out there before I brought the book home. They could never even have thought about coming into my house.

18

. . . .

The dream began that night. Did I usually dream in color? I never noticed. But in this dream the colors were so intense they looked like Day-Glo. I was walking up a hill to a small cottage. I knocked on the door, and an old woman opened it. "He's ready," she said and went off to fetch an old, blind man. They said good-bye tearfully: It seemed clear the leave-taking would be permanent. The old man and I started walking down the hill.

At the bottom of the hill, he asked me if she was waving. I turned back to see, and the old woman was hanging by her neck from the tree. Her face was blue and her body was swaying in the wind. I paused. "Yes," I said after a moment, "she's waving." He smiled and turned and we went on. I woke up frightened and with something nagging at me.

"The problem," I told Carlotta the next day, "is that I don't have dreams like that. I don't have glorious, symbolic, illogical, bizarre dreams. I have dreams that are weird because they're so normal. I go grocery shopping. I go to work. I sit in meetings.

The worst that happens in my dreams is that I double-schedule a client. There is something very strange about that dream."

Carlotta shrugged. Dreams aren't evidence. Lawyers don't spend a lot of time worrying about them. What matters in court is what you can prove, not what you think, much less what you dream. Carlotta might have a lot of "frills" in her house, but when it comes to the law, her thinking is stripped down and to the point. Her opinion of the unconscious is that it ought to stay that way. It is odd in a way. My house might be a lot more streamlined than hers, but my head just might be a lot more cluttered.

Carlotta was sitting in her kitchen wearing perfectly pressed white satin pj's and drinking hazelnut decaf. I had gotten up my courage to go back to work, and today was a private practice day. The TV cameras seemed to be gone, and if there were any reporters out there, they were working undercover as pigeons. Thank God the media had the attention span of a gerbil.

I had come an hour early to have breakfast with Carlotta. I am addicted to her coffee; on the other hand I still can't make my peace with her clothes. Why don't things work for her like they do for the rest of us? If I sat down in pj's like that—much less slept in them—they'd look like used tissue paper when I stood up. Maybe she sleeps in a T-shirt like I do and then, before she steps outside her bedroom door, changes into freshly pressed pj's. I have a fantasy of hiding a camera in Carlotta's room and catching her at six A.M., ironing satin pj's.

Not a chance. When I lived there, I had once run into her in the hall going to the bathroom in the middle of the night. She was wearing pressed white satin pj's. Who knows? Maybe she puts them on to go to the bathroom. I laughed out loud. Carlotta was eyeing me patiently over the top of the coffee cup. The look told me she knew that my reverie and mindless laughter probably had something to do with her.

Why am I so obsessed with the way Carlotta dresses? I'm more obsessed with it than she is. Is it jealousy? I don't really think so. I know what jealousy is. I feel it every time I see someone on a grand prix jumping course. The last three strides before the jump, I climb right into the saddle with them. Yes, lengthen that stride. Yes, or you'll chip for sure. I feel the leather in my hands, throw myself forward for the surge as the horse takes off, shift my balance back, and collect the horse for the turn to the next jump. Which line to take? Well, he's doing good. I'd go straight down the hill. Uh-oh. He's getting strung out coming off the hill. Pull him up! Get him in your hands!

It's the gospel truth—as Mama would say—that I'd rather own a great horse like Calypso than be with any man on earth. I can salivate just thinking about Calypso. In his prime, he was a horse so even-tempered and calm he took naps between grand prix rounds. While the other show jumpers foamed at the mouth and kicked their grooms, Calypso had to be tapped on the forehead to wake him up for his next round. And yet, and yet, put him on a jumping course, and eat your heart out, Baryshnikov. I shook my head at the fate that denies me such a horse. No, I know jealousy, and whatever gets under my skin about Carlotta isn't it.

Carlotta was still eyeing me silently and, I thought, with a kind of wry amusement. We were having one of our nonconversations. Lots of stuff was going on in my head, but I kept forgetting to share it. One thing's for sure: Carlotta is a patient woman. Sort of like Calypso in her way.

I gave up my reverie and headed to my office. We had cut a door into a side wall so that clients could enter and leave without going into the personal parts of the house at all. In the office wing, I had a therapy room for adults, a playroom for children, a very small waiting room, and a bathroom. Once I was there, I closed the door on the rest of the house and immediately forgot all about it and the world outside. I might as well be on another planet when I work. I have learned to focus so intently over the years that sometimes I get tunnel vision.

My first client today was a four-year-old. She had short brown hair—silky with wisps that curled around her ears. She was a big, sturdy girl for four, the kind that are always assumed to be older than they are. Unfortunately in her case, this was not a help. It meant the gap between people's expectations and her behavior was roughly the size of the Grand Canyon.

I saw her mother for ten minutes alone at the beginning of the session. "She pulled up everybody's plants in the preschool," she said. "You know how they cut milk cartons up and all the kids grow their own plants. Well, she pulled up everybody's, and the teachers are threatening to throw her out again. They don't say it like that. They say they're not sure they're the right setting for her, but that's what they mean." Mom ran her hand through her own silky brown hair to catch a stray wisp. She alternated between being empathic with Jeannie and exasperated. Most days she understood why Jeannie acted the way she did, but some days she came close to shaking her and screaming.

Jeannie hit the room like a tornado. Within minutes the puppets were all over the floor, the Magic Markers all over the couch, and Jeannie was strangling a doll, something she had never done before. Carefully I sat down beside her. I could hear labored breathing, a sound that is only present when she is acutely anxious. When I first met her, I couldn't believe breathing that loud in a child so young could be due to nothing more than anxiety. I had asked her mother to have her evaluated for asthma. Nope—it was, indeed, one hundred percent anxiety.

But what on earth was going on today? I hadn't heard the sound of that breathing for months, not since the day she described sexual abuse by her dad. And there was something here today that had never been here before. They say animals can smell fear. Can people smell it, too? It's almost like an odor in the room. Am I losing it? Making things up?

Jennie's hands seemed locked on the doll's throat. The knuckles were white from the effort of squeezing. Her hands were shaking, maybe from the effort. I had never seen her so focused and intent. The only sound in the room was her labored breathing.

I said nothing. I couldn't think of anything I could say that wouldn't somehow lead her. And, anyway, I needed to see where she would go with this on her own. Abruptly she dropped the doll. "I need to go to the bathroom," she said.

We headed to the waiting room, where Jeannie declined her mother's help in the bathroom. She went off while I checked in with mom.

"Well, something's going on," her mother said. "I'm telling you. She's been impossible. I've been eating Xanax to cope with it. I'm right on the verge of driving her to my parents for the weekend and just taking off. I don't know how much more of this I can take."

"Did she hear anything about the murders?" I asked. I knew that hearing that two kids had been murdered in their beds probably wouldn't make my young clients—all of whom had already been traumatized by something—feel any safer in the world. A certain resurgence of nightmares and general fears was probably to be expected. And as for strangling the doll, maybe she had heard the children were strangled.

"Good Lord, no," her mom said. "I couldn't even watch the TV coverage. I kept her completely away from it."

"Are you sure?" I pushed. "She goes to preschool. Other kids might have been talking about it. It was all over the papers. She might have seen a paper at school or heard something."

"Maybe," mom admitted. "But with anything that upsets her I usually hear about it—a lot. You know Jeannie. The clerk at the grocery store hears about it, and anybody who gets in the elevator with us hears about it. But she's never mentioned the murders. I just think she doesn't know."

"What else is going on?" I couldn't get over the change. Although, come to think of it, her last session had been somewhat odd, too, and that had been before the murders. "Are you going back to court? Has she seen her father?"

144

"No, but her dad has won supervised visitation with her brother. I still think he abused him, but how is a two-and-a-half-year-old supposed to report it? Jeannie stays home with my sister when I drop Tommy off and sit in the car while the minister supervises the visitation. She knows Tommy and I are going to see her dad. The son of a bitch could give a shit how it affects her—or Tommy either, for that matter."

That was probably true, although I wasn't going to say it. Feeding people's hatred for their ex-spouses isn't all that helpful—even though there are times when the hatred has been earned.

Mom went on. "You know, I still don't get it. The lousy bastard never paid any attention to Tommy when he lived with us. He yelled and screamed at him over nothing. He called him you little shit so often that—I know you won't believe his—at one point right before Tommy turned two, someone asked him his name and he said you little shit."

"With Jeannie he was all sweetness and light. She was his angel. She could do no wrong. But now he can't get at Jeannie any more so he's desperate to see Tommy. It makes me want to throw up."

I understood mom's frustration. None of this made sense to her. Unfortunately, I see it every day. The problem is that not everybody who is desperate to keep their children is desperate for the right reasons. Half the time they want their children to take care of them. Judges almost never get this. In court, they see a parent crying that their poor babies have been taken away, and they give them back, thinking the parent loves the child. Maybe they do, or maybe they just feel like their left arm has been taken away. Your arm is part of you. It needs what you need. It has no existence except to serve you. You can't even imagine it having needs of its own. When you treat children like your left arm, bad things happen.

Unfortunately, Tommy's dad is one of those "I-can't-live-without-my-left-arm" folks. He needs Tommy to meet *his* emotional needs, to keep him from being lonely. If I asked him what Tommy needs, odds are, he'd tell me what he needs himself, instead.

I thought about the visits between Tommy and his dad. Was it enough to set Jeannie off like this? The strangling business gave me pause. I'd never seen her do anything like that before, even early on in therapy when she was most anxious over disclosing the abuse. And there had never been any indication her dad was anything but a "grooming" offender, one of those types who manipulates children into sex, but who isn't physically violent with them.

Jeannie came back, and we went back to the office. She picked up the doll immediately and stripped off its clothes, muttering things so low I couldn't hear them. Suddenly she threw it on the floor. I picked it up. I didn't know Jeannie saw me—she was half turned away—but she immediately said, "She's bad."

"She's bad?"

"Yes, she's very bad." She said it almost primly. She dropped the sand toys in her hands. "Can we draw now?" The little girl who hesitantly asked seemed much younger than the grim tornado who had trashed the room earlier.

"Yes, of course." We moved over to the art table.

"What makes her bad?" No answer. "Did she do something bad? Or say something bad?" No answer.

Then she said softly, "I said 'stop' 'cepting he didn't." She didn't look up, but seemed intently focused on her drawing. She didn't appear to even be talking to me. Her face held unmistakable sadness.

"Oh," I said. "He didn't stop, even when you said stop." I was being very careful. I didn't want to put words in her mouth or make assumptions about what she was trying to say, so I stuck pretty close to whatever she herself had said. Usually when you repeat what kids say, they will continue talking, but Jeannie didn't. She stayed silent for a long while, then dropped the drawing and went back to the sandbox. She looked at the shelves holding the toys for the sandtray—a two-foot-by-three-foot sandbox set on a table. There are people and buildings and animals and rocks and trees and all kinds of paraphernalia for making worlds. She carefully selected all the spiders and snakes, then made a scene filled with snakes and spiders and carnivorous predators.

When the session was over, Jeannie went to the bathroom again, giving her mother and me another moment of privacy. "She didn't even want to come today, which is rare for her," her mom volunteered. "Usually she asks when she's going to get to see you. I finally told her I'd come with her, and that's the only way she'd come."

Yes, of course. I had forgotten that mom usually had the GAL bring her. Mom works in the records section of the local hospital. Every second she takes off from work is docked from her pay or from her two-week annual vacation. "I took the whole morning off, which is not going to help things at work, but if Jeannie doesn't settle down, I'm going to be too nervous to work, anyway." Mom was pretty close to overwhelmed when Jeannie was at the top of her form.

It happens all too often. Single-parent family. Two small kids. Not enough money. No child support. These dads never seem to pay, and the courts never seem to make them. Too much work at work. Too much work at home. There isn't time between the washing and the drying and the constant house cleaning and the shopping and the cooking and the shuffling children back and forth to day care—time to exercise or take care of herself. There isn't time to get sick. Add sexual abuse and an angry, acting-out child tearing up the world, and there isn't enough resilience left in mom to handle it. And what happens if mom can't work anymore? Too scary for me to contemplate, much less for her to. So, I didn't feel much pressure to figure out what was going on with Jeannie and help her calm down. Right.

I was still thinking about Jeannie ten minutes later when Kiwi came in. Traumatized children, adult survivors—one way or the other I am always dealing with violence of some kind.

Some days I long for a child to come in because she isn't doing her homework or for an adult to come in because he's considering a career change.

I looked at Kiwi. Oh my, it was hard to believe the woman was living in L. L. Bean country. She had on a white linen suit with a black silk blouse buttoned neatly to her neck and black patent leather heels. The black patent leather heels told the tale.

I always think in every relationship there is a signature moment that contains, like the proverbial raindrop, the entire DNA for the relationship. A client had once told me about her marital troubles. Her husband had quit wearing his wedding ring during a period in which they seemed to be constantly fighting. Later, when things were better, she asked him if he would start wearing it again. He said yes—with some prodding on her part—and went off to look for it. My heart broke for her when I heard where he was looking: in old boxes with rusty nuts and bolts. She didn't think her marriage was over, but I knew it was.

With individuals, it is often a gesture, an article of clothing, a defining moment. For Kiwi, it is the black patent leather heels. They are the exact mixture of little-girl innocence (the shoes look exactly like the kind little girls have been wearing for decades) and adult sexuality (little girls don't wear three-inch spike heels) that Kiwi blends. Kiwi absolutely believes that there is nothing sexual about her way of being in the world. She is astounded at the frequency with which men come on to her. And I'd be hard pressed to explain it to her. And yet, the perfectly bleached hair, the touch of lace always peeking out of her sweater, the constant tan, her way of sitting primly with her knees together, even the small pocketbook she clutches. All of the little-girl gestures she makes. Kiwi oozes vulnerability.

"We were driving toward his parents' house in Lyndonville. We had the RV because he doesn't like to stay in their house, and we were supposed to be there for the weekend. Nothing happened. I mean, we didn't argue or anything. He just seemed to get angrier the closer we got. I wasn't saying much. When he's like that I can't seem to win. If I'm quiet he says I'm ignoring him, and if I say anything he says I'm nagging at him. Finally he pulled into a rest area, and he decided to have sex." Tears started falling, but Kiwi didn't seem to notice. Maybe she had cried so much they just seemed like part of her face. "I didn't say anything. I'd have gone along with anything to just calm him down, but he was so rough. He didn't give me a chance to get—you know—ready, and it hurt so much, and then he just pulled it out and put it in my bum, and that was so painful I yelled, and that made him really mad. And he started saying I belonged to him and he could do anything he wanted, and then he got a cucumber, and he stuck it in. And afterward he wanted to just go on to his parents, but there was so much blood. He split something, and it hurt to move or sit, and I told him I had to go to the hospital, and he acted like there was something wrong with me and it was all my fault."

"That sounds awful, Kiwi. He's back to raping you again."

"Well, I wouldn't say he raped me. I didn't say no."

I felt a wave of rage that I desperately tried to control. I wanted to reach across the room and shake Kiwi. I know it isn't politically correct, but it is only my second impulse to comfort people like Kiwi. My first is to shake them while screaming at them to throw the bum out.

I didn't do it, of course. Instead, I tried to think where to start. "Kiwi, did you say yes?"

"Well, he didn't give me a chance. I would have."

"Because you wanted to have sex with him?"

"Well, no, not when he's like that." Kiwi tried to rub the streaking mascara from her cheeks, but she was still crying, and the mascara seemed to smear faster than she could clean it. How much was she wearing, anyway? "I mean I like to have sex with him when he's nice. Well, I used to, anyways. But it's always awful when he's mad."

149

"Then why were you willing?"

Kiwi started sobbing. "Why do you think? Because he would have beat the living shit out of me if I hadn't."

"Kiwi, that's called rape."

"I don't like to think of it like that."

There were a lot of things I wanted to say. I wanted to say, "If having sex with someone because they'll beat the shit out of you if you don't isn't rape, exactly what is?"

I wanted to say, "That's what high-powered rifles are for." But that was definitely out. Women like Kiwi take an amazing amount of crap, but every once in a while one of them turns around and loads up her shotgun. And as they get closer to the edge, it is easy to misread a joke as a suggestion.

Maybe what I really wanted to say was, "Do you do this just to torture me? You waltz in here week after week. My personal all-time low was the time he broke your jaw. And week after week you dump all this on me and make me just as helpless as you are. I DON'T NEED THIS IN MY LIFE." Then I realize this *is* her life, and I'm even more depressed.

Why didn't she want to think of it as rape? I knew why. She liked to think she had a choice. She liked to think what she chose mattered. She didn't want to believe she was as helpless as I made her sound. When you don't have choices, the illusion of choice is sometimes all that's left.

Kiwi continued her retreat. "He's really not a bad guy. He just gets frustrated. And I'm no saint. I'm sure I make mistakes, too. It's not all his fault."

I rarely take battering cases. I rarely take them because it is conceivable I am the worst therapist in the world for battered women. Battered folks need people who are slow and patient, who help them build, session by slow, painful session, enough self-esteem, enough belief in themselves to think that what happened to them mattered. Instead, I spend my time wondering if death squads would be such a bad idea, if only you could hit the right people.

My day didn't get any better. The last phone call of the day was about a six-year-old boy who had been soiling following sexual abuse by his uncle. He was soiling, it turned out, to try to keep the uncle from raping him. He thought having poops in his pants would make him so disgusting the uncle would leave him alone. The uncle was undeterred, and Johnny, in panic, had eventually told another child, who told his mom. The soiling had stopped instantly once his uncle stopped hanging around, and it had never returned.

Johnny's mom practically exploded on the phone line. "It's started again. It is absolutely unbelievable. It brought every-thing back. All those trips to the pediatrician. All the different counselors we saw. All the advice. I just cannot go through this again. And he was doing so well," she wailed.

What was going on here? My entire caseload appeared to be falling apart. "How long has it been going on?"

"He did it two weeks ago, right before he left to go see you, but I just tried to tell myself that anyone could have an accident. I mean it had been months. But he did it twice this week. So it's back. And with all the court stuff coming up and all the different interviews and depositions and all that, I just can't imagine how we're going to get through this. They're going to say it has nothing to do with the abuse. I mean, before it always happened when his uncle was around, so the prosecutor said it was a way he could prove Johnny wasn't just making up a story—that he had symptoms, too, but now what? I'll tell you what. They're going to say the fact that he's doing it and his uncle hasn't been around for months means that it didn't mean anything the first time."

"Well, they can try, but that's not necessarily true." I had put the best face on it I could, but she had a point. "He's having to talk about the abuse for the depositions. It may have brought the whole thing back up. He may be remembering the abuse and soiling out of anxiety." But I was talking through my hat. I didn't have a clue why he would start this up right now.

I dragged home. Work is a definite high when things go well. Successful court cases, kids who get protected, kids who get better, I can float on the endorphins. But nothing makes me feel lousier than everything turning to dust in my hands. I hadn't seen anybody all day who was doing well, and worse, two kids were going down the tubes and I didn't know why.

19

. . . .

I had the dream again that night. It is a frustrating business knowing your psyche is trying to tell you something, but not being able to figure out what. There is an old saying among psychotherapists: "Don't worry if you don't understand your clients' dreams. They'll dream simpler and simpler dreams until you get the point." But my unconscious wasn't putting anything on sale. I guess my psyche thought if it played this particular tune enough times, I'd figure out the lyrics. I knew where the crux of the dream was: It had something to do with the moment I turned and saw the old woman hanging by her neck. But meaning what?

I woke up with an early-morning depression—the worst kind. I hate feeling depressed before I even remember why. It took a second to remember the Southworth kids, and then the depression just settled in. I was really going to flip out if anything else horrible happened that I could have prevented. If only I could figure out my own dream. I decided to go talk to

Marv. Maybe it would be obvious to someone else. Maybe I was too close to it.

I fidgeted and paced til nine A.M. For Pete's sake, surely he'd be up. Nine o'clock was late enough for anyone to sleep. I had a pang of guilt when the phone rang four times. Well, it didn't mean he was sleeping. He might be out. But on the fifth ring a sleepy Marv answered.

I was immediately contrite. This wasn't exactly an emergency. I could have waited until nine-thirty. But it was too late to back out: Marv had caller ID. Even if I hung up, he had my number right in front of him. I had caller ID on my home phone also. One thing any therapist wants to know before they answer the phone is who's calling.

"Uh, Marv, I'm sorry. I tend to forget normal people don't get up at six A.M. on Saturday."

"What's up?" Marv sounded worried. No wonder, given what the last bad news had been.

"Nothing really. I just had a bad dream." It sounded so foolish I laughed out loud. "I'm sorry, Marv. I sound like the client from hell. I swear to you I don't usually wake people up on Saturday morning to tell them I had a bad dream."

Marv laughed. He knew exactly what I meant. It is amazing what some people will call you about on the weekend, on vacation, in the middle of the night. When I worked emergency, one woman called me up at two A.M. to ask me if she could turn her television off.

"Come on over," Marv said. "I've been wanting to talk to you about this case, anyway."

I thought about Marv on the way over. He hadn't made me ask. He even suggested that he was the one who wanted to see me. More than anyone I know, the man has a profound graciousness about him. He uses his considerable astuteness in the service of that graciousness, and the combination of the two produces some interactions that feel as natural as good choreography.

I had heard a story about him once. A CEO of a major, major company had come to see him. This was apparently one of those companies that make more money each year than do most of the world's nations. This particular CEO was apparently a fitness buff—exercise programs for his employees, bonuses for those who stopped smoking, contests for losing weight. So there was the CEO, sitting in Marv's waiting room: a good-looking man, impeccably tailored, tan, and fit, waiting for his first appointment with his therapist, the man who would help him put his failing marriage back together—the one black spot in his otherwise spectacularly successful life. Exactly on the stroke of the appointed hour, Marv's office door opened and out came Marv: short, potbellied, rumpled, and not—by anybody's standards—tan, impeccably dressed, fit, or good-looking.

The CEO recovered quickly—after all, he was a professional negotiator. But not, apparently, quickly enough. Marv looked up, caught the disappointment as it passed over the CEO's face, and said gently, "Well, why don't you come in—anyway." Things went very well after that.

I picked up croissants and vanilla coffee on the way. I held them up at the door for amends. Belatedly, I remembered that my last interaction with Marv hadn't done him any favors, either. I wasn't sure which infraction to apologize for first. But before I could decide, Marv gave me a big kiss, put his arm around me, and welcomed me as though I were doing him an extraordinary favor by dropping by. So I didn't go on and on about it.

"I'm sorry for bugging you. At least it's out of character—not my usual shtick. What's new?" I said, glancing at his walls. Marv has a three-story town house, and every single wall and every surface is covered with objets d'art that take your breath away. Supposedly Marv has a little family money and psychiatrists generally do pretty well, but the paintings, sculpture, and pottery in this little town house aren't anything ordinary mortals can aspire to acquire.

He had taken a month off every year for the last twenty-five and scoured the ends of the earth for native art. He had begun long before it was popular or expensive or even valued. He had taken pack animals into the Andes and emerged with pre-Columbian artifacts. He had backpacked into islands you couldn't find on a local map and emerged with pottery made before recorded history. He is blessed with an infallible eye, a gift for languages, minimal needs for comfort. He had used those gifts to do what probably could never be done again.

"Well, I did pick up a little something at Alice Springs last summer." Marv walked over to a small painting with absolutely stunning colors. "Aboriginal art has picked up, of course, but I still don't think they're charging what it's worth. And of course, there's so much bad stuff out there now it's gotten trendy that lots of it is just tourist crap. But there are some wonderful pieces if you just persevere. I was on my way to Tasmania—they make wonderful baskets, and I hadn't been for several years—when this dealer I've dealt with before caught up with me and persuaded me to make a side trip."

I couldn't help smiling. Marv was standing directly in front of the painting, practically basking in its rich hues, wearing a pair of mud brown sweat pants with a red turtleneck top. I'm a fan of red, myself, and I think it's hard to make a bad red, but if it were possible, Marv had found it. He had on black slippers with some kind of satin purple emblem on them. If you saw Marv on the street, you'd think he was color-blind. The contrast was incredible: the tautness of the colors in the painting versus Marv's sweet, rumpled and jumbled, confused-looking, seemingly color-blind self. But if you looked at him looking at the painting, you no longer would feel like laughing—holding your breath, maybe, but not laughing.

Would anybody ever be even remotely likely to look at me that way? And how would I feel if they did? I used to think Marv was gay. He just never seems interested in women. He never goes out with them. He never talks about them. But as far as I know, he feels the same way about men. However, when I watched Marv watch the painting, I felt like a voyeur—like you do when you're around two people who have just started sleeping together and there's all that electricity still crackling.

"It's lovely, Marv," I said softly.

"Yes, well then." Marv broke eye contact with the painting reluctantly as he ambled toward the couch. "Come sit down and tell me what's happening."

Thank God I had gotten Marv involved in the case. He had come in originally as a second opinion, and mom had signed a permission form to let him look at my records and discuss the case with me. But the permission was broad, and it had neither run out nor been revoked. It was a good thing. If I had had to ask Sharon Southworth for permission at this point for anything—like maybe getting up in the morning—it wasn't likely she would give it. Not that what I had to say had all that much to do with the original case. I'm not sure I needed permission to talk to Marv about the murders.

I sat down across from Marv and put my feet up on the coffee table across from his slippers. "Well, for starters, I don't think Sharon Southworth did it."

"Based on?"

"Based on her psychological testing, on her interviews, based on how she felt about those kids. She may be fairly crazy vis-à-vis her ex, but she definitely wasn't crazy regarding the children."

"So why is she in jail?"

"Well, she did have motive, they say, as well as opportunity and means. Have you read *Beloved?*"

"No, I confess I've never cared much for fiction. The stuff we see seems stranger and more interesting."

"If anybody might change your mind it would be Toni Morrison. Can you imagine making a case for murdering children? I don't mean the usual stupidity that violent folk pass off as thinking, I mean a real case. *Beloved* is a story about slavery, and it's such a gut-wrenching account that you end up believing the stories she tells about going off to a cabin where her characters show up to tell her their tales.

"Anyway, the heroine flees slavery, and the plot goes on, and she thinks she's safe, when one day out of the blue the slave trader shows up to take her and her children—one is just a baby—back. So when she sees him coming, she cuts the baby's throat and tries to kill the rest. And Toni Morrison has given you such a clear vision of what waited for them if she hadn't done it that you end up in the middle of the night trying to figure out what you would have done."

Marv said nothing. He just sipped his coffee quietly and listened. We both knew a book about a dead baby was a little more loaded for me than most folks, but I didn't comment and neither did he.

"So, believe it or not, our killer cut the page that describes this scene out of the book. Let me rephrase that. Our killer cut the page that describes this scene out of my book." Marv got very still. His facial expression, his reach for the coffee cup—everything just stopped for a moment. Then he sat back, having forgotten all about the coffee cup.

"Yes, out of my own little copy of the book. And then the killer took page 149 of Toni Morrison's masterpiece and pasted it into Sharon Southworth's diary. Or, if you buy the easy version, Sharon Southworth pasted it into her diary."

"Well, now," Marv said. "What do we have? The idea, I gather, is that Sharon was supposed to have killed her children to keep them from going back to an abusive father. That's very interesting, but it doesn't fit the facts."

"No, it doesn't. Sharon Southworth never did believe her husband abused the kids. But that got lost with the judge. Mark Twain said once that when a fact and a theory collide, people think the theory will give way. It doesn't. The fact gives way every time. That's basically what happened. The current zeitgeist is back to blaming the mother. Sharon could have shouted her head off that she didn't believe the report of abuse—

actually she did shout her head off—and it didn't made any difference. A child made a report of sexual abuse during a custody fight. These days, if you're the mom, you can kiss your chances good-bye of convincing anyone you didn't put them up to it."

Marv just sat for a minute. Finally, he spoke. "If it's not Sharon, it's someone," he said finally, "who is literate and could get access to both your book and Sharon Southworth's diary. That's a bit concerning."

"I'd say. Downright hair-raising, actually. It kind of does in any hopes it was a stranger. Odds are that you and I both know, and probably know well, a sadistic child murderer. And we call ourselves clinicians. Do you know anybody just off the top of your head whom you've suspected of being a butcher? Someone who murders children for the thrill of it? For that's the MO; that's what dear old Willy tells me. And he probably knows a lot about that sort of thing."

Marv shrugged. "You don't have any reason to be down on yourself, Michael. You know as well as I do. These people are invisible. Until they get caught, nobody suspects them."

"I think I suspect somebody, but I don't know who." And I told him about the dream.

M arv wanted to think about it. I knew that was his way of doing things, but I was still annoyed as hell. My impatience made no difference. Marv wouldn't be pressured into making a hasty interpretation of the dream. He'd probably mull it over until we were all sitting in an old-age commune, rocking back and forth sitting on a green porch in our white rockers. And Marv would say, "You know that dream you asked me about?" I drove home so annoyed I didn't notice Jack's car in my driveway in time to back out. He was leaning against the back door and saw me before I could.

I stopped the car and tried to figure out what I wanted to do. Jack walked up and put his hands on the door and leaned in. "Well, girl," he said, "I came to blow a little sunshine up your skirt." I laughed in spite of myself. Jack had once tried to say something about blowing smoke and had gotten his metaphors mixed up. We both knew why "up your skirt" was on his mind, but I couldn't remember if we ever figured out how the sunshine got in there. I got out of the car. Jack put his arm around me as we walked in, and I didn't shrug it off. I had almost forgotten how nice his arm felt.

"How's your mother taking all this?"

"My mother?" I said surprised. "What does my mother have to do with this?"

"Didn't she once solve a murder? I thought she would have been up here by now nosing about."

"She didn't exactly solve a murder," I said acidly. "She decided a neighbor must have done it because he had the worst manners of anyone she knew."

"But she was right."

"That's beside the point." The whole thing was ridiculous, but around town it had certainly added to Mama's notoriety. And added, too, to my exasperation. My mother's logic is often, well, creative, and it drove me crazy when she was right in spite of it.

I should have left it at that, but I couldn't. What I just said sold Mama short, and the same thing that makes me meticulously accurate in court made me unable to leave Jack with a false impression of her. "Well, almost beside the point. Mostly beside the point." Jack looked at me quizzically. "All right, she did sort of figure it out. But, she only picked that particular guy to work on because of his manners."

What on earth had made me tell Jack about my mother? No doubt it had been one of those evenings with the moonlight coming through the skylight on my bed. You say things you don't expect to be held accountable for in broad daylight.

I should consider taking up drinking. You could blame stupidity like that on alcohol. If you don't drink, you have to take responsibility every time you go to bed with someone or tell someone something you wish you hadn't. Why the alcohol people have those wimpy little ads is beyond me. I could write better ads. "Need an excuse now and then?" "Tired of being Rita Responsible?"

Jack plopped down on a couch while I went to make some ice tea. As I walked back into the living room, I took stock of him. Long and lean—I had played b-ball too long to appreciate any other male body type. But where Adam looks solid, Jack has a catlike slouch and moves with an ambling grace. If he played basketball, I thought, he wouldn't block you out, he wouldn't set a pick that you'd hit hard, he'd slip around you and be all the more dangerous for it.

"So, what exactly is it that your mother did?"

"Nothing, really," I replied, in what I hoped was an uninviting tone. Jack said nothing, just sipped his tea.

"Look, it's not a big story or anything. My mother picked out Elrod because of his manners. Then she sort of made a habit nosing around about him. One day she saw him in a pair of alligator shoes. She raised holy hell, telling everybody those were real alligator shoes, and everybody knew that Elrod never had a dime to his name. He had drunk up every dime he ever had or he ever hoped to have, Mama said, so what was he doing with real alligator shoes? Harvey was the only one in those parts who had any money—which was true—and Harvey happened to be the dead body.

"Mama knew, of course, that Elrod did some work part time for Harvey as captain of one of his fishing boats, that sort of thing. To make a long story short, Mama raised such a fuss, the police looked into it, and, yes, Elrod had been cheating Harvey. Harvey had gotten wind of it and had made the mistake of confronting Elrod when Elrod was drunk and without benefit of his better judgment, probably without benefit of any judgment."

I didn't tell him the rest of it. What nobody around town could figure out was how Mama knew those alligator shoes were real. Nobody around there had ever seen real alligator shoes, so how did she know? It didn't bother me. I figured Mama had a close relative in that alligator and most people recognize their own.

"Well," Jack said, mercifully dropping Mama, "how are you doing with your new notoriety?"

"I'm waiting for Mike Wallace to call."

"You could call him. He'd know who you are."

"There's a thought."

"It's a lousy deal, Michael. It's hard to imagine something like this happening. It's like one of those deals where one of my colleagues cuts the wrong leg off."

"You seem to think I was wrong."

There was a pause. "Well," Jack said slowly. "Sharon South-worth is in jail for murder. I assume you didn't think she was a potential child murderer when you recommended she keep custody of the kids."

"It's still not clear she's guilty, Jack." I sighed. "Although it's also true I could just be in denial."

Jack sat up, put his ice tea down, and said, "Turn around. You need a back rub."

I was in no shape to turn down a back rub. I was never in shape to turn down a back rub. Jack started kneading my shoulders. I hadn't realized how tight the muscles were. He began gently and then slowly started working deeper; the steady rhythm of his fingers rolling and kneading the muscles reminded me of something, but I couldn't remember quite what. I can't think when I'm getting a back rub. I have watched animals having their stomachs rubbed and understand exactly the look in their eyes. Jack spread his fingers and ran them down each side of my spine. At the waist he pulled my shirt out and slipped his hands under it. Ah, the feeling of a man slipping his hands under your shirt. The X chromosome started flashing like a neon sign.

I couldn't get my eyes open. His fingers were warmer on my skin than seemed possible. His hands started moving up again, he paused at my bra, and the clasp sprang open. My breasts were suddenly free and felt very exposed and vulnerable. Jack put his head in my hair as he started sliding his hands forward around my sides.

I hadn't made up my mind what to do about Jack. It wouldn't exactly be a crime to figure it out later. I couldn't think of a reason I had to sort it out right now. Jack's fingers cupped my breasts, and I could feel his breath on my shoulder. His breathing was getting louder. There's nothing sweeter than an interested male—if it's the right male. Jack flattened his palm and made small, lazy circles against my right nipple. I arched my back against his palm.

"What if I loved you?" he said quietly in my ear. I felt myself stiffen. "What if I started loving you?"

I sat up. I didn't know what to say. Jack dropped his hand. "You're just like a deer," he said. "Always ready to bolt."

"Jack," I said, expecting something to follow. But nothing came out of my mouth. I never ran out of words. I must have something to say about this.

I covered my eyes with my hands and then dropped them. "What are you saying?"

"Nothing you want to hear," he said. He got up, took his ice tea glass to the kitchen, and left.

I sat for a while, then went off to the hot tub to brood. This was not my fault. How was this my fault? I was not responsible for Jack. I never promised him anything. I never asked for anything. I was definitely the aggrieved party. Codependent guilt aside—this was Jack's issue, not mine. I even picked a married man. How much safer can you get? You'd think he'd have a little more loyalty to his wife.

Usually if I stroke my conscience enough I can get it under control. But the damn thing had been listening to Carlotta. Ever since she yelled "treating people like blowup dolls" over the phone in North Carolina, the phrase had been pestering me.

What bothered me was that Carlotta isn't a goody-two-shoes. We usually think more or less alike about such things. The problem was, I decided, that responsibility is a slow-growing virus. It doesn't get big enough to detect in adolescence, but by the time a normal person is forty, it has strangled your life. Maybe Carlotta just has a worse case of it than I do. Of course, the other option is that she was right.

As for Jack—most of the men in the Western hemisphere would like to have an affair with no strings, and I have to pick the one man in six states who doesn't? Nobody else had gotten hooked on me. How was I to know Jack would? This was not my fault.

The phone rang, and I dragged my depressed little body out of the hot tub to get it—more to interrupt my train of thought than anything else. "Dr. Stone. This is Chief Bowman."

This was getting really ridiculous. It was evening. Was this Dr. Stone routine permanent?

"Good evening, Chief Bowman," I said, sounding more irritable than I meant to. "Working late?"

There was a pause. A long pause. All right, all right. Maybe I shouldn't take my Jack-anger out on Adam. "Yes, actually I am. The fingerprint results just came in. Sharon Southworth's prints are not on that book. And neither is anyone else's except yours."

"Adam . . ."

"This is not a surprise, Dr. Stone. You owned the book. We would expect your fingerprints to be on it somewhere. In fact, they're only on the inside pages where you turned them. The cover has been wiped clean. The killer just didn't have a reason to wipe every individual page."

I wasn't at all prepared for what Adam said next, even though I should have been. "I do hope you realize what this means, Dr. Stone. It means there is a very good chance the killer is not in jail and, if not, that it is almost certain that you know him—or her. And he knows you and knows you well enough to know what books you read. He knows your method of underlining things. He knows where you keep things. He knows this court case very well—well enough to compare it to *Beloved*. And he or she may well know where you live and how to get in and out."

He hung up, and I looked up at the glass wall in front of me. I was standing there nude, dripping on the rug. It had never been a problem before. There is nothing but woods across the stream, and I'd never heard of a voyeur deer. I hung up, picked up a throw, and wrapped it around myself.

I looked at the door. There was no reason I couldn't go back to the hot tub. No reason at all. The killer had a thousand ways to waylay me. On the way to the car. On the way from the car. It wouldn't do any good to just start hiding in the house. I didn't have any reason to think he was after me, anyway.

I sighed. I was not going to handle this the way most people would. The problem was I couldn't not go back to the hot tub. Though I didn't even want to go anymore. Who wanted to sit there waiting for a stone-cold killer to step out of the shadows? It kind of changed the tone of things. But I despised being intimidated.

I knew it was my Achilles heel, but I couldn't change it. I always go under the boards when I play ball, no matter who is there. I've had the broken noses to prove it. And I had done crazier things. I had once inadvertently taken a parking space someone thought he had seen first. He turned out to be certifiably insane. He had gone berserk, pounding on the windows until his ring dug chips out of the glass. He had to be restrained from destroying the car. All the time he was screaming at me to leave and give him the parking space.

It could be argued that it would have been the smart thing to do. Did I need an argument with a violent, out-of-control male over something I didn't care about in the slightest? I couldn't leave. I'd have laid my life down over a parking space I didn't even particularly want.

I started for the door, then turned around. There were smart ways to do this and stupid ways. I went up to the loft and retrieved the fanny pack with the .357 Magnum in it. My dirty little secret is that I not only have guns, I like them. I just feel comfortable with them. Very weird, but they definitely make me feel safer—depending, of course, on which way they are pointing.

I walked to the door and opened it. If he killed me tonight this was going to look bizarre. The papers would love it. "Woman found dead wearing nothing but gun." I took off the fanny pack and climbed into the hot tub, putting the gun on the table next to it. I sat there grimly staring out into the darkness. Now let me see if I have this straight. I was sitting in a hot tub I didn't even want to be in because a killer could conceivably be out there in the darkness.

What would Mama have thought about this? Mama would not have understood what the problem was. I couldn't remember ever seeing anything in Mama that even vaguely resembled fear; mostly everything and everybody that runs into Mama is afraid of her. Maybe it is easier being Mama than being Mama's daughter.

Adam's comments had shaken me. He was right; I had to know the killer. Maddingly, the dream came to mind, fleetingly, and I didn't know why. Except for Nathan Southworth, there wasn't anybody to suspect, and there didn't seem to be any way to link him to the murders. Had I done enough time in the hot tub to satisfy my adolescent stubborn streak? I climbed out and took my tired, nude, gun-toting little body straight to bed.

21

I jumped every time the phone rang all weekend waiting for Marv to call. I drove to work on Monday glancing constantly at my car phone. It had nearly killed me to get a car phone, even though it only counts as one of my two hundred and fifty items. Ordinarily, I don't like people being able to reach me in the car; I feel as if I'm worse than those people who have phones in the shower. But I deal with very violent folk at times, and I have a way of annoying them. I had finally gotten a car phone when Adam threatened to buy me one as a present when the husband of one of my battered wives decided I was the reason she left him, which was ridiculous. Clearly, I had nothing to do with her leaving him. If I had had anything to do with it, she'd have left him years earlier. With Adam threatening to buy me a phone, I felt I didn't have a choice. I can't stand expensive gifts.

I was heading for my private practice office. I was trying to catch up on some of the clients I had cancelled when the children were killed. Besides, I wasn't quite ready to tackle my office in the department. I might run into my esteemed chairman. Absence might make the heart grow fonder, but whoever said that didn't mention how much absence. I thought several millennia might work with Toby.

The first thing I saw when I pulled up in front of the office was Tom Gaines leaning against his red MG, his considerable girth practically obscuring the car. What was this? National waylay Michael week? Doesn't anyone call ahead anymore? And if he was here, why wasn't he waiting in the office? But, of course, I knew why. I had worked for Tom and against Tom, depending on the case, for ten years. I guess he knew my habit of not returning unpleasant phone calls, so he didn't bother calling. He must also have thought that I would have been likely to keep going had I spotted his car outside without him. That could be true, too. He was Sharon Southworth's attorney, and I wouldn't look forward to talking to him right now.

I was caught. I got out of my car and walked up to Tom. "Are you suing me?" I said. Tom raised both hands defensively.

"We're not," he said. "I can't speak for Nathan."

I grumbled, but took him inside. I am better at avoiding people than refusing to see them once they are standing right in front of me, and I was a little bit curious anyway. Tom walked into my office and settled his bulk into the couch. He made my couch look small and crowded, which is roughly what he did to his sports car. Tom driving that car looked a bit like a Great Dane perched on a tricycle.

I couldn't help liking Tom no matter which side he was on. Maybe it was because he is so good at what he does. Maybe it was because he speaks in a Southern accent, and I think in one.

"Well, Ms. Michael, I must say you are looking mighty fine today."

"Now, now, Mr. Gaines," I replied. "These days that kind of comment is sexual harassment."

"Lawdy, Ms. Michael, if the day has come when a Southern gentleman, far from his own kind, can't compliment a fine specimen of Southern womanhood without being accused of sexual harassment, then the world has come to a sorry state.

You know our mothers taught us to be kind to the ladies before they weaned us."

"You're full of it, Tom. My mama taught me never to trust a man with a silver tongue and a gold watch—and I believe that's a Rolex you're wearing. But to tell you the truth, I found myself thinking about you the other day. I couldn't figure out why a good Southerner like you would live in these cold northern parts, and I realized that if you were in the South, they'd spot you in a nanosecond. You'd have about as much cover as an alligator walking down main street, but up here they just cannot get over the notion that anyone who speaks with a Southern accent must be stupid—not to mention the general belief that anyone who weighs what you weigh is deranged. You win case after case after case, and they still underestimate you every time you walk into the courtroom."

It was true. Sharon Southworth's case was one of the few I had ever known Tom to lose, and there he was up against a bigger prejudice—the bias against mothers in sexual abuse cases.

"Now don't go spreading any nasty rumors about me." Tom said. "I do believe I'd have grounds for slander."

I laughed. "No, I figure if your colleagues can lose time and time again and still think Southerners are stupid, they deserve what they get."

"You overestimate me, Ms. Michael. I'm a simple country lawyer."

"Right. That's what Sam Erwin used to say when he ran the Watergate hearings. Out of curiosity I asked the clerk of court. He said you have the best won-lost record in the county. The only thing I don't understand, Tom, is do you practice with tapes to keep your accent that pure? I lost mine in a few years without trying. I figure somebody would have to go to some lengths to keep one that thick."

Tom looked horrified. "First of all, Ms. Michael," he said sternly, "you know as well as I do that it is extremely parochial of you to assume that the northern brogue you are currently affecting is accentless and what I speak is an accent. A northern accent is as much an accent as a Southern one. Your ability to sound like wherever you are, Ms. Michael, is a character flaw. Your accent has no integrity," he sniffed.

I was enjoying this. I almost never get the better of Tom—neither does anyone else—and it was a novel experience to see him off balance and annoyed. "But we digress," I said innocently. "What was it you wanted?" I hated to get back to the main point, but I knew I should quit while I was holding my own.

"Well, Ms. Michael, I hope you owe me a favor because I'm going to ask one. But first I've got to ask you to keep what I say to yourself."

"I'll have to decide that, after I hear it," I replied.

"What kind of deal is that?" Tom snorted.

"You're absolutely right," I responded, getting up, opening my office door, and holding it open. "It's a terrible thing to suggest. It's an awful idea, and I'm sorry I raised it. Well, that's that. Catch you later."

"Very funny," Tom glared at me. He said nothing more, but he didn't move.

I gave up and shut the door and sat down. "Look Tom," I began, "you're not my client or my lawyer so you don't enjoy any kind of privilege. I don't know what you're going to say, and I'm not going to get in a position of withholding something that looks and smells like evidence. Not that I'm incapable of such a thing, but in this case I have friends doing the investigating, and they would take it personally. So don't put me in a bind. If I can keep it confidential, I will. If it has to do with your client's innocence or lack of innocence, then I won't."

"What if it has to do with me?" Tom said. Oh, Jesus, I just hoped he was running away with the local harp player or something and that it had nothing to do with this case.

"I don't know. If you killed the kids or know who did, you're out of luck."

"I want you to go talk to my client."

"What?" I said. "I don't mean to be insulting, Tom. But you've been hitting the french fries again. You're getting fat cells in the brain."

I don't know how I got to tease Tom about his weight. Nobody else does and I don't do it with anybody else. But somehow things have evolved that way. I kid him about his weight, and he kids me about being a "card-carrying, bra-burning, man-baiting" feminist. I don't mind the teasing but it is annoying that Tom seems to think the two are equivalent.

"Nevertheless," Tom said, unperturbed.

"Tom, I am on your client's permanent hall-of-fame list of assholes. Put mildly, I am certain your client doesn't want to see me." I stopped, suddenly worried. "What's up? Why do you want me to go see Sharon?"

"Well, Ms. Michael. It seems to me lately there's been a change in the weather. I don't know what the police have or they don't have, but offhand I'd say they've got something that points away from my client."

"What makes you think that?" I couldn't tell Tom what I knew.

"Well, they're a whole lot nicer to both of us. If they just didn't have enough evidence but still thought she did it, they'd be sullen and hostile, but all of a sudden the music starts and the flowers come out when I arrive. I am the belle of the ball. The guards have even stopped making lawyer jokes when I come in. By the way, what's the difference between a dead lawyer in the road and a dead skunk?"

"The skid marks in front of the skunk."

"Why don't sharks attack lawyers?"

"Professional courtesy."

Tom raised his eyebrows. "I see you've been hanging around the station house. In any case, the DA's office is dropping hints that they won't oppose bail. I think they may even drop the charges soon, but think it will make a whole lot less fuss if she's already out of jail."

I had to smile. "So?"

"So, I want to be sure I won't be reducing my client's life span if I get her out of jail. She's been on suicide watch most of the time she's been there, and I'm not sure the good old boys are over-reacting."

"You want a referral? I'd be happy to give you a referral. I know countless folks in this area who can assess her for suicidality."

"She won't see them. I've tried. The good lady flatly refuses to have a psychological evaluation."

I was silent for a minute. "Tom, let me get this straight. You want me to sneakily and underhandedly go in to see Sharon on some other pretense—God knows what—and without doing anything direct or asking her any relevant questions that might tip her off, find out if she's going to kill herself if you get her out on bail. I like this. You're not just asking me to predict the future, which, I might add, is problematic enough, but you are asking me to do it using my peripheral vision. Not to mention that this is not the most ethical request I've ever gotten."

"You do have a way of putting things in the worst possible light, Ms. Michael."

"No."

"You are turning me down?"

"I am turning you down."

"Then I need a consult. Exactly what would you recommend?"

"I don't know," I said. Tom said nothing. "This is not my problem." Tom still said nothing. "Oh, hell, Tom, I don't know what you should do. First of all, you're not even supposed to be thinking like this. Your job is to do whatever your client wants, not what you think is in her best interest. Isn't that how you guys put all those thieves, murderers, and rapists back on the streets? What is going on that you are taking care of Sharon instead of representing her?"

"You are absolutely one hundred percent correct, although I

find it a bizarre argument for you to be making, Ms. Michael. I have absolutely no business second-guessing my client, who is dying, so to speak, to get out of jail."

I rolled my eyes.

"But unfortunately, I find it impossible to go through the Jackson case again."

I had forgotten about that. The judge was the one the newspapers focused on, but I remembered now that Tom had been the lawyer involved. He had skillfully talked a judge into setting bail for a battering, stalking husband, even though the the guy was anything but remorseful. Jackson had left the jail and driven immediately to his ex-wife's house. He had raped her in front of their kids, forced her into his car, and driven both of them into a bridge abutment at one hundred miles an hour.

I didn't say anything. What could I say? I knew how something like that would have affected me. Also, I knew firsthand that mothers could get suicidal after their child dies—not to mention two children, not to mention finding them murdered. Tom was a fellow Southerner, a colleague, and a kind of friend.

"I doubt I could tell, Tom. I can't exactly ask her directly."

"Do what you can," he said. "I can't think of anything else to do."

"So exactly what is my excuse for going?"

"You might try telling her you're sorry her children died," Tom said dryly. "After all, you knew them well and you knew her. A simple condolence call."

Now it was my turn to feel horrified. He was absolutely right. It was the first thing I should have done. And I had been so riddled with guilt, it had never occurred to me.

22

I thought about it all the way there. I hate feeling guilty, and I can't seem to avoid it. Guilty for things I did. Guilty for things I didn't do. I have withdrawn from most of the people I know, shucked nine tenths of my possessions, simplified my life as much as possible, and I still feel guilty for something half the time.

As far as I can tell, half the world has too much guilt, and the other half has too little. I haven't met any triple murderers lately who have a whole lot of guilt, although they all tend to feel sorry for themselves. Yet I remember a case study of a guy who claimed his depression was due to the fact he cheated fifty cents on his tax bill twenty years ago.

I'm not an ax murderer, but that doesn't mean I have nothing to regret. A child's death is such a devastating thing that it is appropriate to put aside old divisions. So what if Sharon Southworth was furious at me for supporting her children's claims of sexual abuse. My worst critic had come to Jordan's funeral, and it had meant a lot. In some ways you're as connected to your enemies as your friends.

So yes, I was an intimate in Sharon Southworth's life, and I never really believed she murdered them. I could rationalize my silence if I had thought she murdered them—you don't send a note of condolence to a child murderer—but the truth is I just hadn't wanted to see her. Carlotta told me Sharon blamed me for her babies' deaths because she thought I was responsible for the loss in court. But so what? I could have sent her a note or flowers if I hadn't wanted to see her. I should have done something. But I had had trouble seeing straight, looking with one eye through the lens of my panic that I was somehow responsible for these children's deaths and with the other eye only seeing Jordan. Bottom line—I hadn't wanted to see a mother whose children died. Simple as that. It just brought up too much stuff.

I walked into the jail and saw a couple of the deputies gathered around looking at *Playboy*. "Reading the articles?" I asked as I walked up.

Gene, a middle-aged deputy, shook his head. "I don't know what you women's libbers have against sex," he said. "If God hadn't wanted men to look at women, he wouldn't have built 'um the way he did. Besides, you can't be a women's libber, Michael. Everybody knows those women's libbers are so uggg-ly they couldn't get laid in the middle of the exercise yard at Attica." He flashed a hopeful grin.

"Uh-uh," I said. "Did you guys hear the news about the birth at Jefferson Memorial?" I asked.

"No, what news?" he asked.

"There was a baby born at Jefferson Memorial last night that was both male and female."

"Both male and female?" he said incredulously.

"Yep," I replied. "It had a penis and a brain." The deputies laughed and cried foul.

"Sure, and you never made a joke about an airhead female, right? Come on, you guys. Tear yourselves away from those deformed mammary glands and take me down to visit Sharon Southworth."

Sitting in the visiting room waiting for Sharon, I quit joking. I really didn't want to be there, and I wasn't sure what kind of reception I'd receive. In a few minutes a guard opened the door at the far end, and Sharon walked in.

Seeing her made it obvious the real reason why I hadn't thought to visit her. She looked dreadful, and she looked achingly familiar. How much weight can a human being lose in a week or so? I didn't eat for five days after Jordan died. It didn't look like Sharon had either. And what happens to a face when trauma hits it. The light had died in hers as I'm sure it had in mine, and she looked as drawn and gaunt as I remember feeling.

I was visibly shocked by the sight of her. Fortunately, she had a room to cross before she sat down on her side of the glass wall separating us, and I had time to recover. "Oh, Sharon," I said. "I am so very, very sorry."

"Why did he kill my babies?" she asked. "He won. He already had custody."

If someone was traumatized enough, they forgot all about the social amenities. There weren't any hellos or good-byes, and there sure as hell wasn't any small talk.

"I don't know whether he did or not, Sharon," I replied. "And if he did, I certainly don't know why. What sense does it make for anybody to kill them?"

"Did he hate me that much?" she asked. "Could you hate someone that much to kill their children?" I didn't know what to say. It was a pretty bizarre thought. At least I hoped it was. That kind of hate is hard to imagine.

"Look," she went on. "I know you think I'm crazy, but there was something wrong in that house. Nathan was always so secretive and fake. After a while I realized nothing he said or did was real. Something was going on, and I knew it. It drove me crazy trying to figure out what.

"I've done a lot of thinking since the babies died. I think I just got on the wrong track. I think you were right. Nathan wasn't running around with other women; he was sexually abusing the kids. But why did he have to kill them?" She started crying, and within minutes the crying turned to hard sobs. The glass wall made me feel so ineffective. I couldn't reach her in any way. Of course, the same thing would have been true if the wall hadn't been there.

I thought about what she said. I had never heard her sound so sane. For the first time I wondered what role Nathan had played in her paranoia.

But what about her theory? Could someone kill children just to get back at a parent who loved them? It certainly was the most effective way in the world to devastate that parent; nothing else would even come close. But these children, I was convinced, had been killed for the thrill of it. That's what sadism was all about, and the way they were laid out spelled sadism.

I got on to why I was there. "Sharon," I said gently. "I'm concerned about you." Which was certainly true enough. "Do you feel you have anything to live for?"

"What does it matter?" she said. "What does it matter if I live or die?"

"I'm sure it matters to the people who love you," I said.

"Pleaase," she said.

I decided to be blunt. "Sharon, are you going to be all right if you get out of here?"

"No," she said. "I am never going to be all right. How can you even ask a question like that?"

I had other questions I could have asked. I could have said, "Have you picked out the hose? Have you tried it on the tailpipe to see if it fits? Do you have the pills at home? Have you taken the gun out and stared at it, Sharon? Like I did." But what was the point? Sharon didn't know if she was going to live or die. She had a raging fever of grief, and there wasn't any way to tell yet if it was going to kill her or not.

I walked out feeling Tom wouldn't like this. I couldn't tell him anything definitive. But yes, if he sprang Sharon South-worth from jail, she might truly end up dead.

I waited for the steel door to open at the end of the corridor, and when it did, looked up to find myself face-to-face with Arthur. He was obviously coming in to visit Sharon. He looked surprised to see me. Clearly, no one had told him I was there.

"Hello, Michael, what brings you here?"

"A condolence call," I said. "Just telling Sharon how sorry I am about the kids. What about you?"

"The same," he said. "It only seemed humane. And I gather there's some doubt about her guilt. I couldn't bring myself to come when it seemed she was the killer. Just too awful a thought. Are you all right, my dear? You don't look well."

"Oh, I'm all right." I didn't want to talk about it—not about Jordan, not about the lost time after she died—which was all I could seem to think about. "By the way, I spoke with a colleague in Boston the other day who knew you."

"Really?" Arthur seemed surprised.

"Yep," I said. "She said you were on some kind of child abuse council down there. I was impressed, Arthur. I thought you just hung out with all those corporate types. Come to find out, you were a secret do-gooder all along." Thank God I could still change the subject with the ease of a White House lawyer, even when depressed enough to qualify for interavenous Prozac.

"Michael!" Arthur sounded slightly horrified. "What kind of a prejudice do you have about 'corporate types'? My word. If anybody tried to stereotype women or disadvantaged children around you, I can't even imagine the reaction. But I gather 'corporate types' aren't supposed to be on child abuse councils." Which was fair enough.

"I'm sorry, Arthur. I probably do still have some of my old counterculture ways, but mostly I'm just out of sorts from seeing how depressed Sharon is."

"Well, what do you think?" Arthur said. "Is she going to be all right?"

"No, Arthur, she is never going to be all right. Look, I've got to go. I think I've been in jail just about as much as I can stand today." Arthur seemed to want to talk about Sharon, but I really didn't have the heart for it.

I got all the way outside the building and then stopped and sat down on the steps. Grown-ups never stop and sit on the steps like kids do. I used to sit on a lot of steps in North Carolina, waiting for Mama to pick me up—from school, from sports, from Girl Scouts. Mama wasn't exactly prompt—she came when she felt like it—but still I was lucky if it was Mama. If my sweet Daddy was supposed to pick me up, I had to hope he wasn't in a drinking frame of mind, or I'd end up walking home.

When I start thinking about Mama, something has to be wrong. Well, something was wrong. I felt queasy. I felt as if I had escaped from jail rather than walked out. Why did the air seem so close in there? Why did I feel as if a two-hundred-pounder had hit me under the boards? Maybe seeing Sharon made the children's deaths real. Surely seeing her had brought up Jordan's death again. Maybe I was going into another grief spasm. Oh, good. Depression is bad enough—it feels like trying to move around with weights attached to every limb. But grief— grief feels like someone is beating you to a complete and utter pulp.

Maybe it was something else. Maybe I was just beginning to appreciate the limits of my education. I learned a lot from Mama—how to survive a nor'easter in a small boat, how to look at a dead body without flinching, how to hold your own—but I never learned anything about deception from Mama. Mama just figures anyone worth their salt will naturally stand up for who they are.

So I was over my head with this deception business. No doubt Adam was right. The killer wasn't a stranger. And if he was right, someone had fooled the hell out of me. I hated this shit. Under the boards you know where you are and you get to see the people who run into you, no matter how big they are. But this business—it was like going to sleep with a friend and waking up to find a rattlesnake's head on the pillow next to you in the night.

How would Mama deal with this? Mama recognized real alligator shoes. One thing about Mama—she knew real when she saw it. Did I? It didn't look like it. Great. One of my mother's few unequivocally good traits, and I don't get it.

And yet. The dream kept coming to mind, especially the part where I turn and see the old woman hanging by her neck. She was supposed to be fine when the old man left. But she wasn't. She ended up hanging from a tree. She was much worse after he left. The last sentence lit up like a neon sign when I said it to myself. She was worse, much worse after he left.

That was real, somehow. I was all confused. Some things were real — like Sharon Southworth's grief over her children. That was as real as the steps I was sitting on, as real as a pair of alligator shoes. But something else around me was fake. And I could almost touch it. All I knew was it had to do with something being worse, much worse after he left.

23

....

I drove aimlessly. The wind was picking up. It was a fall wind, snapping at critters, rattling things. I stopped by a pasture, got out of the car, and watched some yearlings wheel and buck in the high wind. A spirited crew, each colt seemed to be trying to outdo the others. Suddenly, a feedbag blew off the ground, and all the yearlings scattered, all save one. He picked up the feedbag and — to my astonishment — chased the others with it. He tossed his head, and the paper bag waved wildly. The others scattered in all directions, literally falling over their feet to get away. King of the mountain. Lord of the paper bag. I laughed out loud, and the laughter just seemed to float off with the wind. My hair whipped around my face like a scarf. Had I laughed? Had I actually laughed since this whole thing began?

All right. So I was having a few problems getting the kids' faces out of my head. You never know what will stick. I kept seeing Andrew quietly sitting in my office — grave and somber and unchildlike — carefully straightening out a crooked toy on the shelf and all the while his cowlick is forcing his hair every which way. Adrienne—I kept seeing her sit up and ask me for the turtle. It was the first time I caught her eye and saw that imperious, demanding, full-of-life part of her. She'd have done well in the world. Now that Tom had suckered me into going to the jail, I could add Sharon's. And Jordan. No, I was not going to think about that.

My little secret—my problem—is I don't understand mean, and I'm supposed to be an expert. Nonetheless, I don't get it. I can't even bear to think about what the killer could stand to do, wanted to do. Like the monolith from *2001,* it's some kind of language the rest of us don't speak.

And I try. I read about it. I talk to people like Willy about it. But I could study it for the next hundred years for all the good it would do me. In my heart of hearts, I think the mean-violent-sadistic types, the real bad actors, must be aliens. I shook my head. With that kind of logic, I'd qualify for a diagnosis of paranoia.

I got back in the car and drove again. I gave the car its head, and it just seemed to naturally mosey up toward the Green Mountains, giving me time to filter all this through. So what do we have here? Sharon's out of the picture. She is not the killer. I may not know mean, but I do know grief, and she's got it oozing from every pore. It's carving lines in her face the depth of the Grand Canyon.

Nathan certainly had means and opportunity. He had the kids. Who's to say they left his house alive? He could have killed them at home, then transported them to Sharon's in the night. No one searched his house when he reported them missing. It's pretty clear he's a child molester. How do I know he isn't a sadistic child molester? Maybe he got carried away and killed one by accident: kept his hands on a small neck a little too long; pulled a plastic bag off too late—whatever. He could still have a key to her house. Maybe she never thought of changing the locks. Just because she thought he was a son-of-a-bitch womanizer doesn't mean she thought he'd ever sneak into her house. So maybe he saw an opportunity to divert attention from himself and hurt his ex-wife profoundly at the same time.

What do I really know about Nathan? Not a whole lot. So who would? Doctors spend most of their lives at the hospital: The nurses sometimes spend more time with them than their wives do. I perked up at the thought. I knew some OR nurses pretty well who would have worked with Nathan. I screeched to a halt, whipped the car around, and headed for the hospital.

If everybody has a signature gesture that gives their essence away—if my poor battered Kiwi has her Mary Jane high heels and Andrew had his way of straightening a toy on the shelf—could I hear something, talking to enough people—something about Nathan, some gesture, some anecdote, some comment that would carry the scent of sadism? It was a long way from a conviction, but I wanted some of Mama's certainty. I wanted my map of the world back. I wanted to know where the snakes were.

I had never actually gone searching for a snake before. No doubt there were those who would question the wisdom of such a project, those who would think getting as far away as possible was a better idea. My common sense was kicking up again, telling me that annoying a snake could be risky. I gave it serious consideration. I thought about it from all angles. I looked at the pros and cons. But I did notice the car didn't slow down at all.

24

. . . .

I parked in the lot near the tunnel entrance. The hospital is built on a split level. The front and side entrances are all on the same level, but the road to the parking lot behind dips down so that the lot itself is on the same level as the tunnel entrance. Patients and most staff climb the steps to the ground-level entrance. I never do. You'd think I come from a long line of moles, I like the tunnels so much.

I walked in, and the door closed behind me. Immediately, there was quiet. The sound of the wind didn't carry into the tunnels; the sounds of a busy hospital never penetrated. The entire ceiling was covered with pipes. The whole lifeblood of a working hospital was running over my head: steam pipes, condensate conduits that returned spent steam, water, and oxygen, electrical conduits, communications cables, compressed air, propane for the kitchens and the labs, even a vacuum system for cleaning out wounds in the OR. All around me, everything was sleek and bare: the concrete walls, the floors, the pipes, nothing was painted. My footsteps were so loud in the tunnel I sounded as if I were wearing tap shoes.

I like the tunnels because they are honest. There is no pretense in the tunnels: no decorator colors, no elevator music, no receptionists trained in "guest services." Everything is functional, and when medicine gets functional, you see what it really is: body plumbing. The only reason doctors have higher status than plumbers is because pipes don't make the rules.

I headed for an inpatient unit where Tessie, a nurse I knew, usually worked when she wasn't in the OR. I couldn't exactly crash the operating rooms looking for her, so if she wasn't on the inpatient unit, I'd just have to come back another day.

"Where's Tessie?" I asked. "Is she working today?" The unit secretary barely glanced up, just long enough to make sure she was talking to a regular.

"I think so," she replied. "Somebody said she's subbing in the ICU. Anyway, she's not on this floor."

I walked across the hall and into the doctors' room. Three docs were sitting there: two making phone calls and one writing notes. Every floor has a communal work space. There's no place in the hall to write notes, and even institutional medicine—which has never won any kudos for sensitivity—recognizes it wouldn't be a good thing to have a patient walk by while you're on a hall phone getting the results of their malignant biopsy. The doctors' room is a communal work area in which doctors make phone calls, write notes, consult each other, bicker among themselves, all with some degree of privacy from their patients and none at all from each other.

No one looked up when I walked in. Like any communal place where people work in parallel, the rules are different from the outside world. People don't say "hello" when they come in; they don't say "good-bye" when they leave. The normal social exchanges just don't occur. If someone's best friend walks in, it would be completely normal for neither person to speak. In the absence of physical walls, other kinds of walls have developed to insure some kind of personal space.

"What brings you up here, Stone?" I turned around to see Dr. Ruth walk in behind me. Ruth wasn't her last name, but Dr. Ruth was all anyone ever called her. It started with the kids, who tend to use your first name with Dr. if they like you. Of course, "Dr. Michael" didn't ring any bells with adults, so it didn't get picked up. "Dr. Ruth" only had to be said once for it to stick.

"Hanging around trying to make a nuisance of myself," I replied. "What are you up to?" The woman I was now facing was a stocky woman in her forties with short blond hair. She was dressed in casual, baggy pants and a knit shirt.

"Kid tried to die on me this morning," she said, shaking her head at the audacity.

"Heck of a thing," I said sympathetically.

"Some days you just don't get no respect," Ruth went on.

"Did this ungrateful child succeed?" I asked, just to give Ruth a chance to talk about it. Ruth wouldn't be joking if the child had died.

"Certainly not," she sniffed.

I walked over to the phone. I love the abrupt way doctors terminate conversations. They walk off all the time without warning. When I first started working with docs, I would finish discussing a case and find myself staring at the phone when the doc simply said, "Okay, good-bye," and hung up. Now I can warp-speed my way out of conversations with the best of them.

I called Intensive Care and found that, yes, Tessie was working today. I turned to leave and realized the other docs had left. Ruth and I were alone.

"Ruthie, do you know Nathan Southworth?"

"Sure," she said, without looking up from the chart she was writing in. "What a nightmare, huh? Is it true? Did his wife really kill their children?"

"I don't think so," I answered. "Anyway, what's he like?"

"As a surgeon? He's pretty good. I had a case with him last time I was on the ward." Ruth sat up and stretched. For the first time I realized how tired she looked. "A teenager was driving his dad's tractor, one of the McKay kids over in Charleston. It fell over on him and crushed his chest. Nathan was good. He did a good job on the chest, and he did a good job with the kid. Our hot-rodder was scared out of his mind and didn't want anybody to know. Nathan was very patient with him. Explained things carefully. I was impressed. He even asked him how he felt."

"Whoa," I said, and we both laughed. I had come bitching to Ruth the day I walked out of a depressed surgery patient's room and heard the chief surgery resident describe my patient to Crookshank. "You may not want to go in there, now," he said. "She's depressed." For some of the surgeons, emotions were the messy part of dealing with people.

"By the way," Ruthie said. "You got room for another case?"

"Not really," I replied. "What is it?"

"Do I have a deal for you," Ruthie said. "No incest. No alcoholism. No suicide attempt. Not even an adolescent kidnapper and car thief," she went on, reminding me of a former case of mine. "Just a family that could use some support."

"Aw, I don't know. Doesn't sound like my kind of thing, and I'm overbooked as it is."

"It'll wait," Ruthie said. "One way or another they'll be around for a while." Ruthie never gave up when she wanted something for one of her patients.

I headed for the ICU. I was irritated, and it had nothing to do with Ruthie's case. That son of a bitch Nathan. Does he have the whole world fooled? But that wasn't fair. Being a child molester didn't mean he wasn't a good surgeon, and that's all Ruthie was talking about But there's some preadolescent part of me that wants bad guys to be bad guys all around and wants everybody to know it. Gray is supposed to be the color for grown-ups, but I still prefer black and white.

I took the stairs to the ICU floor. Once on the floor I had to pass through the waiting room to get to the unit. Only family members are allowed in the ICU and then only for brief visits.

Relatives and friends mostly camp out in the waiting room, sometimes for weeks.

It is always a pretty glum scene. No patient is in the ICU for a good reason. Nobody there is stable, or they would be transferred to another floor. Nobody there needs to die—is terminally ill or just too old and worn-out to live. Those folks are no-codes and stay on the floors or go home. The ICU is for people who shouldn't die, who don't have to die, who—if they get through this whatever—can go on living. The ICU is the place where medicine gets aggressive. For the families, it is place where they hang out in a small waiting area with a television that blares the soaps all day—caught between the tedium of waiting and the fear the waiting will abruptly end.

I hit the squares on the wall ten feet from the ICU doors, and the doors flew open. There are no handles on the doors themselves: They are built for stretchers traveling at speed. Once inside, I looked around. Like the tunnels, the ICU is medicine without the window dressing. Technology is God in the ICU. There is enough equipment in that room to launch the next space shuttle.

I made the mistake of glancing into the first glass cubicle on my way to the nurse's station. The patients are in private rooms in the ICU, but the walls are made of glass to allow constant monitoring. A small form lay motionless on the bed. My feet stopped—I hadn't planned on it, but children aren't that common in the ICU. Unfortunately, they were getting more common—common enough that a PICU, a Pediatric Intensive Care Unit, was being developed, but it wasn't here yet.

I walked into the cubicle. The small form in the bed appeared to be about five or so, although who could tell? I could see nothing but a small part of the face. The head was swathed in bandages. A respirator tube was running down his or her nose, and the mouth was taped shut. I could see shut eyes, a nose, and only part of the cheekbones. The rest was hidden by sheets. There was a small forest of IV drips and monitors surrounding the bed. They were whooshing and popping and beeping. A number of the lines went under the sheets. How many lines were attached to this child? I counted the lines. Sixteen lines. Sixteen somehow connected to this one tiny form. When medicine gets aggressive, it gets aggressive. Who was I to argue? Without it, this kid might be in the morgue right now.

I picked up the chart. Some docs more or less ask me to help out on any kid I have time for. Other docs wouldn't call for a psych consult if their patient were psychotic. I looked for the doctor's name on the spine of the chart. This was Ruthie's case. Ruthie wouldn't mind my looking at a chart of hers. I wondered if this was the case she wanted help on.

I opened up the chart. Stupid truck accident. Somebody put a six-year-old girl in the back of a pickup and stopped suddenly. The kid had gone flying, of course, and banged up some vital parts.

I scanned the numbers. There was a sea of them, as usual. Heart rate. Blood pressure. Blood gases. Electrolytes. White counts. Medication orders. The tale of living and dying in the ICU is always told in numbers. This is up. That's down. To anyone who knows the code, the numbers sometimes say, "Read my lips. This child is going to die," as clearly as flashing neon.

I didn't know what all the numbers meant, but I knew some of them. I knew enough of them. The wrong numbers were going down. The wrong ones were coming up. If this was the case that Ruthie was talking about, her relief might be short-lived.

The child wasn't moving at all. She was snowed with a morphinelike medication. She couldn't breath entirely on her own, so they had used medication to paralyze her lungs to keep her from fighting the respirator. Panic sets in when you paralyze people's lungs; thus the morphine to keep her so stoned she wouldn't notice.

I didn't want to get involved in this. There was no reason I had to get involved in this. This might not even be the case

Ruthie was talking about, and, besides, I had already turned that one down. I had enough dead children trailing after me: Jordan, now Andrew and Adrienne. I didn't need another.

Then there was the fact that there was nothing I could do for this child. I couldn't protect her. Not that I did such a great job of protecting Adrienne and Andrew, either, which wasn't the point, really. The point was I've spent my entire professional life protecting children, and when it came down to it, I couldn't protect my own. And I had learned it is not true that if you take care of other people's children, God will take care of yours. I quickly picked up the chart to read on, but I was too late. Grief clipped me from behind like an NFL linebacker making an illegal hit.

I tried to ignore the mental images and kept skimming the chart. There were lab results, medication records, progress notes, and results of consults ("prognosis grave" wrote the neurologist), and all the other dry shorthand of medicine at its most technical. In the middle of the progress notes from doctors and nurses I found a small four-word note from this morning. "Kept vigil," Ruthie had written. "All night."

Jesus Christ. There wasn't anything Ruthie could have done for this child last night that the nurse or the intern or the resident couldn't have done. What was Ruthie doing sitting up all night?

Just what she said, I suppose. This child was dying, and it was on Ruthie's watch, so she kept vigil. I don't know a lot about that kind of thing: keeping vigil, bearing witness. I know about playing people a lot bigger than myself under the boards. I even know about getting a county doc to straighten my nose—using his fountain pen as a guide—and going back into a game under the boards. But I don't know anything about sitting in a room with a child who is just slipping away and keeping vigil. How could anybody do that? How could Ruthie sit in a room with a dying child and not break something? Oh, shit, I didn't have that many cases. It wouldn't kill me to take on another one.

I put down the chart and went off to find Tessie. I had to yank my head away from the girl in the glass cubicle. Which set of stunned faces in the waiting room had she belonged to? I found Tessie in another cubicle and waited until she came out. By then I had gotten my head a little straighter.

"What?" She said when she saw me. "A shrink in town in August? Aren't you people all supposed to be on the Vineyard?"

"We are," I answered. "But you know how much I like to act out. Let me put it this way. If I were lesbian I wouldn't play softball."

Tessie laughed. She was gay and had once told me her new partner had been shocked that she didn't play softball. "But you have to play softball," she was told. "It's PC."

"No zucchini this year," I told her. "I'm locking my car. And no leaving them on the hood like last year."

"What are friends for," she said, "if they won't take your zucchini?" Tessie is one of those folks—like my Aunt Sally—who lives to garden. She works three twelve-hour shifts at the hospital so she can spend four days gardening. Winter doesn't slow her down at all. She has flats with sprouting seeds all over her house.

"Can you take a break?" I asked. "I want to talk to you about something."

"As a matter of fact, I can. Things were so hectic this morning I haven't eaten yet today. If I don't eat soon, I'll faint."

Tessie went off to find the other nurses to clear her belated lunch, and I waited at the door. We headed out together. I always feel huge walking with Tessie. She is barely five-two and slight. With her reddish brown hair cut to within a couple of inches of her head and her petite size, Tessie looks like Peter Pan in white.

We took the stairs to the cafeteria. Most staff never take the elevators if they are within three floors of their destination. The elevators are so slow, rumor has it they have lab rats running on treadmills in the basement to pull them up.

We walked into the cafeteria and looked at the food. How do they dare to have this place on a different floor from the cardiac unit? Everything in sight was either fried or deep fried. Fried chicken. French fries. Doughnuts. Onion rings. Every hospital I have ever been in has food like this. It's a biosphere kind of thing. The cafeterias create patients, and the rest of the hospital treats them.

Tessie didn't seem to mind. The stress of the ICU is not conducive to dieting. She picked french fries and a hamburger from the wilting buffet without apology. I had to admire her. Not many women would eat a french fry without mumbling something about a diet, not even if they were Tessie's size.

We sat in a booth by the window, and I looked around to see if we were within earshot of anyone. You never knew who knew whom in a hospital. "Tell me about Nathan Southworth," I said. "What kind of doc is he? What kind of person is he?"

"Well," Tessie said, shrugging. "He's not a rip-and-tear surgeon. And he doesn't throw his instruments." It sounded like a joke, but it wasn't. There are surgeons who have temper tantrums in the OR and throw their instruments. I always wonder what kind of liability the hospital will face when one of them hits a nurse in the head with an orthopedic hammer one day. "He's a pretty good surgeon. And he's not even all that arrogant professionally. Actually, he treats staff pretty well. What do you want to know about him?"

"I don't know, Tessie. You know I'm involved in a weird case. Everybody in the universe knows. I just need to understand Nathan better to make sense of some things, and I'm not sure where to start."

"You might try Athena."

"Athena?"

"Ah, you've missed Athena. That's because you're female. None of the men have missed Athena. Athena joined nursing a few months ago and has worked her way through every physician she can find—particularly the surgeons. She's a scream, really. She rates them, if you can believe it. It's one to ten, and she has categories. Foreplay, I remember is one of them. Style. Vigor. I can't remember them all.

"She tells locker room stories. I remember her saying one of the surgeons wants his partner to lie perfectly still. She thinks he prefers women unconscious. She claims another guy's idea of foreplay is unzipping his pants; another thinks he's on a rowing machine. I know it's crude, but it's so damn funny to see the shoe on the other foot. A friend of mine was talking to a college student in the clinic the other day. Did you know one of the frats has a special room where the guys take girls to screw on-camera—without the girls' knowledge, of course—and they show the film to the whole house later."

"Unbelievable," I said. But it wasn't. I had heard worse. "But Tessie, how many docs go along with her?"

"You'd be surprised. She's not doing that badly, although she does get turned down. She had the nerve to approach Crookshank, and he stared a hole through her. When she strikes out, she gets pretty vicious. I don't think we're dealing with a well puppy here."

"So, what about Nathan? Was he on her list?"

"That's the weird part. I know she went after Nathan, but I don't have a clue what happened. No ratings. No locker room stories. No viciousness. No nothing. If you ask her about Nathan, all she'll say is he's a very nice man."

"That's it?"

"That's it. I don't get it either."

"Wait a minute. This woman's got a system. If they sleep with her, she's disdainful. If they don't, she's hostile. How did he beat her system? Are you sure she's gotten around to him?"

"Positive," Tessie said. "She's like those pool sharks who call their shots in advance. She announces who she's going after." I had an image of Athena pointing to a man the way Babe Ruth pointed to left field. I couldn't suppress a grin. Tessie was right. What Athena was doing was crude and obnoxious, and I had no business laughing at it, but there was a sick kind of humor in seeing the shoe on the other foot.

Tessie pushed the french fries away. Oh, damn. She wasn't going to eat them all. I have a weakness for french fries, which I try not to indulge. The great UCLA coach John Wooden might be right: You can't coach quick, but you sure can slow it down with french fries. I have a little bit of quick on the b-ball court, and I want to keep it.

"Do you think he's blackmailing her or something?" Tessie said.

"Victims don't usually describe their blackmailer as 'a very nice man,'" I answered. "Besides, she sounds a bit blackmail proof. Exactly what kind of thing would Athena want to hide?"

"Drugs?" Tessie offered.

"Maybe," I said. "He could be supplying her with drugs. She'd lose her license, her livelihood, not to mention access to her hobby."

"There's another thing," Tessie said. "I had a strange experience with Nathan once. Have some french fries." Maybe she noticed me salivating. I shook my head.

"What?"

"Well, you know how polite he usually is. One night after work I went back to the outpatient clinic to pick up something a friend of mine had left. Anyway, nobody was in the whole place except Nathan and his wife. They were in his office, and he was screaming at her with such incredible rage, I mean out of control. It shook me. I thought about calling 911. I really thought he was going to attack her."

"Really? What happened?" I asked.

"Nothing that put anybody in the hospital. She said something—I don't know what—and he grabbed her arms and held them down and spit in her face. I couldn't believe it. She just seemed to crumble, and then she ran out. I doubt they even knew I was there. Anyway, it was strange. I don't think I've ever been around anyone that angry in my entire life. Nothing, and I mean nothing, like that has ever happened with him at work. I could never think of him in quite the same way after that."

I didn't say anything. What did it mean? It was standard sex offender chameleon behavior, but was it more than that?

Maybe it was the grief. Only part of my head was engaged with Nathan. The rest of it was caught somewhere between the small form in the glass cubicle and a much smaller form in the ED some time ago. In b-ball you're supposed to let every play go as soon as it's over because if you're thinking about the last one, you're going to screw up the next one. And that's what I did. My poor head had slowed down to a snail's crawl. I had lost my quick and didn't know it. If it hadn't, it would have been obvious how Nathan had silenced Athena.

25

I was hoping to make it back to my Department of Psychiatry office before Tanya, my three-o'clock client, arrived. My secretary, Melissa, got so anxious around Tanya I wasn't sure which of them to treat. It would have been better, at least for Melissa, if I had seen Tanya in my private practice, but she needed the backup of a twenty-four hour emergency service, and I saw clients like that at the department.

I could see Melissa from the door of the waiting room. She was sitting stiffly at her desk and had a slightly frozen expression on her face. I didn't need to walk into the waiting room and glance around to know Tanya was there.

I turned around to greet Tanya. The woman I faced was dressed almost entirely in black: black pants suit, black silk blouse, large black hoop earrings. The only color in her outfit was a tie with brightly colored cartoon figures all over it. The effect was whimsical and oddly charming. It was quite a contrast to the last time I saw her. She had been wearing L. L. Bean hiking boots with gray sweatpants and an oversized, somewhat ratty sweater. She had looked somewhat like the last survivor of an expedition up K-2. The woman in front of me, with her black eyeliner and her rose lipstick, only remotely resembled the woman I saw last week.

Tanya came into my office and immediately lay down on the couch, carefully placing a couple of small, square pillows under her head first. No personality of Tanya's had ever lain down on the couch before. From the way she took over the space, I had the feeling this part of Tanya might be a tad flamboyant. I had to smile. Nobody ever lay down on my couch; it was only there to provide extra seating for family sessions. If Freud could see me now. I finally had a client on the couch.

I waited for her to start. This might be the same body that came in last week, but it wasn't the same personality. Tanya was a multiple personality, and when the alters showed up, they usually had an agenda. Things went best if I let them start off.

"Call me 'baby,'" Tanya said, smoothing her hair back. It was pulled into a bun at the nape of her neck. "That isn't my name, of course. But that's what the gentlemen always used to say. 'Baby, baby, baby,' they'd say. They were nice to me, those gentlemen. Always bringing me presents, always calling me 'baby.'"

She was silent for a moment. "If I could find a tie with babies on it, I think I'd be cured. Don't you agree?"

I wasn't sure how to answer. A tie with babies on it was not going to fix Tanya, but there wasn't any point in saying so. People place their hopes on peculiar things, but hope, itself, is a pretty valuable commodity. I tend to step lightly around it lest it be more fragile than I know. I waited too long to reply, and Tanya took my silence negatively.

"Your secretary agreed with me. But, unfortunately, she has never seen a tie with babies on it so she couldn't tell me where to find one. She did say she'd keep her eye out for me. Well, if I had a tie with babies on it, I'd be good. It would remind me to be good. Babies aren't bad, you know, not like that bad girl. She deserves to be hurt. But I don't want to talk about that now. Let's talk about you."

"I don't think talking about me would help you at all," I replied. "But what gentlemen are you talking about? I don't know anything about them."

"My daddy took me. He told me to be a good girl and do whatever the gentlemen wanted. I tried. I really tried, but I wasn't a very good girl because they hurt me."

"Where was your daddy?"

"He left. He went off with another little girl. He liked her better."

Was this a child sex ring? There were clubs, I knew, where the price of entry was bringing a child under five. I once had an offender who specialized in setting them up. He not only got access to the kids. He charged a fee and made money from it. If it wasn't that, what was it? Was there any possible innocent explanation?

Suddenly Tanya grabbed her crotch and yelled, "Ready, ready, ready." She started trembling, and—when I collected my wits—I realized she was staring out the window.

I got up carefully. Tanya looked disoriented and seemed to be having a flashback. I knew not to get too close to her. People having flashbacks are reliving a trauma, and if you get too close, they can mistake you for an attacker. I moved gingerly to the side, trying to see what she was staring at out the window. There was a man outside at a bus stop, smoking a cigarette.

At first I thought it was the man that set things off. Maybe he looked like someone she was talking about. Maybe it was just that he was a man combined with what she was talking about. But then the bus pulled up, and the man turned slightly and threw the cigarette away in the general direction of the window. Tanya gasped and pulled back. "Ready," she said, staring at the cigarette on the sidewalk. "Me ready. Me be a good girl."

I felt sick. "Tanya," I said, then stopped. She wasn't Tanya anymore. Tanya was an adult, and so was the personality who called herself 'baby.' But this didn't sound like an adult. "It's safe now," I said. "There are no men here. Nobody is going to hurt you."

She seemed to calm down slightly. She turned from the window and looked around the room as though seeing it for the first time. "What's your name?" I said.

"Carrie" Tanya answered. "The men are gone?"

"All gone," I said.

"I was a good girl."

I didn't comment on that. "How old are you, Carrie?

"I'm three," Carrie said holding up four fingers. She looked across the room at the Magic Markers. "Can I draw?" she asked.

"Of course," I replied, and Carrie got up and went over to a small table to draw. The flashback seemed to be over, but it had evidently tripped Tanya into a child alter. She sat down in one of the small chairs, picked up a Magic Marker, and laid her head down on her other elbow while she drew. It was odd seeing an adult body curl over a drawing like a three-year-old. Carrie held the Magic Marker awkwardly and slowly drew a head. The head had eyebrows and eyelashes, hair, ears, mouth with lips and teeth, a nose, and even nostrils, but the body was a stick figure with clothes.

Everything about the drawing was wrong. If a real three-year-old had drawn a person, she would have drawn a circle for the face and two lines for the legs. Even if she had drawn a full stick figure, it would have never have had clothes. Clothes and facial details go with two-dimensional arms and legs. It wasn't just that the drawing was older than three, it didn't go together developmentally. The drawing came across as an adult trying to imitate a three-year-old's drawing and it was. The books were right. The problem for multiples isn't that different personalities actually inhabit one body. The problem is the person believes they do—and believes it deeply and unconsciously. This was not a real three-year-old I was talking to, in any sense, but it was one confused, lost soul of an adult.

Carrie stayed most of the session and told me about the

cigarettes and what happened to her if she didn't do what her daddy wanted. She told me, too, about going to the place where the men and the other little girls were and where you had to do what the "gentlemen" said.

"Carrie," I finally said toward the end of the session, "it's time for you to rest now and Tanya to come back." Letting this adult woman wander out of the building thinking she was a three-year-old was not a good idea. For one thing, Carrie couldn't drive.

"No," Carrie said.

They don't teach you this kind of thing in graduate school. I never heard a lecture titled "How to Get Your Multiple Personality Clients to Switch into a Responsible Adult Alter Who Can Drive." And yet what are you supposed to do with a child alter who doesn't want to leave?

But then, there are a lot of things you didn't learn in graduate school: Not having a course called "How to Keep Your Antisocial Clients from Killing You When You Tell Them You're Going to Call the Police About Their Intention to Kill Their Wives" was, I thought, a particularly significant oversight.

"Close your eyes, Carrie," I said. "It really is time for Tanya to come out now because she can drive and you can't. If it's too scary to close your eyes, just look up at the corner of the ceiling. I'm going to count backward from ten." I counted slowly and rhythmically. "Ten . . . nine . . . eight—you're feeling very comfortable and safe, and you're beginning to fade away a little, and Tanya is beginning to come out—seven . . . six . . . five—you're very safe and comfortable, and you're slipping into a pleasant sleep while Tanya is waking up." Carrie had closed her eyes. "Four . . . three—Tanya is almost here, you're barely awake—two . . . one. Tanya, open your eyes."

It always amazes me that this works, but it does. Tanya's eyes flew open. She looked down at her clothes and shut her eyes again. "I don't believe this," she said. "What am I wearing?" She sounded weary. I could understand it. Hell of a thing to wake up and try to figure out who you are for the day.

What a world! The most damaged of trauma victims has a fragmented consciousness with specialty personalities: one, perhaps, to contain the rage, one to remember the abuse, one to protect the child alter, maybe another for self-hatred. In the meantime the poor host personality might wake up in a supermarket and find a man following her, calling her by a name she doesn't know.

Then there are the offenders. They have continuous memories but fragment other people's experience of them: The victim sees an abuser, the job sees a "responsible" worker, the community sees a civic-minded asset to the town. And the offender, well, he sees a world where you change your presentation to fit the circumstances—liked other people change clothes.

It comes down to the fact that people are always fooling themselves or fooling each other, and the biggest difference I can see has to do with who picks up the tab.

I explained to Tanya who showed up and what they said. "Do you remember any of it?" I asked.

"No," she replied, fingering the tie. She kept looking down at it. Maybe she just liked the way it looked, or maybe it stood for all the things about herself that made no sense.

"I don't know what she was talking about."

"Which one?" I asked.

"Either," she answered, finally looking up. "I don't remember any of it. I don't remember any men. I don't remember being called 'baby.' I don't think any of it ever happened. Probably Carrie was just looking for attention, the lying little bitch."

She bit into the last words, and the force of them caught me by surprise. I decided not to confront her with the self-hatred. This was not one of her better days. She had had one major flashback and several personality switches, and I suspected she was pretty fragile.

"What do you remember about the preschool years?"

"Nothing." She seemed embarrassed, like someone stopped

by a cop who doesn't have her driver's license. I suppose losing your memory is a lot like losing your driver's license.

"Nothing at all?"

"Nothing." She looked down at the tie again.

"Christmas?" I asked. "Birthdays?"

"I mean nothing," she said. "The memories start in first grade." She paused, and I waited. She went on tentatively, "Even then I remember school stuff, but not anything at home. I don't have home memories till years later."

"What were you like in elementary school?" If the scenario Carrie described was true, there was no way Tanya wouldn't have been symptomatic.

"I don't know. I don't think I had a lot of friends. And I remember I was terrified of a male teacher in one of the classes. I had a lot of nightmares. I had one for years and years. I still have it sometimes. There is this large bird with a huge beak who swoops down on me beating his wings. Then other birds come, too, and they all peck me. It's a little worse than that. They sort of tear off bits of flesh and take them away and then come back for more. I hope you don't make too much of all this. I don't think it means anything."

Sure. Everyone dissociates into alternative personalities and grabs their crotch when they see a man with a cigarette and yells "Ready, ready," plus they are completely amnesiac for most of their childhood—at home, that is—and have a recurrent nightmare of having bits of their flesh torn off. No reason I should make anything of that.

"Things got better." Tanya seemed anxious to reassure me. "They did."

She correctly read my skepticism. Given the state she was in as an adult it was hard to imagine things had gotten a whole lot better. "Okay. Tell me about it."

"I don't remember a lot about it. I just remember I was less afraid. The nightmares slowed down. Somewhere around fifth or sixth grade, I remember noticing that I didn't want to die anymore. It was sort of funny. I remember thinking that there was something wrong with me that not wanting to die was this big, new thing. Before then, wanting to die was so constant that I hardly even noticed it. I don't know what happened."

"Were there any changes in your family? Did anybody quit drinking or go into treatment or get put into jail or anything?"

"Not really."

"Was your dad any different that you can remember?"

"I don't know. Mom and he separated when I was ten or so."

Jesus Christ. The things you have to drag out of people. A cardiologist told me recently that no one who has a heart attack smokes. "Used to," they all say. "I've quit." He's learned to ask when. "Last night," they say. Things got better when her mom and dad separated. No reason to make anything out of that.

"So when did things get bad again?" The history Tanya had initially given me had been of being sexually molested by an uncle around age thirteen or fourteen. I hadn't known anything about the possible preschool abuse until today. Early abuse would make sense, though. Almost nobody develops a multiple personality from abuse that starts as an adolescent and—as bad as the adolescent abuse was—it never sounded to me like enough to create a multiple.

"Jeannie, what do . . ." I stopped. Why on earth had I called her Jeannie? Jeannie was my little client who had strangled the doll. I despised making mistakes in therapy. How could I possibly have called Tanya by the wrong name? Good grief, she had enough alters that if I had picked a name at random it would probably have been one of her alters. How did I come up with one of the few names she'd missed?

I didn't think she'd let it go, and she didn't. "Jeannie? Unless you know something I don't, there isn't any Jeannie here today."

Not surprisingly, she had an edge in her voice. She didn't feel she mattered worth a damn. What a help to have a therapist who didn't know her name. "I'm sorry. I have no idea where that came from."

After she left, I thought about it some more. Where did it

come from? I believe the opposite of most therapists. I don't think my clients' slips of the tongue in therapy always mean something, but I'm pretty sure mine do. What did Jeannie and Tanya have in common? Pretty clearly, Tanya ran into a sadist somewhere along the way. Nobody burns a child with a lighted cigarette when they don't spread their legs fast enough unless they are well and truly sadistic.

But Jeannie's offender had been one of those sickly sweet, manipulative, betrayal-of-trust types, supposedly. At least that's all Jeannie had ever described. But that couldn't be right. If that was right, why was Jeannie strangling a doll in such a compulsive and riveted way? I thought back to the reports on Jeannie's offender. He had molested a bunch of other kids, too, and there hadn't been a report from anybody that smacked of sadism. Had I missed something? Again?

Maybe the connection between Tanya and Jeannie was something else. Multiple offenders? A lot of people — more than the general public have any clue — run into more than one sex offender. Once a child has been abused, their self-esteem is usually down and they're easy pickings for predators. It looked to me like Tanya had run into a sadist — maybe her dad — in her preschool years and an ordinary, garden-variety pedophile uncle in her adolescence. Had something like that happened to Jeannie? But Jeannie was still a preschooler. How many sex offenders could one child run into in five years? Too many, I thought, remembering back to some of my other small clients.

Both Tanya and Jeannie had been doing well for a while, and both got worse. Tanya had gotten worse because a new offender had entered the picture. Was that why Jeannie was decompensating? But I had several kids who were deteriorating. Was it possible that half my caseload was being molested by a new offender? Couldn't be. Too much of a coincidence. Not starting at the same time. Not unless . . . I froze.

The phone rang, and I picked it up absently. Did the kids who were deteriorating have anything in common? Did they go to the same youth group or have the same music teacher? But I was pretty sure they didn't. They were different ages and lived in different neighborhoods. Really, they didn't have anything in common except me.

I snapped out of my reverie when Melissa said that Gene, the deputy at the jail, was on the line. Had something happened to Sharon? Oh, Christ. I didn't want more bad news. Was this going to be like the phone call from Carlotta telling me the children were dead? Gene came on the line.

"Michael, this is Gene," he said. "You got a minute?"

"Sure," I said, holding my breath. "Is everything all right?"

"Yes and no," he said. "I've got a sister up in the Northeast Kingdom, and if her fourteen-year-old doesn't kill her it'll be a miracle."

"Good Lord, Gene," I sighed. "You scared me to death. I thought something had happened to Sharon."

"Sharon?" Gene sounded puzzled. "Sharon's fine. That guy Arthur is visiting with her." The way he said "Arthur" didn't sound like they were bosom buddies.

I settled back in the chair. "I'm sorry. Tell me about your sister."

"She's the sweetest kid, and she's always had it hard. She raised all of us after mom got sick. There were six of us, and I don't think any of us lifted a finger to help her. Then she married that asshole flatlander who left her when she was pregnant with Cheryl. She's raised that girl all by herself, working two shifts at the Ethan Allen factory most of the time. You'd think the kid would be grateful, but all Cheryl does is scream at her. She's staying out all night and running with a fast crowd. My sister's at her wit's end. I told her to go to court, take out a CHINS petition. Tell the judge she can't control Cheryl and have her put in a detention center. But she won't listen."

"Whoa, Gene, slow down. Maybe it'll come to something like that, but that ought to be way down the line." Something was bugging me about this conversation, too.

"Okay, how can I help? Are you looking for me to see her or

refer her to someone or what?" Time to cut to the chase. I can't deal with vague conversations that amble along and never go anywhere. I am a poor choice for those people who just want to ventilate.

"Oh, this is too far for her to come," Gene said. "Her car doesn't work that well in the winter. I just think most counselors aren't worth shit, and I thought you might know someone up there who knew their ass from a hole in the ground."

"And you're willing to trust a referral from Gloria Steinem? Good thing for you we feminists aren't as crazy as you think."

I gave him the name of a good, solid, no-nonsense counselor in the Northeast Kingdom, but all the time I was wondering why I felt so uneasy. Maybe it was just my latest wave of paranoia over my small clients' deterioration. Maybe I was turning into a crazy lady. Oh, for Carlotta's sense of perspective.

"When you going to let me take you hunting, Michael?" Gene surprised me by asking. "One of the guys said he saw you at the shooting range, and you were hammering the target."

"When a deer shoots at me, Gene, I plan to shoot back. Until then, we have a truce."

"Michael, don't tell me you're opposed to hunting, too. We're just thinning the herd. If we don't do it, nature will."

"Well, if you guys are just thinning the herd, you're doing it all wrong. Last I heard, nature picked on the old and the sick. You guys are after the twelve-point bucks. Since when did you help a herd by taking the biggest and the best out of it?" I had had it with people who rationalize killing. No doubt when we finally figured out who killed Andrew and Adrienne, they'd have an excuse for it, too. People always do.

Gene gave up, and I hung up. What wasn't right about that conversation? Something about the niece? Something about Gene?

I picked up the phone. "Gene," I said when I got him on the line. "How do you know Arthur?"

"I don't know him. What do you mean?"

"You said that guy Arthur like you knew him, but you couldn't know him from the jail if it's his first visit."

"I don't know where you got the idea it was his first visit. He's been coming here two or three times a week since she got here."

Had he now? Funny thing. I was pretty sure he said it was his first visit when I talked to him. So why lie?

I hung up and chewed on it. What was the point of Arthur's telling me it was his first visit, or had my memory gone psychotic? A friend told me once that in your forties you don't have Alzheimer's, you have "sometimers." Maybe my memory had taken a "sometimers," but I really thought Arthur said it was his first visit.

That wasn't all of it. Why had Gene sounded so disapproving when he mentioned Arthur? Surely he didn't object to Sharon's having some support. I picked up the phone again.

"I swear, Gene. I won't bother you again. I just have one more question."

"You're not bothering me, Michael. I'd talk to you all day."

Gene's voice always has a funny kind of energy in it when he talks to me. You can feel the standing waves of eagerness, but nothing else. Why is it that when some men hit on women, the whole thing is so curiously devoid of warmth—no matter what words are used? Does Gene see any real difference between me and a twelve-point buck? Probably he'd like to see my head mounted right next to the deer's. Well, maybe not my head. "What do you think of Arthur? Really."

There was silence on the line. "I don't know anything about him. He doesn't seem to have much to say to any of us. I don't have anything against him. It's just . . ."

"Just what?"

"Well, he gets her so upset."

"What do you mean?"

"I don't know. When anybody else comes to see her she's

all right afterward. She's always crying and stuff like that, but it's nothing different. But when that guy comes, she gets really upset, and then she stays upset. People notice. The night shift say they can tell when he's been here. She gets up a lot more in the night."

What sense did that make?

I stumbled through the rest of the day, my mind elsewhere. If the clients I saw that afternoon paid by what actually happened in therapy—this much for interpretations, that much for empathic comments, so much for reframing a dilemma—I'd have ended up owing them (assuming vague grunts didn't count). I felt like I had in high school when my mind was always elsewhere and I was always desperately trying to hide the fact. I told myself my absorption wasn't entirely my fault. When people lied to me it was all right to get curious about it— although some would say total oblivion to the rest of the world was going a bit far.

The last client finally left after a therapy session that had a half-life in the decades. It was after six when I stepped out of my office, and outpatient psychiatry was closed for the day. The hall was as quiet as the sound of one hand clapping, to coin a phrase. The stillness seemed just right. Sometimes when the inside of my head is racing, I do better when the outside isn't.

I was walking out when I saw the light on in Marv's office and the door partially ajar. No doubt, he was working late, as usual. I paused, then knocked gently and felt heartened by Marv's cheerful invitation. His office, like its occupant, has an air of rumpled comfort. Charts and papers are piled high on the desk. There are several pieces of small, interesting artwork on the wall, nothing large enough or flashy enough to dominate the room or even alert the unknowing to their quality. One small bronze sculpture stands on the table, slightly behind and to the side of the chair the clients sit in. I had never noticed before that the piece was placed so Marv could see it, without getting caught looking at it, when he was talking with a client.

I don't know why I feel so comfortable in Marv's office. There is more stuff in that room than I own. But comfort is where you find it, and I sank into Marv's stuffed armchair with my usual sense of relief.

"Man lied to me today," I began.

"What a surprise." Marv observed wryly. "Was he a sex offender or a lawyer?"

"Maybe both," I said. "What do you think about Arthur as the killer?" I told Marv about the number of visits Arthur had made to the jail and went through the pros and cons of his being the murderer. I didn't tell him about my Freudian slip with Tanya. I wasn't sure what to tell him since I wasn't sure what I thought of my confusion of Tanya and Jeannie. I'd sit with it a while.

I went on. "He meets all the criteria that Adam outlined. He certainly knows the case. He knows me pretty well. He's frequently been in my office, and he could have filched the book. He knew the children. Heck, he was their GAL, and he spent a lot of time with them. They would probably have gone with him had he gone to pick them up."

Marv didn't seem impressed. "But how would he—or anyone except Nathan or Sharon—have gotten into Sharon's locked house?"

"I don't know, but think of it. He's very literate. He's the only one I know in this case who is sure to have read Toni Morrison.

I have a vague memory I may have even discussed it with him."
I didn't say it but I thought I might be making that up.

Marv had been brewing some tea in a small Chinese teapot while I spoke. I took some just to look at the intricate blue cup he served it in.

"I think you're working too hard," he finally answered.

"What?" I asked, with some wariness.

"You know the medical saying, 'When you hear the sound of hoofs, don't look for zebras.' You're looking for zebras."

"What zebras?"

"Arthur's a zebra," Marv explained patiently.

"So who's the horse?"

"Nathan. He's been the obvious one all along. He's a child molester, and he despised his ex-wife. Perhaps he was furious at his children for disclosing the abuse. The children were in his care at the time they were murdered. He probably had access to his ex-wife's house. Why did you consider him so briefly and then pounce on Arthur? There isn't much that implicates Arthur."

"He lied to me."

"Foolish," Marv said, smiling wryly, "but not proof he's capable of murder. Suicide, maybe, but not murder. Perhaps he had other reasons for lying to you. Besides, what are you suggesting is the connection between his visiting Sharon in jail and his supposedly killing the children?"

"I don't know."

"My point exactly. So why did you let Nathan off the hook so quickly? You're working terribly hard to avoid seeing him as the killer."

"That's crazy," I blurted out. "I'm hoping he's the killer."

Marv said nothing. He took a sip of tea and waited.

I didn't say anything either. I surprised myself. I hadn't realized what I said was true until I said it.

"Nathan would be easy for me," I said slowly. "My private, not-for-circulation opinion is that he's a scumbag. The son of a bitch molested those children, then said they were liars when they called him on it. If he killed them, it only means he was worse than I thought, but that's all. I won't feel blindsided if it's Nathan."

"And if it's not him?" Marv asked.

"Then I'm blind as a bat." I was pretty sure Marv was way ahead of me on this and had been all along, but I said it out loud anyway. "If it's not him, it's someone I know and maybe even like or something. We both know it isn't a stranger."

"So why do you want to blame the butler, the cleaning lady, and the children's stuffed bunny?"

"Well, I've got a personal reason for wanting it to be Nathan, so I don't trust I'm objective." I lapsed into silence. It hit me how foolish that was. Mama may have thought Elrod was the killer because he had bad manners, but that didn't change the fact that he actually was the killer.

Somehow I bet this kind of thing is easier for Mama. I just can't see her having spasms of self-doubt and second-guessing her own motivation. But maybe Mama has too little doubt, and I have too much. Or maybe doubt is just one of those genetic things that skips a generation now and then.

Marv said nothing. He has a way of making silence as comfortable as talking. Finally, I broke the silence with a laugh and a shake of my head. "It's so weird. Mama decides someone is a killer just because she doesn't like him, and I decide someone isn't a killer just because I don't like him. Sometimes I wonder if I'm Mama with the polarity reversed."

Wisely, Marv didn't comment. He knew, and I knew, it was the kind of statement that if anyone else said it to me—or even agreed with it—I would start a fight.

He let it go, instead. "Michael, we haven't talked about the loss in court at all. I need to ask you if you feel my rather pathetic performance was a major factor." I looked up from my tea to see the strain on Marv's face. Oh, dear. Had he been carrying that around? Did he think if he hadn't messed up, the case might have been won and, who knows, the children might still be alive?

213

"Absolutely not. You weren't the strongest part of the case, and I did feel really bad about dragging you into it, but you didn't lose it for us. It wasn't winnable. You can only give people the opportunity to believe something. If they don't want to, they won't. The judge had a knee-jerk reaction. He heard the words custody fight and child sexual abuse accusation in the same sentence, and he wasn't going to buy it no matter what the facts."

Marv sighed, and some of the strain in his face eased a fraction. "I don't know how you do it," he said. "Court is the most dreadful, ruthless, unfair arena with which I have ever had the misfortune to be involved. I don't know how you manage to go in the witness box day after day. It's like playing Russian roulette with live ammunition. It appears we lost a case we should have won just because the chamber was loaded. I hope I never sit in a witness box again, staring at a horrible painting of a former governor." Marv shuddered when he mentioned the painting. He sounded more affected by the painting than the questions.

I laughed. I had never even noticed what was on the walls. "For all its obvious flaws," I replied, "it is possible to make a case for court. It's what makes us human."

Marv raised both eyebrows. "Really. I rather thought the opposite."

"Think about it. With every other species on the planet, might makes right. If you can catch it, you can eat it. I know what most people would say: The lion has to eat. Well, excuse me, but so does the zebra. What makes the lion's life worth more than the zebra's? Nothing. But with nature, nobody is going to ask the question of whether it's fair for the lion to save its life at the expense of the zebra's.

"Circle of life. Bullshit. Pure Walt Disney. The lion eats the zebra when the zebra is at the peak of her life with two cubs back in the grass who are now going to starve if they aren't eaten by another lion. The lion eventually dies of old age, and the next zebra munches on the grass he fertilizes. As if the lion cared once he was dead. Any way you cut it, the lion has a better deal.

"Humans are the only species that asks the question of what's fair. You don't see lions and zebras sitting down after the fact to mull over whether the lion should have eaten somebody or not. At least we make an attempt—occasionally a serious one—to hold predators accountable. You've got it backward, Marv. Nature is the most dreadful, ruthless, unfair arena there is. Going to court is a piece of cake compared to living in the wild."

"Michael." Marv's smile was warm. "I've always wondered what makes you tick."

"What? And now you think you know?" I felt rather alarmed by whatever it was Marv thought he knew.

"Let's just say I have a clue."

I felt like shooting something. To be honest, I frequently feel like shooting something, but this time I decided to do something about it. The firing range was open till ten so I headed over. The problem with this whole murder thing was that it was a knot inside my chest that wouldn't ease. I couldn't pull it apart. I couldn't talk it apart. I couldn't even seem to look at it from a different angle.

I pulled into the parking lot next to a pickup truck. That wasn't difficult. Just about anywhere in the lot I could have parked would have been next to a pickup truck. Good thing we weren't playing bumper cars: My little red Honda was dwarfed by its neighbors. Some of those trucks had tires roughly the size of my car.

I pulled my Model 66 .357 Magnum out of the glove compartment—I'd taken to carrying it around lately. Most people think of Magnums as large guns, but mine was about the size of my hand. I've actually seen a .45 that was smaller—not much larger than my palm—but the shorter the barrel, the shorter the sight radius, the harder to shoot. I wasn't planning on shooting anyone from a great distance away: It seemed to me that anyone attacking me would likely be in the same room. But still, if things were serious enough to pull the trigger, it probably wasn't a good idea to miss.

Then there was the matter of the kick. The smaller the gun, the larger the recoil. Even my size Magnum kicked so much with .357 ammo in it that I tended to use .38 Special Plus P.

I have trouble understanding my relationship with guns. The .357 feels right in my palm. The weight feels right. The curve of the stainless steel feels right. I get along with guns; I confess I'm comfortable with guns—which makes no sense, given that I dislike violence.

I walked in the front door of the indoor firing range and breathed in the sharp, bitter smell of burnt powder. Back in the lanes, there would be a faint blue haze hovering. No doubt the residue of burnt powder is roughly as carcinogenic as asbestos, but it smelled good to me. There was a faint smell, too, of ammonia from the cleaning solvents used and a much stronger smell of cigarettes—also hovering in blue haze quantities— which I could do without. Even from the lobby, the noise coming from the lanes was considerable.

There was a counter in front of me and a small waiting area off to the side. Sitting in the worn-down chairs were two young women watching television. They were giving zero attention to a toddler who was playing on a floor that had never met a mop. The whole scene irritated me. What in hell was a baby doing here at this time of night among the noise and the cigarette smoke? That kid should be home in bed. God sure didn't hand out babies according to who could take care of them. And why were these women sitting there while their men were shooting, anyway? Who did they think would be attacked—the men?

It was probably the New England version of the two-step. She had the steady job. He worked at plowing or logging or construction when it was available. He made the payments on the pickup truck. She paid for everything else, which included the house, the snowmobiles, the motorcycles, the RV, the groceries, and, no doubt, the guns. Good grief, was I down on everybody and everything today. I reminded myself of the old Joplin song, "And I don't like anybody very much."

I walked up to the counter. "Good evening, Michael," the attendant said. "You're in luck. There's one lane left."

I had brought my gun and the ammo, but rented the ear protectors and bought some targets. You could go with circles or silhouette targets, and I took the silhouettes. I actually like shooting circles better. There is something queasy-making about pointing a pistol at a human form, but let's not kid ourselves. Women buy guns to protect themselves from crazy males. If I do ever have to shoot somebody, I want the aiming part to become instinctive. It takes three- to five-thousand repetitions to make anything instinct, and I haven't fired at anywhere near that many silhouettes.

I put on my ear protectors and opened the door to the lanes. The noise, considerable in the lobby, would have been deafening without the ear protectors. The best thing about being in the lanes is it is too noisy to talk to anybody. It's the very best place for me to go when I'm in an advanced stage of grumpiness. I walked behind the shooters to lane four and hit the button on the wall. The clip for the target moved forward to where I was, and I put the first target up. I hit the button again and the target started sliding down range.

I took the Magnum out of my fanny pack and popped a bullet into the single chamber that wasn't loaded. I keep one empty chamber in the gun and always leave the gun with that chamber up. It is a compromise. If I need a gun, I clearly don't want to be taking time to load it. On the other hand, I can't quite bring myself to walk around with a bullet in the firing chamber.

I leveled the gun at arm's length, holding it with both hands, and steadied it. I focused on the front sight and filled the rear sight. Sighting is very simple. The tiny protrusion on the front of the barrel needs to fit exactly in the notch on the back. Every time I breathed, of course, the sight moved off center.

They say that Olympic shooters can squeeze the trigger between heartbeats. I am a long way from that level. All I manage to do is shoot between breaths. Slowly, I squeezed the trigger, pulling it to within a fraction of an inch of firing and then steadied the sight again. I fired six shots with a couple of seconds between them. Wyatt Earp I'm not: There is nothing fast about the way I shoot, but you don't gain anything by shooting fast and sloppy. Speed will come.

I hit the button and waited for the target to come up. All six shots had hit an area about the size of my palm, and all were pretty much exactly where the heart would be. I shuddered. Maybe I'd go back and pick up a couple of circles for targets. The silhouettes had never seemed all that real before, and I hadn't thought that much about it. But this time I had a feeling I was really practicing to shoot someone.

A half hour was enough. I don't shoot that much, so my trigger finger gets worn out pretty easily since I was trained to shoot double action only. Not to mention I don't have any plans to be in a gunfight that lasts more than half an hour. I handed in my ear protectors and noticed the attendant looking at my targets. I looked around. The two women were gone at last. Too much to hope somebody was cooing over that baby now and rocking her to sleep. There were a number of men standing around talking, and a couple looked at me with interest. Strange, though. No one ever hits on me in a firing range.

I headed for the car with my gun securely tucked in my fanny pack. Sad to say, but the only woman in the world who can cross a deserted parking lot at night without being afraid is one with a loaded gun. A gun will only take you so far, however. You don't stop feeling sad or angry that the world is the way it is. But at least you don't feel scared and helpless, too. And, as Joplin said, "that was good enough for me."

I got in the car and started up the engine. Nothing more to do about this business today. The shooting had calmed me down. There is something Zen-like about the stilling and steadying you have to do to shoot well. Besides, concentrating that much on anything tends to wipe my neurons clean. What I needed now was some time in the hot tub looking up at the moon through the evergreens. What kind of moon was out there tonight?

I started to pull out, but a car suddenly drove up very close beside me in the parking lot. It startled me—the lot wasn't full, and there was no reason for a car to be next to me, much less inches away. I turned to look at the car as the window on the passenger side near me rolled down and the driver called my name. When I realized who it was, every muscle in my body spasmed. Carefully I rolled my window down and looked over at Nathan Southworth.

"Dr. Stone, I hear you've been asking about me at the hospital. I just wanted you to know that if you say or do anything to slander me or harm my reputation, I will sue your ass off. And loss of reputation for a surgeon means loss of income, which is to say, I could take you for everything you have."

To my astonishment there were two children in the car with him. I wanted badly to look at the small boy sitting between Nathan and me, but I kept my gaze firmly on Nathan. Even with peripheral vision I could tell the boy was four or five, maybe, with brown hair and eyes like small, dark pools. His face seemed to hold nothing at all—no light, no animation. Maybe he was tired or sick. Maybe he was dissociated. He looked back and forth from Nathan to me, and his expression didn't seem to change. You couldn't have told which one of us he knew. A girl, maybe six or seven, leaned forward from the back seat. She was staring at Nathan, and her mouth was slightly open. Maybe she hadn't heard him angry before. I hoped not.

The son of a bitch. His hand was on the back of the seat, inches from the boy's shoulder. The goddamn narcissism of sex offenders. He couldn't resist showing off.

"You need to take whatever legal action you feel is justified," I said, trying to sound matter-of-fact and unflappable. "That's

up to you." As I spoke, Nathan casually dropped his hand on the
boy's shoulder. I ignored it. "Hopefully, if the case drags on
long enough, somebody will surface to back me up." Slowly,
Nathan started stroking the boy's arm. The boy didn't flinch or
pull away; he had no reaction at all.

I felt frozen. I was looking at Nathan's face, but every neuron
in my brain was focused on that child's arm. I couldn't believe
Nathan was practically fondling a child in front of me. It
actually crossed my mind that I had a gun in the car. This case
was going to make me certifiably insane.

I gave up ignoring it. "You know, Nathan," I said, trying to
hold my voice steady. "They'll all tell, eventually. In five years,
in ten years, sooner or later, they'll tell." For the first time I
looked directly at the boy. "If this man touches you in a way
you don't like, tell someone and keep telling until someone
believes you." Nathan dropped his hand. About the only thing a
pedophile fears is disclosure. I barely got the last words out
before his car accelerated. I could see the girl in the backseat,
her head turned to look at me as the car sped away. She kept
looking at me all the way out of sight.

Peace of mind can be fleet of foot. I watched mine disappear
with Nathan's car. Whose children were they? A new girlfriend
already? His kids are barely dead and he's riding around with
new kids, which no doubt means he's grooming if not already
molesting them? Sharon isn't even eating, and her ex-husband
is already up to his old tricks. Maybe Marv was right. Maybe he
did kill them. And exactly what can I do about it? The very
thought of his getting away with it made me crazy.

I rode home obsessing about the case. All this time I had been
worrying about who did it, but never really thought about what
happened if I found out. What a misery it was going to be if I
ended up knowing Nathan killed the kids, but nothing ever
happened to him. And worse yet if he knew I knew and taunted
me with it. Then there was the fact we both work at the
hospital, so I wouldn't be able to get away from him. I couldn't
imagine working with someone who had put his hands around

a child's throat. Maybe I had better talk with Adam. I needed him to tell me they were making progress on this case.

I pulled into my driveway, then backed up. There was a letter halfway protruding from the mailbox. What was a letter doing in my mailbox? All of my mail goes to Carlotta's. No one has my new home address. I don't even get junk mail.

I turned on the car light and stared at the letter. There were initials instead of a name in the upper left-hand corner, and they were written quite precisely, more like calligraphy than handwriting. I knew who wrote them. At one point Willy had let me read some of his journals, and his handwriting was unmistakable.

This day was deteriorating by the hour. Let's see. Sharon looked like a survivor of Auschwitz. Arthur had inexplicably lied to me. Somewhere in the back of my head, a woman who thought she was a three-year-old was saying "Ready, ready, ready." Nathan was out molesting again and wanted me to know it. Why not finish off with Willy? What did Willy have to say? Wearily, I tore the envelope open. A saner woman would have waited till morning, but I am the kind who speeds up to get through intersections.

"Dr. Michael, I have taken the liberty of writing you because I believe I have information of some interest in regards to the Southworth case." Willy's tone was as formal as the handwriting. "I would come to you, but present circumstances are somewhat inhibiting. Please call upon me at your earliest convenience."

So he knows where I live. Where did the son of a bitch get the address? Nobody had it to give to him. Not to mention hinting that he'll come to see me when he can.

Still, he had me; I'd go see him. I wanted to know who murdered Adrienne and Andrew more than I wanted to stay away from Willy, and I couldn't take a chance that Willy might really know something. Great, I can end the evening knowing I'm at a sadist's beck and call.

I took the Magnum out of the fanny pack and walked into the house with it in my hand. I made some ice tea and headed for the deck—drink in one hand and gun in the other. It seemed to me I was carrying the gun around a lot these days. Living alone in the country just didn't have the same homey feel it used to.

I sat down in the rocker on the deck and looked up. The branches of the overhanging pine trees formed a black lace canopy against the moonlit sky. Finally. I thought I'd never make it. This day was the living proof of Zeno's paradox, which says you can never get from A to B because first you have to cover half the distance and then to cover that half you have to get through half of that half and so on. Theoretically, you never run out of halves. In short, this day had gone on for decades.

The stream chortled its way through the rocks, and I waited for things to ease inside my head. All of it—the lace above my head, the breeze I lifted my face into, the sounds of the stream—were about as close to the promised land as I was likely to get.

I waited. It took me a while to realize nothing was happening. Not just my head—my entire body was so tense that if I tried to lie down, I'd probably bounce. There are some things you can't shoot away, things you can't soothe away.

I went back in and picked up the phone. It wasn't that late, not really. "Carlotta," I said when she finally answered. "Did you know what Freeman Dyson's job was in World War II?"

"Not exactly. Who's Freeman Dyson?"

"A physicist. A seriously smart, as in world-class, physicist. His job was to do calculations to decide how close the British bombers should fly to each other. The closer they flew, the more accidents they had running into each other. The farther apart they flew, the easier they were for the Germans to shoot down. He had to decide how close they should fly. Hell of a job."

"This means something to you?" Carlotta said. Somehow she didn't seem to have her usual patience with me.

"Willy," I replied. "It has to do with Willy and how close you can swim to one snake to catch another. The problem is, I don't think I'm as smart as Freeman Dyson."

"You don't have to be as smart as Freeman Dyson," Carlotta said. "You just have to be as smart as Willy."

Maybe it was the day I'd had. Somehow it didn't sound a whole lot better.

28

I woke with a start. I had remembered something in the night. What the hell was it? I jumped out of bed and flew downstairs and into the kitchen. Good grief. It was there. A coffee cup was sitting in the dish drain. The problem was I hadn't put it there. I only have four coffee cups, and I always use the same one—an old favorite Carlotta gave me. I had filled it yesterday morning and taken it with me. I was sure there had been nothing in the dish drain when I left.

I sat down and tried to think. How could I not have noticed it—consciously noticed it—the night before? I had gone into the kitchen and made ice tea. It had been sitting there. Clearly my unconscious had noticed it, because I had woken up with it on my mind. But the rest of me had swept right by it. And I think I'm paranoid? I don't have enough hypervigilance to cross a street without an escort.

I got up and walked over to the phone. The call was ridiculous. Carlotta had a key, but she wouldn't stop by without letting me know. I called anyway. Her phone rang an interminable period of time, then a sleepy voice came on the line. "Too much sleep gives you cancer," I said.

"Good thing I've got a friend like you," Carlotta answered. "I'll live forever."

"Did you by any chance stop by my place yesterday?"

"No, why do you ask?" Carlotta's voice had lost its sleepiness.

I backtracked and minimized and downplayed. It didn't do any good. Carlotta didn't like the sound of things, and, no doubt, that meant she would mother-hen me to death for a while.

After a few minutes I decided to try Jack. What the hell. Maybe I had lent him a key in some fit of insanity I couldn't recall. I paged him at the hospital. All the docs have beepers, and it is more private than calling Internal Medicine and asking for him. He called me back immediately. Doctors call anyone back immediately who isn't a patient.

Maybe I could do a better job on this one. "Hi, Jack," I said. "Do you have a minute?"

"Sure." Jack's voice sounded vaguely anxious. I don't know what he expected.

"I was poking around the hospital yesterday trying to get a better sense of Nathan. I can't get a feel for him. Supposedly he's the most gracious man in the world, yet one nurse said she heard so much rage in his voice yelling at his wife, she thought he'd maul her. How well do you know him? What can you tell me about him?"

"I've worked with him on a few cases. He's very competent technically. But . . ."

"But what?"

"To be honest, I've never known what to make of him. He is incredibly polite, almost obsequious around women, but if he's in the men's room or the locker room, he tells unbelievably hostile and demeaning jokes about them. The two sides don't seem to fit together." No, of course not. Not if you don't know sex offenders. And Jack didn't because he would never let me talk about them. He favors the ignore-the-problem-and-it-will-go-away method of dealing with sex offenders. For Jack, the less said about them the better.

Jack's voice had relaxed, and that eased things for me, also. Jack and I always work well together on collegial stuff—working on cases together was how the whole thing got started. I like Jack. It isn't a crime to climb into bed with someone you like. Show me where the Ten Commandments say you have to love someone to have sex with them. Still, I felt guilty every time I talked to Jack now. He had gotten serious, and I hadn't, and somehow that made me feel like a jerk.

I turned back in and realized Jack was still trying to explain his reaction to Nathan. "I know a lot of men who are like that one way or the other. It's just I've never seen both sides so clearly in the same person. It's always made me uncomfortable. I don't know which one is the real Nathan. Maybe he's a nice guy who worries about the size of his penis and tries to be macho in the locker room. Maybe he really dislikes women and overcompensates when he's around them. I don't know. It's more your territory than mine. Does any of this help?"

"It does. I think the evidence is in about what he thinks of women. By the way," I said casually, "did you by any chance stop by yesterday?"

"Stop by where?"

"The house." There was a silence.

"Why would you think that?"

"Nothing really. It just looked like maybe somebody stopped by."

"What do you mean it looked like somebody stopped by?"

"It's nothing, I tell you. I just wasn't sure if you stopped by." Jack didn't say anything. "It's no big deal. I've got a memory like a sieve these days. There was a dish in the dish drain, and I didn't remember leaving it."

"In your dish drain? That doesn't sound like you. Have you talked to Carlotta?"

"Yes, it wasn't her."

"Don't you lock your house?"

"Yes, of course, I lock my house." Well, more or less. I didn't tell him I wasn't that religious about it until after the children died. I used to sort-of-mostly lock my house. "Look, I'm telling you it's no big deal. It's probably my imagination working overtime."

There was another silence.

"I wouldn't classify you as the hysterical type. Why don't I come stay for a few days? I can sleep on the couch if you prefer."

This time I was silent. For a moment. "And your marriage? This would not exactly help your marriage."

"Nothing is going to help my marriage. The point is there is someone running around who thought nothing of killing two children, and you were very close to those children. Maybe he thinks you know something." I hadn't heard Jack like this in a long time. He was like he was when a patient crashed: clear and decisive and forceful. Between us, things had gotten so muddled and so mushy lately I had completely lost touch with this side of him.

"Don't blow this out of proportion. If somebody had been in my house who shouldn't have been there, you don't think they'd leave a cup out, do you?" But, actually, I could think of several people who would leave a cup out. More than once over the years I had met the type of perpetrator who liked you to know you'd been had. That type would see leaving something obviously amiss as a calling card of sorts.

I hung up and stared at the phone for a while. A calling card. That was Willy's style. On impulse I picked up the phone and started to dial the number of the prison. I stopped myself and put the phone down. What was wrong with me? What was I going to ask—whether Willy escaped last night? If Willy was out of prison for any reason, I would have heard about it. I sat down slowly. I was getting hysterical. I needed to think a little.

This could be Willy. It was like him. And he didn't need to do it in person for it to be Willy. There wasn't a logical reason in the world for Willy to stalk me, except for the small fact that he had no capacity for attachment and he got giant chemical explosions in his brain from other people's fear. The high he got was motive enough. "Better than crack," he told me, "better than cocaine." And then there was the fact he made sure I'd come see him. Frightening people was no good if you didn't get to see the reaction. Great, if I was Willy's newest project, it was going to be a big problem.

On the other hand, if Jack was right and the killer was worried about what I knew—which was unfortunately nothing—then I was probably worse off. Heck of a thing. My best hope was that I had early senility and had left the cup there myself.

I got up and walked through the house. I had put it off as long as I could. I needed to know if anything else had changed, and I really didn't want to.

I held my breath while I checked things out. Good thing to have only two hundred and fifty things if you're going to hold your breath while you check all of them.

Nothing looked different, but then, nothing had looked different when the book disappeared, which—I now had to consider—really could have been taken from the house. If it was, maybe he was making a habit of being in my house, a very comforting thought.

Everybody needs a space that is inviolate. The lucky ones have it inside their heads. I used to before Jordan died. But grief has cut up the internal structure, and this small, fiercely private house has became my sanctuary. I don't let mail in. I can count the people on one hand I'll let visit. Most people don't even know it exists. It is the place where the outside world stops. So now somebody had somehow gotten into it—again, maybe— and was taunting me. Or else I was losing what was left of my neurons.

Nothing to do about it. Carlotta would want me to move in with her for a while. Jack would want to move in with me for a while. I couldn't do either. This whole thing was playing to my worst weakness. I had all the guile of a redcoat, marching forward in full view. My opponent—and it was increasingly obvious there was one—was clearly a sniper. The track record of redcoats against snipers is—last I heard—a bit problematic.

29

The drive to the prison rolled past old New England farms and dairy barns. Nothing in Vermont is flat for more than a hundred yards, but things goes up and down slowly. The valleys the road looks down on, the hills it looks up at—in a good mood, I think the landscape serene. Today I decided it was the scenic equivalent of a barbershop quartet.

I fussed and grumbled and stewed for a while, cranky and ill at ease with just about everything that was happening. But somewhere along the way I dropped it all and just let my head freewheel. The talk with Willy was too important for me to get in my own way. I needed to have all my gears meshing, and I'd discovered how to do that best: quit working them to death and let my engine coast for a while. There would be time enough to put them back in gear.

I got all the way through the front door before I took control of the wheels in my head again. As I was handing over my keys and driver's license, I decided not to bring up Willy's mail arriving at my home. He either did or didn't know how remote and private my home is and how few people know where I live. If he didn't know, I certainly didn't need to tell him. If he did know, I certainly didn't want to emphasize my sense of violation. Anything I said could and would be used against me.

The guard at the desk called down to the sex offender program for me. Willy works part-time in the education center, and he was there now. Why was I not surprised? It is the only place in the prison where he can get access to computers.

I signed in for the education center at the front bulletproof, glass-enclosed kiosk and started working my way through the maze of steel doors. First one door opened, and I walked in. That door shut behind me, and the second door opened. I was in a slowly advancing mobile cage. Long ago, someone had had the bright idea that—if there is a steel door blocking the way at all times—no one could escape. Good idea. The truth is, between the steel doors, the armed guards, the cell bars that rotate on the outside with a separate core that rotates on the inside, and the razor wire, not a whole lot of people escape from prison anyway. It's generally a lot easier to con your way out of prison through the parole board than it is to make a run for it.

I had made up my mind about strategy by the time I entered the education center. I spotted Willy working on a computer and sat down across from him. "Good morning, Mr. Willy."

Willy looked up with feigned surprise. "Well, Dr. Michael, you are certainly up bright and early."

"I've got a busy day, Mr. Willy. And I did want to find out whether you had thought of anything that might be pertinent in the Southworth case." I put a slight emphasis on "whether," which Willy ignored.

"Straight to the point, as usual, Dr. Michael. Don't you ever get sidetracked?"

"Not by comments like that." I waited. I considered glancing at my watch and decided against it. No need to get theatrical.

"Well, maybe we should talk when you have more time. It will take a little bit of explaining, and I wouldn't want to leave anything out by rushing." Willy leaned back and crossed his arms, waiting for my response. We both knew what he was saying. "I'll tell you what I want to tell you—in dribs and drabs—when I'm damn good and ready. It's my way or the highway." I did not like this deal. This would not be a good deal to take.

"Mr. Willy, if you have anything to say, say it now, and I'll listen. And if it's important enough, I'll come back when I have more time to discuss it further. But I'm not going to yo-yo up and down this highway while you futz around. Besides, while I have the greatest respect for your knowledge of the subject, it's not real clear to me you could know much of anything about this case. You've got nothing more than newspaper accounts to go on." If my Achilles' heel is my redcoat mentality, Willy's is his narcissism. He would not like my thinking he had nothing to offer.

"Very well. Has he made contact yet?" I felt my stomach drop a few stories.

"I beg your pardon. . . . With me?"

Willy nodded, his eyes sparkling like a glass in a Calgon commercial.

"Why should he make contact with me?" I got my voice level at least.

"He will, if he hasn't already." Willy turned back to his computer and started casually typing as he spoke. "But I suspect he has. It all has to do with the timing. The timing wasn't an accident, you know."

"Timing of what?"

"The events. The encounters. Whatever you call them."

"I call them murders, Mr. Willy."

"Whatever." Willy leaned back, put his fingertips together, and began to hold forth.

"Think of it. Why then? So dramatic. Just as the court case concludes—within hours—the children die. Why was the timing important? The only person who was affected by the timing was you."

"I was affected by the timing?"

"Consider, Dr. Michael. What would have happened if the children had died before you testified? You would have been off the hook. You would never have committed yourself in court that the mother was a good parent and should have custody. Then consider what would have happened if the children had died two months later. Your testimony would have been too remote from the events to make the news. No, the only way you could be discredited was if the children died on the heels of your testimony."

"That's very interesting, Mr. Willy, but blaming the mother didn't hold up very well. True, she's still in jail, but it's getting clearer all the time that she didn't kill them."

"I think you'll find, Dr. Michael, that her release will be on page ten whereas her arrest was on page one. In short, the damage to your credibility has already been done."

That was a cheerful thought.

I couldn't help it. "Surely you're not saying two children were murdered just to discredit me?" I realized I was gripping the chair arms. I slowly let go.

"Tsk, tsk, Dr. Michael. That is a surprisingly egocentric comment for you to make. Of course not. You're not that important. You don't listen nearly as well when you're . . . upset. I said the timing was determined by the desire to discredit you, not the killings themselves." He'd missed a chance to inflict pain. Later I'd have to think about why.

"This is very interesting, Mr. Willy. But I'm not a very likely target. There is no one in this case who even has a grudge against me." Except Nathan, that is, although I didn't share that with Willy.

Willy laughed. "In your case, no one needs a specific grudge against you."

"Why not?"

"Your righteous indignation, Dr. Michael, your sense of moral superiority, your arrogant faith in your own efficacy—all in all it would be difficult not to target you." There was an undercurrent of something in Willy's tone that sounded extremely unpleasant. "But, actually, there is another option even more compelling."

"Which is?"

"Consider this. Someone close to you—very close to you—wants to continue on his merry way, doing things you are quite intolerant of. Voila! He can't count on you not stumbling over his activities sooner or later. After all, you are involved with some of the people he is involved with—witness the Southworth children. So, he plans his most flamboyant episode in such a way and at such a time as to discredit you to the point where any future accusations would be fairly worthless."

I thought about it. "So why would he make contact?"

"It would take supreme discipline to win and not have your opponent know you had won. Also, you know—or you should by now—there's such excitement in taking chances. It exponentially heightens sensation. Besides, who's his audience if not you?"

"The police. Why not make contact with the police? Fooling the police ought to be a bigger thrill than fooling me."

"I don't think so. You're the one he was worried about catching him. You're the one he has some kind of relationship with. All right. Fair is fair. Has he made contact?"

"Maybe," I replied.

On the way back, I considered it. There was another possibility. Willy was jerking me around. What if Willy had arranged for someone to get into my house, then spun his maybe-somewhat-plausible-but-probably-not tale. He gets to scare the bejesus out of me, violate my privacy, become my confidant, and monitor his success all at once.

And it would have nothing at all to do with the murders because Willy surely didn't kill the Southworth children. Not that he wouldn't have liked to and not that it wasn't his style, but Willy was a hands-on killer. Being there was the thrill for him. For Willy, hiring someone to kill for him would be like a normal person hiring someone to make love for them. Not likely.

Hiring someone to scare for him was a different story. The thrill was in seeing my reaction, not in leaving the cup. All right, how much did I reveal? Hard to answer.

The trip back seemed a lot quicker than the trip there, and I felt a whole lot lighter. It wasn't just my feeling that a crony of Willy's—and not the killer—just maybe was the person who penetrated my privacy. It was the realization that Willy really didn't know me.

All that stuff about my arrogance and my faith in my own efficacy? Willy was right—once upon a time. But he wasn't right anymore. Jordan's death wiped out any sense of efficacy I ever possessed. I was sure Willy knew I had lost a child. It had been in the newspapers, and they are easily accessible these days by computer. Clearly, however, he doesn't know what losing a child means to me. With no capacity for attachment, he has none, either, for grief. So bizarre. I have a place Willy can't go. And look where it is. Another great deal.

30

Carlotta was waiting for me when I got to my private practice office. As if there was any chance she wouldn't be. She sat down on the couch as though she planned to stay for a while. Fortunately, I only had a few moments before my first client showed up. "So what's the deal?" she asked. She can get to the point quicker than I can when she wants to.

"All right, I think someone did get into my house, but I don't think it was the killer." I told her what Willy had said and what I thought about it.

Carlotta thought for a while. I can think for a minute before I speak. Carlotta can think for light-years. Just once I'd like to see Carlotta do something impulsive. Maybe that's why her pj's are never wrinkled.

At last she said, "What if Willy's right?"

"That's the beauty of Willy's kind of thinking. He could be right," I allowed, "but I don't think so."

"Because you don't want to think so?"

"Maybe, but I've also spent a lot of time around him. This just sounds like him."

"You know, he's enough of a son of a bitch to know you'd think like that. Would Willy like to see you hurt?"

"Probably. I don't think what I know is going to make a lot of difference if he never gets out. But he definitely wouldn't like to see me interfere with his 'activities.' That's the thing, Carlotta. Everything Willy said was true of him. He hates my 'moral superiority.' He doesn't want me interfering with his activities. He'd like to see me discredited just in case he ever gets out. I just think he was talking about himself."

"And what if you're wrong and Willy's setting you up? What if he's trying to lull you into complacency because there really is a killer out there on your tail and Willy wouldn't mind seeing him blindside you. What if Willy knows talking to you is just going to make you suspect *him* and leave you that much more vulnerable to the Southworth killer?"

"Then Willy's a lot smarter than I am, and I suppose I could get hurt. Not that I'd know what to do differently even if I thought the Southworth killer *was* making contact. All I'm saying is I don't think I have to panic about someone's getting into my house. I really think it's Willy playing games with my head. But what can you do, Carlotta? You take your best shot and go with it."

"Goddamn it, Michael," Carlotta snapped. "If you don't give a shit about yourself, think about your friends. I don't want to lose my best friend through sheer stupidity. We are not talking about taking chances on cross-examination. We are talking about taking chances with someone who has killed two children."

"Don't yell at me," I said. "I am not taking chances. Even Willy didn't think the guy was out to hurt me."

"What! Michael, for Christ's sake, if Willy's right, the person invading your home is a killer. Think about it. Do you really believe it's safe for him to be getting in and out of your house —

maybe while you're sleeping? Quit dreaming. Are you staying here tonight?"

"No."

"Then you are taking chances."

"I've got a client."

Carlotta looked like she might refuse to leave. I had to get her out of the office. "I'll think about it, okay?"

She shook her head, but she got up. I didn't know why she was so upset. "Michael, there is no reason on earth you have to stay alone in the country tonight."

"Yes, there is."

"What?"

"I live there."

"Asshole." She started to walk out, then turned around. "Do you remember that poem Carl wrote for you?"

"Carl? The poet with the wife in New York?"

Carlotta just looked at me.

"Vaguely," I said.

"I just think it's relevant," she said.

I couldn't believe Carlotta remembered it. I started to go to the door to look for my client, then turned around and went back to my desk. It was in there somewhere. I rummaged around and, amazingly, came up with it.

> At best,
> It is the face of a racehorse.
> Pale
> With intelligence.
> Carved clean
> With the fear of losing.
>
> Bold
> With that deep stubbornness
> Found only
> In thoroughbreds
> And Southerners
> And brain-damaged children.

I laughed. What could I say? I had forgotten all about it, but I could see it might be relevant. I heard the door to the waiting room open and went out. Instead of my client, Arthur was there. "I was supposed to transport Joseph," he said, "but he refused to come. I'm terribly sorry. He just flatly refused, and I couldn't really make him come. The day care provider and I both tried to persuade him."

Great. Half my child clients were deteriorating, and the other half were refusing to come see me. "Arthur," I said impulsively, "what about lunch? I don't have any clients for a while." Why not? I needed to talk to him about lying to me.

Arthur agreed — it seemed to me a bit reluctantly — and we headed off for Sweet Tomatoes. It was definitely the right choice. If you have to confront someone, better to do it over Sweet Tomatoes pasta. That way you'll enjoy lunch no matter how the argument turns out. We settled in, and I congratulated myself on my restraint. I said nothing at all about the issue until after we ordered.

"Arthur, I have a question," I said with as much politeness as I could muster. "How often have you gone to see Sharon since she's been in jail?"

Arthur looked down and straightened his fork carefully. "Why do you ask?" he said.

"I was just curious how often you've gone to see Sharon. Is there some secret about it?"

"No, no. It's just . . . Well, I have gone to see her some."

"As in two or three times a week?"

"I doubt that much."

"The guards don't. My problem, Arthur, is not how often you've gone to see Sharon. It's why you lied to me about it."

He looked up for the first time, surprised. "I didn't lie to you."

"Actually, you did. You said you couldn't bring yourself to go see her until it was clear she wasn't the killer. Meaning, quite recently. So why lie to me?"

Arthur put the fork down he was fiddling with and folded his hands on the table in front of him. He looked embarrassed. What was going on?

"Sharon and I are . . . friends," he said simply.

"Friends," I said, "as in lovers?" I was more than surprised; I was floored. I don't know why. He is older than Sharon, in his sixties or so, but that isn't all that unusual.

"Good heavens, no," he replied. "It wouldn't have been appropriate. Being friends is problematic enough."

"Is there some law against being friends?" I asked.

"More or less if you're the Guardian Ad Litem doing a custody evaluation of the children."

"You mean you've been friends . . . how long?"

"Too long from the judicial system's point of view. But I swear it didn't influence the custody evaluation. Nathan really is a child molester, I believe that, and she should have had custody. It's just . . ."

"Just what?"

"It's just that if the court knew we had a relationship, they would have discounted the report."

"Discounted the report," I said, loudly enough that people at an adjoining table turned to look at us. "That's the least of your problems. You could be disbarred. You should be disbarred. You should have withdrawn as the GAL the moment you became personally involved."

"I know," he said, "but . . ."

"But what?"

"But I was afraid—Nathan was so slick—I was afraid someone else might not see what was going on and give him custody. It would have killed her."

"Arthur, the whole thing is moot because the judge didn't listen to you or me and the kids are dead, anyway, but what were you thinking? If she had gotten custody, Nathan could have gotten the ruling overturned on the basis that you were biased."

"He wouldn't have found out. I was prepared to walk away permanently to keep him from knowing. Nothing happened, Michael. I mean nothing happened because of this. It didn't matter."

"It matters now. I have to report you to the State Bar Association's Ethics Committee."

"Why? I swear to you. I would have made the same report if I hadn't been Sharon's friend. The judge didn't take my recommendation anyway, and the case has evaporated, and nothing that happened to the kids had anything to do with my relationship with Sharon."

"Are you in love with her?"

He looked me squarely in the eyes for the first time. "That's none of your damn business," he said.

We both fell silent. Great. He was obviously in love with her, doing some kind of crazy white knight number trying to protect her.

"Look," he said. "I'm prepared to withdraw permanently from being a GAL. If I do that, can't you let it go? Sharon's had enough pain and suffering."

"I don't know, Arthur. What's bothering me is that if you had been on Nathan's side, I'd definitely report you. If I would have reported you if you were on the other side, how can I not report you just because you were on my side? I can't start treating one side differently from the other, or I'll end up as biased as the defense attorneys try to make juries think."

I hated this shit. No matter how this came out, Arthur's days as a Guardian Ad Litem were over. Either he was going to withdraw voluntarily, or I was going to report him. What a shame. He had been an effective voice for children, and there weren't many. Did the whole thing have to cost him his license to practice, too? I'd have to think about whether I could let it go.

Arthur dropped me back at the private practice office, and I saw a couple of clients halfheartedly. I used to be a good therapist. I used to think about what I was doing when I was in a therapy session. Now I was lucky if I could remember my clients' names. By late afternoon I decided to call it a day. I had to do some work on some legal cases, but I might as well do it at home.

I headed home with my head still bouncing back and forth between Willy's speculation and Arthur's revelation. Arthur's story made sense except . . . except what? Except for Gene's comment that Sharon was always worse after Arthur left, a lot worse. Why? People aren't usually worse after a close friend leaves. They are sustained by friends, not depleted.

The more I thought about it, the odder it sounded. On impulse, I turned the car around and headed for the jail. Sharon was the only person who could tell me. Arthur might not even know she was worse after he left.

Gene looked pleased to see me. "Michael," he said, "don't tell me—you've changed your mind about going hunting."

"Not in this lifetime, Gene. Didn't you ever see *Bambi* as a kid? Don't tell me. You're the guy who shot his mother."

Gene laughed. "You're a card, Michael. Here to see Sharon?"

"Yep, if that's okay."

"You're just making it. Visiting hours close in fifteen minutes."

"Don't worry. She'll throw me out before then."

Gene raised his eyebrows but didn't comment. He took me on down to the visiting room, and I waited for him to bring Sharon up. I didn't expect to be shocked this time—after all, I had just seen her —but in my mind I must have whitewashed her a little because I got a mini-jolt when she came in. How could anyone look that bad? She was gaunt, and her eyes looked distracted and almost disoriented. Grief is a ragged thing.

"Sharon," I said gently. "I'm sorry to bother you, but I wanted to ask you some questions about Arthur. I had lunch with him today, and he told me about your relationship."

"What questions?" she said sharply.

Before I could answer she asked, "Are you going to report

243

him? He said you'd report him if you found out and he'd lose his license."

"I don't know, Sharon. I guess that's partly why I wanted to talk to you."

"Don't, Michael. Don't take away the one thing I have left."

Uh-uh. This didn't sound platonic.

"How long were you having the affair?"

"What did he tell you?"

"I didn't ask about the time."

"I don't remember, exactly."

"Ballpark?"

"What does it matter? I can't believe you've come here. Both my children are dead, and you are worrying about how long I was having an affair? What does it possibly matter now? I'm not going to talk to you about this." Sharon's voice was rising. She was labile, anyway, and I had hit some kind of nerve. "Arthur was a prince. He took a chance of being brought up on ethics charges to protect me. How can you even think of punishing him for that?"

"Sharon, the 'prince' could have waited until after the trial was over to get involved. What he did was unethical, and it could have backfired badly."

"As if that mattered now. He was right. You don't understand. Stay out of this, Michael. You already messed things up enough. Don't even think about reporting him. I love him, and he's all I have left."

She walked out, back to her cell, and I sat for a few moments fuming. Arthur had lied to me again. The son of a bitch had tears in his eyes when he denied having an affair. Two strikes.

31

I thought about calling from the jail, but there wouldn't be any privacy there at all. I thought about calling from a phone booth, but you can never hear from those damn things. I thought about calling from my car and realized I would probably have a wreck. I headed back to my private practice office, then realized my Psychiatry office was closer.

I didn't even take off my coat before I started dialing his number. He had a secretary who chirped, and she chirped cheerfully that he was gone for the day. I put the phone down. It wasn't an emergency. It could wait till tomorrow. I hate it when people call me at home about things that aren't emergencies. There wasn't any need to bother him at home.

I grabbed my Rolodex and then picked up the phone; I was too ticked to wait. "This is Arthur Morrison," the voice on his home line said succinctly. "Please leave a message after the beep." Well, at least he didn't have music on his message. Only a sadist would put music on an answering machine.

"Arthur, this is Michael," I said. "I need to discuss something with you at your earliest convience regarding the Southworth case. I'm in my department office. Please give me a call."

It wasn't too bad. I couldn't keep the edge out of my voice, which sounded, I knew, like I was thoroughly irritated. But then again I didn't tell him he was a lying son of a bitch and I'd break both his thumbs when I caught up with him.

I sat and stewed. I might not hear from him till tomorrow. He might be out of town. The secretary claimed not to know where he was, but maybe if I hadn't sounded like an irate bill collector her memory might have been better. Was there any chance he had a beeper? She didn't volunteer it. Did he have a car phone?

The phone rang. Absently, I picked it up. "Hello, Michael," Arthur said. "You were looking for me?" Surprised, I sat up straight. His secretary pretty clearly had a way to find him and fast. He had a beeper or something. I glanced down at Caller ID. Where was he?

Of course, the damn thing would be broken. And I just got it. Come on, folks. It wasn't supposed to have your number on it; it was supposed to have the caller's. I looked again. Something was wrong. I was at the office, and the number on the machine was my home number.

It hit me. Jesus Christ! The son of a bitch was calling from my house. He was in my home. My home. I swallowed. Too many seconds had gone by already.

"Sorry, Arthur," I said. "You caught me eating a bagel." My voice did not sound right at all. What was he doing in my home? So there had been someone in my home? What was he looking for? How much I knew? Or did he just like the thrill of prowling? "I want to talk with you, but I'd rather not do it over the phone." Get out of my home. "Are you playing ball tonight? I could meet you, say, a half hour earlier at the gym." It was the first thing I thought of. I always felt safe on a basketball court. And you'd look hard to find a more public place.

"Sure," Arthur said. "See you then." I hung up and stared at the phone. I picked it up, then put it back. Clearly, he didn't know I had Caller ID at the office. But why not? He could see it at the house. Maybe he didn't think I had it at the office because I had a secretary there. Actually, that was true. I'd only had it installed the week before because I was putting in a lot of hours when the secretary wasn't there. With a shock I realized he didn't have to guess. He had been in my office as late as a couple of weeks ago. He could have checked it out then and discovered I didn't have it. I started to pick up the phone, then realized I couldn't take a chance he'd do what I did—look at it.

I raced over to Marv's office and threw the door open. I didn't even think about the fact that he might have a client. Thank God he didn't. He had his feet up on his sofa, and he was typing on his little portable computer. "Jesus, Marv, you won't believe this," I said, blasting into the room and grabbing the phone. "I'm going to dial my number. Leave me a message. Ask me to give you a call." I was talking so fast I sounded as if I were on speed. Marv dropped his feet, startled, and stared at me. "Don't say anything else," I said. "Someone's there."

Marv just kept looking at me. God, that man is molasses. I dialed the number and handed him the phone. He got his wits about him. "Michael, this is Marv," he said. "Please give me a call."

I jerked the phone out of his hand and then dialed my access number. If Arthur was curious about the call, hopefully Marv's message would reassure him. When the beep sounded, I pressed seven. I had always wondered what that little feature was for, that allowed you to listen in on a room. I never had a clue why you'd want to use it, but I remembered it because it was so weird.

I heard footsteps over the phone and then what sounded like papers rustling. Unbelievable! He was in my house. I hung up the phone. It almost made me nauseous to think of him rifling through my things. My books, my papers, my bathroom things—all forty of them. I sat down abruptly; my hand automatically went up to my mouth. I felt as if I were being raped. He was in my things.

Marv said, "What's going on?" But I couldn't talk. I was too busy trying to think through what this meant. I hung up the phone and ignored Marv's increasingly frantic inquiries. Of course. That's what happened. If I hurried, I would just have time to stop by and see Sharon to check it out. I jumped up and headed for the door.

"Michael, where are you going?" Marv said. "What's going on?" Even in my haste I could hear how alarmed he sounded.

"I'm going to the gym," I replied, "to play some b-ball. I'll call you later. Thanks." I don't know if he even heard the thanks. I was pretty far away by the time I said it.

I don't think it took very long to get to the jail. My old style of driving came back to me when I needed it. But what is it about hurrying that makes everything seem slower? The faster you go, the more of a hurry you are in, the more time seems to slow. You just can't get some places if you are in enough of a hurry. Maybe that's what relativity is. The perception of time is inversely correlated with the speed at which you move.

Partly to distract myself, I picked up the car phone. There was one person besides Sharon who could tell me some things about Arthur. Miraculously, I got her on the phone. The more she talked, the stupider I felt. Why hadn't I thought to check his story out?

I pulled up to the jail and left the car out front. I ran in. Gene was still at the front desk. I practically skidded to a stop. "I need a favor," I said. "I need to see Sharon again, and yes, I know visiting hours are over, but it is very important, and if you'll let me see her for five minutes, I'll buy you a lifetime subscription to *Playboy*." I believe in a kind of flexible feminism.

Gene stared at me as though a tornado had just blown in the door. "You're on," he said.

I raced down to the visiting room and paced until Sharon showed up. I sat down facing her through the glass wall again. "Sharon, I just have one question," I said. "Tell me the truth. When you were having the affair with Arthur, did you give him a key to your house?"

Sharon looked away. It wasn't good enough. "Well, did you?"

I said. "I don't want to guess, Sharon. Did you or didn't you?" It was probably a good thing there was a glass wall between us.

"I knew that's what you'd think," she said, sighing.

"Sharon, did you or didn't you give him a key?"

"Yes, he had a key, but it wasn't what you think," she said stubbornly.

I discovered I was standing. "And you never told the police!" I practically shouted. "Your children are murdered. The door is found locked with the kids inside, and you don't tell the police you gave someone a key. What were you thinking of? What were you thinking of?"

"He didn't do it," she said. She and her voice rose at the same time. "He would never have hurt those children. You should have seen how much time he spent with them. Nathan never spent that much time with them. He was too goddamn busy making brownie points at the hospital. And I'm sure Nathan kept a key to the house. If I'd told the police Arthur had a key, they'd have hung him with it when it was Nathan, it was Nathan. I knew it was Nathan. I couldn't let him get away with it."

I closed my eyes. I was right the first time. She was crazy as a loon. Hate had metastasized like a cancer. Long ago, it got her heart, and now, it had eaten up her brain. I got up and left.

32

....

I got to the gym before he did. That was good. Shooting a basketball would settle me down better than anything in the world. I starting shooting and getting the rebound, shooting and getting the rebound, trying to get some kind of rhythm established that would slow my heartbeat to, say, double its normal rate.

I was at the top of the key, shooting in a semicircle, when he came in. He put on his shoes silently and took a position under the basket catching the ball when it swished through and throwing it back.

"I've been thinking," I said and put up a jump shot. "How this whole thing came about." I caught the ball, dribbled twice to the right, and put it up again. "A pediatrician told me once. He saw five children in the same year with anal lesions." I caught the ball. "Thought they all must have been constipated." I faked right, dribbled once to the left, and pulled up for a fade-away jumper. "Never occurred to him to find out if they had any connection with each other. Funny thing, though." The ball

250

came back harder than before. "They all went to the same day care.

"Now isn't it amazing, knowing that, I would do the same thing." I faked up and drove. "So there I am, with these little kids who are inexplicably getting worse in therapy." Arthur threw the ball back very hard. "And I never even ask the question of what they have in common. Or who, really."

His face was totally expressionless. The silent, empty gym was beginning to take on the feel of an abandoned warehouse. Arthur just stood and fed the ball back to me, but—it seemed to me—the ball was coming back a little harder and faster each time. I ignored the throws and dribbled into the key, turned my back to the basket, and pivoted into a right hook.

"Amazing. I never even considered all those kids might be being molested again by a new perp—at least I didn't consciously." Arthur threw the ball so hard it almost slipped through my fingers. I had just got there, and I was already glad that other people would be showing up soon. Maybe I didn't need to be alone with him to confront him, after all.

"But funny thing, somewhere in my little brain, I registered that the kids who were seeing you were the ones falling apart, and they were always worse after they saw you. I know I knew it because I had a dream about it."

I started throwing up jumpers from the side. It's always harder to shoot from the sides—no backboards to help out. I missed a couple and wondered if it was the angle or my nerves. I told myself that people would be streaming in very soon. The thought eased the knot forming in my stomach. The silence, the stinging throws, they were getting to me. I went on. "I had a dream in which a woman committed suicide after a man left— which definitely qualifies as being symptomatic, acting-out, whatever. I think my unconscious was trying to ask me who the kids had been with when they began deteriorating. If I'd looked for it, the only person the deteriorating kids had in common was you."

I threw up a series of close jumpers to get my eye back. I

didn't tell Arthur what I had originally thought about the dream. I had just assumed loss was involved—that the woman committed suicide because the guy left. I tend to see loss lots of places it probably isn't.

"The guards said Sharon was worse, too, after you left. But that was different, wasn't it, Arthur?" I had quit shooting and just started dribbling around, switching hands and dancing from side to side. "Sharon was worse because you were feeding on her grief. That's what a sadist would do, and you're a sadist. So what was it? What did you do? Have her describe how cute the kids were or talk about her favorite moments with them? Or maybe you made her describe how she felt when they were born."

"One on one?" Arthur startled me when he spoke. His voice was flat and even, but it definitely had something curling at the edges of it.

"Sure." Did I really want him that close to me? But this was, thank God, a public place, a gym, and I would feel foolish being nervous when the first people walked in the door. And I definitely didn't want him to know I was afraid of him. I threw up one more jumper.

Arthur walked up silently and handed me the ball. I started dribbling again. "And then," I said, "there was the literary touch. That should have given you away." I faked left, drove right, and went up with an underhanded layup under his arm. He chopped my arm, but the ball went in anyway.

Arthur didn't seem to be concentrating on the game. I could concentrate on basketball if I was playing—well, a double murderer. He took the ball and walked up to the top of the key. "Losers keepers," he said, meaning if you hit your shot, the other team got the ball.

He started dribbling. "In this fantasy you've constructed," he said, "why should the 'literary touch' have given me away?" Suddenly, he faked up ever so slightly, then drove left. The fake didn't move me out of the way very much, so I was pretty close when he brought his right elbow out on the drive and caught me in the solar plexus. He knocked me backward as he shot. I didn't say anything. It seemed kind of ludicrous to call a foul on a murderer.

I took the ball and headed for the top of the key. I danced around again from side to side, dribbling. "Sharon Southworth wasn't the sort to read *Beloved,*" I said. "I never saw a book in her house on the home visits, never heard her mention one. I don't think she read at all. But you read a lot, don't you, Arthur? Living alone, no spouse or kids. Easy to remember now. We were in my office talking, after the first meeting about this case. You picked up *Beloved* and made some comment about the ghost in the book being the most believable one in fiction. It was a single passing comment, and for the life of me I couldn't pull up who talked about it."

I faked up once, and he went for it. I went up again when he was coming down; it was easier to get my shot off outside when someone was really getting rough. The ball danced around the edge of the rim. I went after the rebound, faking right and going around Arthur to the left. I was in the air grabbing the ball when he slammed into me.

"I'll take that," I said. All right, maybe I would call fouls on a murderer. I couldn't stand to let him get away with that shit on the basketball court.

I started dribbling. "But of course what the law will be interested in is your past history." I drove in a few feet, turned my back to the basket, faked, and pivoted into a left hook. "I called the friend of mine who knew you in Boston on the way here. The one you were alarmed about when I mentioned at the jail I'd run into someone who knew you."

The ball wouldn't drop. I'd have to do something about that left hook. "No wonder. Pity that in that first conversation we didn't get around to comparing notes. You were never married, Arthur, despite your claims, but you were an outstanding community member. I understand you coached baseball and soccer, took troubled kids under your wing."

Arthur had the ball and walked to the top of the key. "What

are the chances when they start poking, Arthur, that they'll find a victim here and there who'll talk? No wonder you didn't want an investigation by the Board! Who knows what will turn up once anyone starts investigating you." He drove all the way under the basket and put it up on the other side, but the shot was wild. Arthur didn't seem to have his heart in the game. I did, though, to the point I didn't notice that people should have been in there by now.

Arthur caught the rebound and threw up a very poor shot; it seemed almost deliberately poor. I went for the rebound, and this time he hit me so hard he knocked me into the wall. I started to fall, but he followed his shot and grabbed me. He threw me back against the wall, and pressed his forearm into my throat. I couldn't breathe very well.

"You self-righteous bitch." He got his face very close to mine. "So I panicked. It can happen. They would have told. What was I supposed to do? I didn't have any choice."

"Bullshit," I hissed. I couldn't talk any louder with so much pressure on my throat. "No one puts a plastic bag over a child's head because they have to. You did it for the hard-on it gave you. And you loved every second of it, you son of a bitch."

There was some kind of uncertainty in Arthur's face until I said this. I didn't even know it was there until his face settled into something quite different. There was a new sense of calm about him. He seemed almost relieved. Slowly he took a plastic bag out of his pocket.

"Don't be a fool, Arthur," I said. "People will be here any minute."

"I don't think so," he said, "I locked the doors and put up a sign—gym closed. There won't be anyone to disturb us.

"You arrogant cunt. You think you're so smart. Do you know how many times I've been in your house? I could have reached out and touched you in the shower." Arthur saw the question in my eyes and laughed. "It was easy. Carlotta's keys were in her purse. I stole her key and made a copy. I got it back before she even noticed it was gone." Of course. Carlotta and Arthur were in meetings together over legal cases all the time, and Carlotta carried a lot more stuff around than I did. She wouldn't have noticed.

My musing stopped abruptly when Arthur tightened his forearm and cut off most of my wind. "You have no idea who you're dealing with. Now beg me. Yes, beg. Get down on your knees, you bitch, and tell me you'll do anything I want, if I'll let you live."

I could feel the bulge in his pants pressed up against me. I knew it would get bigger if I begged. It would buy me some time. I could scream when I heard someone outside.

I opened my mouth to speak. Arthur let up the pressure on my throat slightly. "If you kill me," I said, "you better never go to sleep again, because I'll put a cold finger on the back of your neck in the dark."

It's what Mama would have said.

Hell, it's what Mama would have done.

Arthur slammed into my throat. I could hear the sound of cartilage cracking. The light began to go. Everything started fading, and I slipped into something like delirium. I thought I saw a big .45 pressed against Arthur's temple. That's funny, I thought. You'd think I'd hallucinate my own sweet Model 66 and not that big, ugly cop's gun.

I heard a voice a long way away saying, "Drop her." Nothing happened, and then the voice said louder, "Drop her, or I'll shoot." Suddenly, I was falling and taking big delicious gulps of air. I hit the ground before the lights came back on. I heard the sound of handcuffs clicking, then Adam was next to me. I noticed right away how grave and serious his face looked—but good, his face looked very good.

"I have to call an ambulance," he said. "I'll be right back."

"No," I hissed. I found to my surprise I couldn't talk very well. "Don't leave me alone with him."

I tried to scramble up, holding on to his sleeve. He put his arm around me to support me, and I got to my feet. We started hobbling to the door. I didn't look at Arthur directly, but I could see out of the corner of my eye he was handcuffed to a bleacher.

I wasn't doing very well walking. I was shell-shocked, and my throat hurt so badly tears were running down my cheeks, and I still couldn't breathe right. I wasn't walking too well. It would have been easier to carry me. But I didn't want that, and Adam seemed to know it. Patiently he helped me hobble outside.

"How'd you know," I said, tears running down my cheeks. "How'd you know to come in?"

"Marv called me," he said. "He said you were acting 'hypomanic' and 'counterphobic.' When I didn't get it, he screamed in the phone, 'Rash, she's going to do something rash.'"

It had been raining, and all the surfaces of things were dark and gleaming. I looked down and saw a puddle of shiny, black water. For once I walked around it. You have to watch out for those pools, I thought. That's where you find them. You find the snakes in that black, shiny water.

I didn't heal as fast as I would have liked. My throat didn't get better, nor did my bruised psyche. I knew all the symptoms of post-traumatic stress disorder, and I had most of them. Within a week I had installed the most expensive alarm system known to humankind, but I still didn't feel safe. I slept in fits and starts. If anyone got near my neck, I gasped.

And I had other issues, too. I had been rescued. A humiliating experience. And yet I wanted to see Adam; I felt safe around him. But I didn't like the fact I didn't feel safe unless I was around him. I felt embarrassed by the whole thing.

Easy to run. It was definitely a choice. Stay away from Adam for a while. Let things settle down. I thought a long time about everything, and then I made two phone calls. I called Jack, and I called Adam.

I waited nervously in the restaurant. He had said he'd come, but I had never actually had dinner with him in public before so maybe he'd get cold feet. Maybe I hoped he wouldn't show.

This would change things between us one way or the other, and who knows if that was a good idea.

He came right on time, and he looked a whole lot more relaxed than I felt. As he walked up, I remembered how much I just liked looking at him, and always had. I looked at his hands and wondered how they'd feel on my breasts. I tried to put it out of my mind. It wasn't conducive to keeping my train of thought.

We talked about the case. He told me he'd heard another complaint of child molestation had come in against Nathan. It seems he had been sleeping with Athena, after all, and he had silenced her by being so "nice" to her kids. Athena's ten-year-old daughter had finally told her mom just how "nice" Nathan had been, and Athena had gone ballistic and, more importantly, had gone to the police. I asked what the kids looked like and finally solved the mystery of that night with Nathan in the car.

I told him I was glad to be vindicated. I would have gone to my grave believing Nathan was a child molester even if no one else did. But somehow, I was more glad that what Adrienne and Andrew had said had been vindicated. They had told the truth, and Fishbein was an asshole for not believing them—judge or not. Nathan was a child molester—just not a sadistic one. And what better place for Arthur to hide—than in the shadow of another perp.

As dinner went on, we talked about where I was at. "I've seen PTSD I don't know how many times in clients," I explained. "I've treated Vietnam vets and rape victims and even a survivor of a concentration camp. But what a difference when you're the one who's got it instead of the one who's treating it."

"What's going on?" he said.

"The memories. 'Intrusive memories,' they're called in the lit. You don't get to decide whether to think about what happened or not. The memories just keep rolling like some kind of split screen in your head."

"Even now?"

"Even now. And I don't sleep. If anyone even puts an arm around me, I freak. I absolutely can't stand anyone near my neck. It's all part of the 'intrusive phrase.' I'd like to switch over to the avoidant phase, where you just numb out and stay away from stuff that reminds you of what happened, but I can't seem to figure out how to get there. And hyperstartle? The phone rings, and I jump big time."

"It would ring less if you answered it occasionally."

"I know. I needed some time."

"I was afraid you'd shut me out."

"I thought about it."

"It might not be a good idea to make up your mind right away. I learned a fair amount about PTSD in disaster training, and it doesn't seem like the right time to make any big decisions."

"Actually, I've made one." Dinner was over, and we were on our second cup of coffee, and I couldn't put it off anymore.

"I'm going away for a while. I'm not getting better fast enough, and maybe I need to just get away from here. I'm going to Kauai. It's a lot more rural than most people think. Everybody thinks it's like Honolulu, but Honolulu is big and urban, and Kauai has little roads and a few restaurants and lots of beach. I've rented a condo on the beach for a couple of weeks, and that's what I'm going to do." I couldn't put it off any longer. I had to say it.

"So I have a ticket for tonight, for a nine o'clock flight." I pulled the ticket out. "Actually, I have two." I put another ticket on the table. "I wanted to thank you for saving me, and I'd, well, I'd like to spend some time with you, but I know it isn't much notice. That's just the way I do things, and I entirely understand if you can't get away from your job with that little notice, or maybe you have a dog or something, and it's not a problem. You see, your ticket is open; mine is closed. I'm leaving at nine tonight, but you can take the trip any time because I really do want to thank you, and, really, I do understand if you can't do it with this little notice. . . ." My voice sort of trailed off, but at least I had shut up, finally.

Adam took the ticket and opened it. Then he shook his head and looked at me. He tapped the edge of the ticket on the table. "Well," he said leaning back in his chair. "Well now." He shook his head again and laughed.